HE'S ONLY HUMAN

Father, if he were alive, would be annoyed by my softhearted decision to let the Cuban live. He always insisted that I be wary of humans, whether they number one or a hundred. *"They're weak but treacherous,"* he taught. *"Remember, it's always better to eliminate a problem than deal with it later."*

But the man is only a human, as weak and powerless as any of the others. Try as I might I can't imagine any way this one man can do me harm. Finally I push him from my mind, concentrate on breathing in time to the surge of the waves as they rush at the island's shore.

Fading off to sleep, I picture myself gliding through a cinnamon-scented sky, spiraling in slow ascent toward the distant shape of my future love.

The Dragon DelaSangre

Alan F. Troop

A ROC BOOK

Visit Alan F. Troop on the web at www.DragonNovels.com

ROC
Published by New American Library, a division of
Penguin Putnam Inc., 375 Hudson Street,
New York, New York 10014, U.S.A.
Penguin Books Ltd, 80 Strand,
London WC2R ORL, England
Penguin Books Australia Ltd, Ringwood,
Victoria, Australia
Penguin Books Canada Ltd, 10 Alcorn Avenue,
Toronto, Ontario, Canada M4V 3B2
Penguin Books (N.Z.) Ltd, 182–190 Wairau Road,
Auckland 10, New Zealand

Penguin Books Ltd, Registered Offices:
Harmondsworth, Middlesex, England

First published by Roc, an imprint of New American Library,
a division of Penguin Putnam Inc.

First Printing, March 2002
10 9 8 7 6 5 4 3

Cover art by Kovek
Cover design by Ray Lundgren

 REGISTERED TRADEMARK—MARCA REGISTRADA

Printed in the United States of America

PUBLISHER'S NOTE
This is a work of fiction. Names, characters, places, and incidents either are the
product of the author's imagination or are used fictitiously, and any resemblance to
actual persons, living or dead, business establishments, events, or locales is entirely
coincidental.

BOOKS ARE AVAILABLE AT QUANTITY DISCOUNTS WHEN USED TO PROMOTE PRODUCTS OR
SERVICES. FOR INFORMATION PLEASE WRITE TO PREMIUM MARKETING DIVISION, PENGUIN
PUTNAM INC., 375 HUDSON STREET, NEW YORK, NEW YORK 10014.

For all the dragons among us.

Acknowledgments

First, foremost and forever, to Susan, my wife and my favorite reader, without whose love and forbearance I doubt I'd ever have completed this or any other book. To Rocky Marcus for her encyclopedic knowledge of literature, her advice and her well timed and well delivered ego strokes. To Jim Cory, wherever you are, a damn good poet and an excellent critic. To Bob Darwell for your help and advice and to Bob Hollander who always wanted to be in a book. And to Jason, David and Leah—dreams can come true if you work hard enough at achieving them.

1

Since Mother's lonely demise on an arid isle beyond the Gulfstream, Father and I have lived alone. He sleeps most of the time now. The years have caught him in their grip and, during those brief times when he's awake, he's become quite fond of repeating that death lurks beyond each labored breath he takes.

I never detect any sorrow in those declarations. Father has lived long enough to savor whatever he wished. When death comes, he'll surely embrace it.

Dignity is all I wish for him. He's always admired those who fought for the joy they found in life. *"And I've always regretted the necessity of their deaths,"* Father's often said. *"Even in defeat, the brave ones surrendered only their bodies."*

But no matter how calm Father's death, no matter how well received its arrival—I fear the loneliness that will follow. *"Don't despair,"* he reassures me. *"There are still others. One day you will find a woman of the blood, just as I found your mother."*

But each year passes without such fortune. Father can doze and dream his memories. I can only wish for my future.

Ours is a large house, made from coral stone. It sits on an island—a small spit of sand stuck between Miami's Biscayne Bay and the great blue wideness of the Atlantic Ocean. As much as I love the salt smell and ocean song that fills the air each day, I dread the thought of a lonely future spent roaming the cool stone corridors, from empty room to empty room.

We've owned this island, Caya DelaSangre, or Blood Key, since Philip II, the king of Spain, granted it to my family in exchange for gold, services rendered and the promise of Don Henri DelaSangra to never return to any portion of Europe. When first deeded to our family in 1589, the island measured eleven acres long and five acres wide. But over the years, wind, tide and storm have eroded our homestead, just as our family has diminished under the weight of time. My inheritance has worn away to no more than nine acres of dry land. Truth is, I wouldn't trade them for ninety anywhere else. My mother gave birth to me here. I grew up in the house Don Henri himself built.

Without a bride of my own, without children, I admit it's an empty kingdom to rule. Still, I pity those poor souls on the mainland who move every few years, from house to house, without any connection to their land, without any sense of their history or their responsibility to it.

The other night Father awoke and grew nostalgic. *"Remember when you were a boy,"* Father wheezed and coughed, *"how you loved to play soldier?"*

I nodded.

"You'd go out on the veranda, climb on its coral parapet and point to the sea—shouting that pirates were coming to attack. Then you'd run, seeking pretend enemies, circling the house until you finally stopped by one of the gun ports cut into the coral and . . ."

"And I'd beg you to move the cannon into position," I said.

Father chuckled. *"Your mother always hated that I kept a few of the old ship killers. When I'd fire one for you, she'd be mad for weeks. She always worried we'd be heard. She never believed we were far enough from land for the noise to go unnoticed."*

It was a wonderful place for a boy to grow up . . . even a strange child like I was. I still like to stand in the great room on the third floor of our coral-stone house and overlook it all, like a captain viewing his ship from the top deck. Usually I dine alone each night at the massive oak table in the middle of that room, Father asleep, rumbling and turning with his dreams in the room below.

From my seat I can survey all the approaches to our island home. To my right, a large multipaned window faces the endless waves of the Atlantic Ocean. To my left, three smaller windows look out across the pale blue width of Biscayne Bay to the South Miami skyline on the horizon. In front of me, two other windows view the swift current flowing through the narrow channel separating us from the bird sanctuary on Wayward Key. And behind me, yet another window overlooks the mile-wide channel between our small island and the green tree-covered spits of land called the Ragged Keys.

When the windows are open, no matter which direction the wind blows, it washes through the room like an unending wave. Always the house smells of sea salt and ocean damp. Always every outside noise washes through too. Only birds and fish can visit our island and escape notice. Don Henri planned it that way when he built this house.

Tonight I choose to dine out far from our home, away from the endless waves and restless breezes that worry at our tiny island. I land our motorboat, a twenty-seven-foot Grady White, at our slip behind Monty's restaurant in Coconut Grove. It's been almost a week since I've come ashore.

I walk down the dock, ignoring the blare of reggae music and the smells of fried fish and spilt beer that always seem to fill the air around Monty's thatch-roofed outdoor patio. Just past the restaurant's parking lot, I pause for the light, and glance across South Bayshore Drive to the green-and-beige concrete tower on the left—the Monroe building—where LaMar Associates, my family's business, keeps its offices.

While I've little interest in the daily functions of the company, I find it difficult to pass the building without giving it at least a cursory glance. After all it houses the company Don Henri founded to manage and grow our wealth.

Studying the office building's sparse, utilitarian lines, I wonder, as I often do, why anyone would pay an architect to fashion such an ungraceful edifice. Just to the south of it, workers swarm around the skeleton of another, taller tower, one probably just as sterile in design.

I curl my lip. I can remember a time when Coconut Grove was a simple bayside village, when a five-story building would have dwarfed everything in the area. Now concrete towers line South Bayshore Drive, the well-designed ones crowded and eclipsed by their inferiors.

Unfortunately I have to give myself part of the blame. My family's corporation probably has some money invested in every building in sight.

A shiny black Mercedes coupe sits parked on the street in front of the concrete tower. I recognize it as belonging to Jeremy Tindall, my family's attorney and the comanager of LaMar Associates. Frowning, I wonder why he's chosen to work late. It's unlike Jeremy to show such initiative.

I toy with the impulse to go upstairs and pay him a surprise visit. But I have little desire to confront him tonight. Knowing Jeremy as I do, I never doubt whether he's plotting against me, looking for new ways to divert some of my family's considerable wealth. Only the vigilance of his comanager, Arturo Gomez, and the threat of my family's power keep him in check.

A long time ago I asked Father why he tolerated such an employee. He sighed. *"Great wealth always results in great temptation and great temptation invariably destroys honor. If I could, I'd do without them all,"* he said. *"But if you have to have employees, it's better to know one is a thief than be surprised by it. I've found in my long life that the only men who could do great damage to me were the ones I trusted.*

"At least with Tindall, I know what I have. I can rely on him to behave in certain ways and because of that, I can control him. But I would never trust him or any of the others, not even Gomez. And you shouldn't either."

I make a mental note to call Gomez in the morning, warn him to be more vigilant, and then I turn my attention to the bustle of the cars, the rush of people going about their business, celebrating another evening in the Grove.

As I cross the street, passing the office buildings, I smile. I've missed the feel of concrete and asphalt under my feet. As the neighborhood turns more residential and I walk past the manicured lawns and the towering trees that fill each yard, I take deep breaths, smell the richness of the vegetation, the sharp tang of newly cut grass and I relax—thinking only of the evening before me.

Detardo's Steakhouse sits on the corner of 27th Avenue and 12th, a good two-mile hike from the bay. Once fashionable, the area's on the wrong side of U.S. 1 now, almost hidden beneath the concrete columns that shoulder the weight of the elevated Metrorail tracks. Only the restaurant's legendary gargantuan steaks at picayune prices continue to lure patrons.

People still come, even though they have to park their oversize luxury cars in an unguarded lot, illuminated by a few murky yellow security lights. They scurry past the dozens of winos who spend their evenings lurking nearby, hidden behind the bushes and crouching in the shadows.

Max Leiber nods to me when I enter, motions me past the waiting crowd. "Mr. DelaSangre," he says, winking a wrinkled eyelid, "the table you reserved is waiting."

The ancient maître d' grasps my right elbow with his bony hand and guides me to a small table in a dimly lit alcove. "You always seem to stay so young," he says as he hands me a menu he knows I won't use and lights a small table candle I don't need. "I wish I knew your secret."

I smile in return, hand him the twenty-dollar bill he's come to expect. "Remind the chef how I like my food prepared," I say, wishing him gone. He smells of age gone bad, weakened bladder and stale cigarettes.

"Maria will be your server. Just give her your order. I'll make sure the chef takes extra care with it." He rushes off to calm his waiting throng.

Everywhere people consume meat. The aroma almost overpowers me. I can close my eyes and still point to which tables have pork or fowl or beef—and where the rarest meat is puddling blood on its plate.

Maria looks almost too young to be waiting tables, a slightly plump girl with wide, strong hips and bright black eyes. She is in her menses. The smell of it floods my mouth with saliva. I have to swallow before I speak.

"I'll have a twenty-four-ounce Porterhouse steak, blood rare. Tell the chef it's for Mr. DelaSangre—he'll know how I want it."

She stares at me, asks what else I want—salad, potatoes?

I shake my head.

Still, she stares.

My own fault really. Father has laughed many times at my vanity. Like all of my people, I'm taller than most men. My muscles strain against my clothes, especially at the shoulders and neck. But where Father's face is angular—his nose, long and sharp, his lips, thin and cruel—my features are softer, more middle-American.

"Your eyes," she says.

I grin at her.

"I've never seen such green eyes . . . like emeralds."

"They run in my family," I tell her. It's true. There's much about ourselves we can change, but no one of the blood has ever been able to conceal their eyes. In the old days that's how they would find us. Thankfully, such knowledge has long been lost.

Maria lingers at the table. "If everyone else in your family looks like you . . ." she coos, then blushes and rushes off to place my order.

I grin again. I can hear Father saying, *"It's your damn ego, calling attention to yourself."*

Father will never understand. He was born well before this time. To him, all human forms are equally unpleasant. *"You might as well admire cattle!"* he says anytime I remark at a human's beauty. But I'm young enough to have been shaped by the movies and later, television. It's only natural for someone like me—brought up in a world where appearances matter more than reality—to choose to improve his looks.

Father laughed most, when, after viewing Kirk Douglas in *Spartacus*, I decided to have a cleft chin. For a creature who can change form at will, something like a cleft chin is a moment's thought—as are all the other shapings I've done. What Maria sees as she bustles around my table is merely an amalgam of years of watching movie heroes.

The steak tastes almost cool to my tongue, thick with its own juices, redolent with blood. I force myself to cut each piece small and eat at a measured pace. Even so, I finish before Maria comes back to check my table.

She eyes my empty plate, cocks one eyebrow. "I guess everything was okay, huh?"

I nod, smile and order a coffee, black. She returns the

grin, lingers, as if she's going to say something, then blushes and rushes off.

There's no doubt she's available but my stomach's full. All I want to do is slouch in my chair and enjoy the warmth of the room.

My eyes are half closed when she returns—my thoughts far away. I smell the coffee and something else. An edge of nervous perspiration and a hint of sexual excitement now spike her aroma. Before she speaks, I know what she'll offer.

She hands me the check and another piece of paper. "My number," she says. "I get off by eleven most nights. I don't live far from here so I'm home by midnight at the latest." She grins. "I live alone, so don't worry if you have to call late."

I return her smile, carefully fold her note and place it in my pocket. "My name's Peter," I say. Tonight would not be a good time to take her. But in a few weeks, before she's forgotten me . . . "Things are difficult now"—I stare into her eyes—"but as soon as I can, I'll call."

Our hands brush when I pay the bill. The warmth of her tempts me. I resist the urge to make plans for later. Too dangerous. As Father always says, what is good will be better later.

Outside, the air smells of night jasmine and car exhaust. Stars crowd a black sky nearly devoid of clouds. Only a yellow sliver of moon breaks the darkness. I wish there was some place to lie down nearby. At home we doze after large meals. I sigh, fight the languor seizing my body and take slow steps away from the restaurant.

The shadows shift at the edge of the parking lot as a man walks out from behind the bushes. "Hey friend," he says, "can you spare a poor guy a few bucks?"

My nose wrinkles. He smells of alcohol, filth and decay. I shake my head and walk on.

"Just a dollar or two . . ." The man blocks my path. His height almost matches mine and he's quite a bit wider. He holds his right hand clenched at his side.

I grin at him. "I suggest you move out of the way." It's only fair, I think, to give the man a chance.

His eyes go hard. "Hey, mister. I asked nice." A metallic click punctuates his words and he shows the switchblade now extended in his right hand. "Now why don't you make things easy and hand me your money."

My heart speeds up and I laugh at the sweetness of the sensation. I'm aware of every drop of blood, every organ, every cell of my body. This threat calls for only a small response and I cup my right hand in my left so it's hidden from the wino's view.

In an instant, I adjust my right index finger—the stretching of skin, the elongation of bone and nail sending a small thrill of pain-laced pleasure up my arm.

Darting forward, I jab out, rake his forehead with the one talon, backing up before he can see just what has injured him.

The man's face fogs with confusion. He gasps, and staggers back as blood wells from the gash and runs down his forehead. "He cut me!" he yells to his friends in the bushes. "He cut me!"

I laugh again, push him out of my way and walk on. Already my finger has shaped back. A small fleck of his blood remains on my fingernail. I sniff it, recoil at its smell and wipe my finger clean on the leaf of a nearby bush. The man's body is riddled with drugs and alcohol.

I'd rather eat offal.

The wind has risen with the night and, across the bay, waves jump in sympathy. No challenge at all for the deep-vee hull of my Grady White. Twin two-hundred horsepower Yamahas thunder from the stern as the boat dances from white crest to white crest.

The night is too black for most men's eyes, the water and wind rough enough to keep most boats in port. But I know there will always be a few fishermen too foolish to stay at home. "It's time to fly!" I shout into the night wind. "Time to hunt!"

The mugger has roused me from my languor; my stomach's no longer so full. It's one of the limitations my people have. Changing takes energy. Even such a simple adjustment as I used in my defense burned as many calories as running several hundred feet.

But no matter, I think . . . before dawn, Father and I will feast better than we have in months. Father will be glad. He's complained for weeks about the lack of fresh meat.

A pale light bobs in the water a few miles to the south of Blood Key. I kill my navigational lights, turn the Grady White and race toward it.

Their boat is anchored just north of Boca Chita Key. I approach close enough to make out the size of it, the dark shapes of two men hunched over their rods. The boat can't measure more than fourteen feet. The men constantly have to adjust their positions to cope with the pitching of their small craft.

I wonder at the wisdom of spending such a rough evening in such a puny craft for the dubious pleasure of hooking a few fish by the mouth. But I'm glad they have. If theirs was a larger, more expensive boat, I would have to bypass them. It's one of Father's rules. He has many when it comes to humans. *"Never take rich ones, if you can avoid it. Their absence never goes unnoticed. The poorer the prey, the less likely the chance of retribution."*

Intent as the two men are on their fishing and as loud as

the wind and water are, I doubt they have any sense of my proximity. One brings in a fish, rebaits his hook and casts again. Good, I think, they have the look of men committed to a long night of fishing. I turn away and rush for home. When I return, it will be a simple thing, both to take them and to upend their craft so they will look as if they were lost to the sea.

The island is a black presence silhouetted against a darker sea and sky. I maneuver the turns of the channel at full speed, caroming from wave to wave, missing the sharp rocks below by inches. There are no markers, no buoys to show the way. No matter. I know it as well as I know my name.

"Father!" I mindspeak. *"Wake up! It's time for a hunt!"*

I have to repeat myself four times before he answers. *"And about time too,"* he says. *"Will you bring me a young one?"*

"You know better than that," I say.

I can sense his disappointment, even though I'm still hundreds of yards from shore. It's an old disagreement. No matter how sweet they may be, I refuse to take children. Just like so many on the mainland refuse to eat veal, I insist on my preferences.

Father snorts at the thought of it. *"You are what you are,"* he says. *"When will you accept that?"*

"You didn't grow up with them. You didn't go to their schools."

"We only do what we must." Father sighs. *"We're no different from the lions that roam the Serengeti. We just happen to favor the taste of man."*

"That doesn't mean I have to eat their young," I say.

"Don't forget. We were rulers of great kingdoms once, slayers of thousands," Father says, *"Ours is a history older than the age of magic—"*

I've heard this lecture all my life. I interrupt, and parrot back the words he's spoken to me so many times before, *"Had we slain a thousand times more of them, we still couldn't have stemmed the explosive growth of humanity. And no matter how strong our power, no matter how long we lived, we were never numerous enough."*

"Quiet!" Father says. *"Don't bother me anymore until you have something to bring me."*

I grin at his dismissal, guide the boat into the narrow channel that slices into our island and then empties into a round lagoon—the two together looking uncannily like a keyhole from the air.

As soon as I tie off the Grady White's dock lines, I strip off my clothes, leaving them piled on the dock. I stand for a few moments and let the night wind caress me, play with my hair. I hold up my hand before me and marvel at its softness, the frailty of the human form.

How such weak beings could ever end up ruling the earth still amazes me. Any one of my ancestors could kill hundreds of them in a single skirmish. But, I know, as Father taught me, once the first of us was brought down in battle, mankind lost its fear of us. So what that it might take a thousand men to kill one of ours? There were always thousands more to try.

"In the end," Father said, *"by the time of the beginning of written history, only a few dozen of our families were left. They learned how to survive in secret and became changelings and night slayers. They called themselves 'People of the Blood.' Mankind called them 'Dragons.'"*

I draw in a deep breath of the salt-tinged night air, let out a slow growl as I will my body to change. Welcoming the pain, the almost pleasure that comes with it, I twist and stretch—my skin tightening, turning to armored scales, my torso lengthening and thickening until I'm more than twice as large as my human form.

My back swells, then splits to allow my wings to unfold. Taloned claws replace hands and feet. Fangs replace teeth. A powerful tail grows behind me.

My heart hammers out each beat. My lungs pump great quantities of air. Saliva fills my mouth. I think only of the hunt to come. The excitement of it, the memory of the taste of fresh prey overwhelms the possibility of any other thoughts.

I stand on my hindquarters, spread my wings to full length and block the wind with their strength. Opening and closing my claws, sweeping my tail from side to side, I run forward, take to the air with a few mighty beats of my wings.

The small boat still bobs in place near Boca Chita Key, the two men hunched over their fishing rods. I circle far above them, letting the winds keep me aloft while I watch and wait.

One of the men yanks on his rod, stands as he tries to reel in a fish, the rod almost doubling over, the boat pitching and yawing as the fisherman moves. The other man puts down his rod and shifts his position to compensate for his friend's activities.

I spiral down, gathering speed as I near the water, zooming forward just above the wave tops, rushing toward the boat from the rear, the wind whistling around me, salt spray coating my scales.

Intent on the battle with the fish, neither man seems to notice my approach. Unwilling to leave behind a bloody boat, I land just behind them so the impact and my weight upset the craft.

I take to the air again as the boat flips, the fisherman dropping his rod, both men shouting as they fall into the water.

Once again I circle above them. I wait until one man attempts to climb up on the boat's overturned hull. I spiral down toward him, snatching him with a clawed foot, slicing his throat with the slash of the other, carrying his still body to Boca Chita's abandoned beach.

I place the body on the sand, pause as the rich aroma of the dead man's fresh blood fills the air around him. I know I should return to the hunt immediately, find the other man before he works out a way to escape, but my stomach convulses with hunger. Lowering my head, I rip a chunk of meat from the body with my teeth and gulp it down.

It only takes the edge off my hunger. I'm tempted to continue feeding, but I know only too well the scolding Father will give me if I bring him a half-eaten carcass. I take to the air again.

I find the other fisherman far from the overturned boat, swimming toward Boca Chita Key. The man uses such clumsy strokes, flailing as he moves through the waves, that I'm amazed at the progress he's made. Circling over him, I admire his persistence, and wonder if he saw me strike his friend. If he didn't, if he never saw me, I think, I could let him go. After all, Father and I could have a perfectly ample meal with just one of them.

But I know I can't chance this one's survival.

I sigh, fold my wings and dive toward him. Leveling out at the last moment, I grab his shoulders with my rear claws, yank him from the water and carry him into the air. He screams, kicks and struggles, fights my grasp even as I dig my talons into him.

Beating my wings to gain altitude, I continue climbing until the water lies far beneath me. I wait until the man shouts again, then release him—the man still wailing and kicking as he falls. A great blossom of white foam and seawater splashes skyward when he strikes the ocean's surface and I spiral down after him.

I find him floating facedown. From the height I released him, the water couldn't have provided much more cushion than concrete. Still he surprises me by gasping for air as I fish his still form from the sea. Holding him with front and rear talons, I seize the back of his neck with my mouth, close my jaws and crush out whatever life remains for him with a single bite.

"*Father,*" I mindspeak as I fly to the beach to recover the other man.

"*Peter? Have you returned already?*"

"*Not quite yet, Father. But I will in a few minutes . . . with fresh prey—two of them.*"

"*There was a time I was the one to bring you fresh prey.*"

"*It's my turn now, Father. It's your turn to relax.*"

"*I was powerful once. You should have seen me then.*"

"*I did, Father. I was in awe of you.*"

"*You'll feed with me tonight?*"

"*Of course.*"

"*I wish your mother could see how well you've turned out.*"

"*I do too, Father,*" I mindspeak. "*I do too.*"

2

Maria answers her phone on the fifth ring, just after her machine picks up. I disconnect and wait a few minutes before dialing again. Recording our conversation would serve me no good.

This time she answers on the second ring. "Hello," she says, her voice small and heavy with sleep.

I smile at the sound of her, picture her lying askew, warm and comfortable in a rumpled bed. "Hi," I say. "You told me to call any time."

"So what time is it?" she murmurs into the receiver, then yawns. "And who are you?"

"Peter. The guy with green eyes . . . you gave me your number a few weeks ago. It's a little past one."

"Mierda. I just got to sleep." She yawns again, rustles her bed sheets. "Peter?" Her voice turns coy. "I remember you. I didn't think you were going to call."

"I told you I would."

"Yeah, guys tell me lots of things . . . sometimes they even mean it."

"Well it's a beautiful night and I was wondering if you'd like to go for a boat ride."

"Now?"

"I have to come across the bay. I can pick you up at the Dinner Key docks in about forty-five minutes. Is that a problem?"

She says, "No, not really."

* * *

The Chris Craft runabout hasn't been used for months. Its motors cough, sputter and die the first few times I try to start them. "Damn!" I shout at the boat, thinking I should have sunk the thing when I first saw it. I don't want to use my Grady White this evening. Too many people on the waterfront know who owns that boat. But then the Chris Craft's motors catch and settle into a purr.

Maria, I think, will like this boat better. It's a rich man's boat, all varnished wood, upholstered seats and gleaming brass—useless, of course, for fishing or serious boating. I chuckle. The boat was too pretty to ignore and the wealthy couple I took it from were just as pretty, just as useless and very, very surprised at their fate.

When I brought them home, Father had been so angry that I ignored his rules that he almost turned down his share. *"You forget, Peter, that we only survive because of our anonymity. You must not put us at risk like this. Hunt over Bimini or Cuba instead. If the authorities here ever became aware of our existence, of what we are, they would never relax until we were eradicated."*

Maria waits for me to tie up the boat and walk up the dock before she leaves the safety of her locked car. "Too many creeps around here," she says.

I nod, hug her and inhale the warm smells of fresh skin, bath soap and fruit-scented shampoo that surround her. She giggles when I stroke her hair. "It's not dry yet. I just showered and didn't have enough time to blow-dry it." Maria laughs again when I kiss her on top of her damp head, and hugs me back.

She smiles, striking a pose when I step back to admire her. She's come dressed sensibly for a late night on the open water. Still, even in baggy, long jeans and a windbreaker, Maria manages to be tempting. It helps that the jacket is open, showing off her tube top, exposed stomach and pierced navel. She fiddles with her belly-button ring. "So? You like?"

I nod and return her smile. But I wonder. Dressed as Maria is, she could be just another adolescent at the mall. "How old are you anyway?" I ask.

Maria laughs, gives me a bad-girl sort of look. "Don't worry," she says. "I just look young . . . I'm twenty-two." She walks to the edge of the dock, examines the Chris Craft. "Nice boat. . . . How old are you?"

"How old do you think?" I step onto the boat's bow. It's low tide and the deck is a good three feet below the dock. Maria allows me to help her down, then makes an exaggerated show out of examining my face.

"I'd say about twenty-six."

"Twenty-nine," I tell her. I try not to look too pleased. If Father were nearby, he'd laugh at my vanity, point out that even he could look young if he wanted to expend the energy. I wonder how Maria would react if she knew I am almost twice the age she guessed.

I steer the Chris Craft from the docks, out the Fisherman's Channel. As we clear the last of the spoil islands that protect the marina, the boat rides up and down on lazy swells pushed north by a gentle southeast wind. Around us, on both sides of the channel, dozens of boats moored in the free anchorage bob in sympathy to the water's slow relentless dance.

"It's beautiful," Maria says. She shivers from the coolness of the night air and presses against me. The top of her head nestles under my chin. I feel her warmth, smell her excitement.

I have no doubt she plans to end the evening as I do—in my bed. I study her young, plump, ripe body and feel lust and hunger grow within me.

We pass the last channel marker and I jam the throttle

forward. The Chris Craft's motors roar, its stern digs into the water, its bow rises high then settles and Maria laughs as we accelerate into the darkness of the open bay—the boat's props spewing white froth into our wake.

"Can I steer?" she asks. I let her take my place behind the wheel, show her how to guide the boat through the water and make sure she holds us on course for my island. The boat skitters across the water, seems to leap from wave to wave, barely slowing at each impact, spraying water to each side.

Near the island, Maria fails to anticipate a particularly large swell rushing toward us and slices through it, taking a solid slap of seawater over the bow. Saltwater spray fills the air around us, coats our faces. She laughs and I can't resist kissing her, mixing the salt taste on her lips with the sweet freshness of her mouth.

Overhead a jet drones its way toward Miami International, and a quarter moon dimly glows in the black sky. I take the wheel, slow the boat and turn into the island's channel. Behind us, Miami's lights glow on the horizon. The island, Blood Key, is a dark shadow to our front.

Maria points toward it. "Is that where we're going?"

I nod.

"It's so dark."

"We'll turn the lights on when we get there," I tell her and hug her close. "Sometimes lights attract the wrong sort of visitors."

She nods. "But . . . wouldn't it make it easier for you to guide the boat in?"

"No. I grew up on that island. I know the way." I slow the boat a little more. The motors' growls subside into throaty purrs and we glide through the water, rising and falling with the swells. A gust of wind rushes around us and I pull her to me, and press my lips to hers again.

Maria holds me, kisses longer than I'd intended, then

backs off and smiles at me. "And just what are we going to be doing on this island of yours?"

I grin back. "Whatever two people do when they're deserted on an island together."

She sighs, leans against me. "It's so beautiful here." The wind gusts again, washes over us. Maria takes a deep breath. "I love the smell of the ocean!"

I breathe in too, savor the salt smell around us, the sharp scent of excitement building around her and then . . . another scent penetrates my nostrils, and makes my heart race. It smells of cinnamon and cloves, maybe musk and something else—pungent, almost rank, disturbing yet somehow familiar. I sniff the air, wonder whether I imagined it—disappointed to find only a memory of it in the air.

I cut the motors, let the boat wallow and I breathe deeply again.

"Is anything wrong?" Maria asks.

"No." I shake my head. "I thought I smelled something."

She frowns, watches me as I sniff the air. "Something bad? Fire?"

"Something strange," I say, finding no trace of the aroma remaining in the air. "Maybe . . ." I let the word hang, leave the thought unfinished. My shoulders suddenly feel tense and I flex my back, stretch my neck and push the Chris Craft's throttle forward. Maria presses against me as the boat regains its forward momentum. I hug her and guide the runabout toward shore.

Dogs bark and growl in the darkness as we enter the island's small harbor. I feel Maria tense beside me, smell the acid aroma of fear building within her. "Watchdogs," I explain. Two thick, dark forms pace and stare, snarl deep growls at our approach.

"Slash and Scar, the two alpha dogs. They lead the pack."

"Sweet names," she says, her sarcasm evident.

I smile at her. "There are at least fifteen others like them out there in the dark. We have them to keep the island private and prevent uninvited guests from disturbing our estate."

Slash and Scar continue to growl, and hold their ground as we approach the dock. I pick up the boat's searchlight and flash it on them. They pause a minute, two black, furry beasts frozen in the beam—their massive teeth showing stark white in the artificial light—then they bolt off, into the darkness.

Maria gasps. "They're huge."

I shake my head, cut the motors and let the boat coast to the dock. "They're no larger than German shepherds. They just have overly large heads and mouths," I say. I hop off the boat and tie the lines to the dock cleats. "But they've been bred to look like that, to guard this island. My ancestor, Don Henri, brought the first dogs to control the slaves he used to build our house. Over the years we've added others, eliminated the weak and timid ones, until we ended up with our own breed, all of them like the two you've just seen."

A chorus of growls comes from the dark shadows just inland of the docks. "Don't they scare you?" Maria asks.

"No." I'm tempted to laugh at the question. These creatures know who is the master of this island. They tuck their tails and cringe before my displeasure. I bring two fingers to my mouth and whistle three times—short, sharp bursts that pierce the quiet of the night. The growls cease, their sound replaced by the rustle of the underbrush as the pack scurries away.

Maria reaches up and I lift her from the boat and place her on the dock. She giggles at the ease with which I handle her, feels my biceps and mutters, "So powerful."

Something about the way she does it makes me feel boastful and I pick her up and cradle her to my chest. She looks up and we kiss.

"Peter," Father mindspeaks to me.

I sigh. *"Father, I'm busy."* I carry Maria down the dock toward the house. She snuggles against me.

"I heard your whistle. . . . It woke me."

"Go back to sleep."

"Have you brought me something? Something young and sweet?" Father asks.

I heft Maria in my arms and she sighs. *"I don't know if I have or not,"* I tell Father. *"It's been a confusing evening so far."*

"How so?"

"There was something in the air . . . a strange scent, like cinnamon mixed with other things. . . . It disturbed me."

Maria shifts in my arms. "Can you put me down? Is it safe? I'd like to see your house."

"It's safe," I say and put her down.

"I knew you brought me something!"

"She's here for me, Father. Go to sleep."

"I may know what that smell was . . ."

"Tell me, Father, then go away!"

His chuckle fills my head. *"Later,"* Father mindspeaks. *"I'm an old man . . . tired and hungry . . . with an ungrateful and selfish son. Wake me when you have something to bring me and we'll discuss that strange aroma you discovered."*

"Father!"

"Later, Peter, didn't you tell me to sleep?"

I feel the emptiness around me and know he's closed himself off. Irritating old man.

"You said, 'we,' before," Maria asks. "You don't live here alone?"

"No." I shake my head. "My father lives with me. He stays in his room mostly. He's very old and very sick."

"Oh," Maria says. "Sorry." She takes my hand in hers, and squeezes it.

We walk to the end of the dock, neither of us speaking, the night silent except for the irregular slap of water lapping at the dock, the whisper of the evening wind rustling through the trees and the rhythm of the ocean waves' gentle rush.

At the end of the dock a massive iron gate, set into an archway made from coral stone, blocks access through the thick, high coral fence that guards the homestead. Maria and I stop in front of it and she waits while I take an ancient key from my pocket and unlock the gate's equally ancient lock.

Maria cocks an eyebrow at the darkness looming beyond the gate, then looks to me for reassurance.

"Wait," I say and step through the gateway, reach for the weatherproof switchbox inside the wall and throw the lever on the side of the box. Maria gasps as the lights come on, illuminating the stone pathway to the house, accenting the gardens my mother planted so many years ago. Floodlights shine on the house's coral walls, throwing shadows that make the three-story building look larger than it is. At the end of the walk, coach lights ascend the wall in tandem with the wide, deep, rough-hewn coral steps that lead upward to the veranda that surrounds the house.

"It looks like a castle," Maria says.

She walks through the coral archway and I shut the gate behind us. Outside the gate, dark forms scurry as the dogs retake possession of the night. Maria doesn't notice. Her eyes are focused in front of her, her mouth open.

I smile at her reaction, proud of the effect of my lighting. Before I started the electrification of the island, Father was content with torches, kerosene lanterns and open fires. At first I just ran lights at night with a single, noisy diesel generator. But over the years I added wind generators, solar panels and, finally, a new, larger, far more quiet generator. Now the house has all the modern amenities, up to and including air conditioning that we never use, and our own satellite TV dish, which brings us shows Father refuses to watch.

Maria follows me up the wide steps, brushes her hand on the wall's rough coral blocks as we ascend. "Slaves did all of this?" she asks.

"Don Henri sent some of his slaves to work at a quarry in the Keys. They cut the coral blocks from the ground, chiseled them to shape and loaded them on his ships. On the island, other slaves carried the blocks ashore and mortared them in place." I turn toward her. "My father told me he treated them well for the times, but still many of them died."

She shakes her head.

"It was a long time ago," I say. "A crueler time." I don't tell her that the remaining slaves suffered an equally dismal fate once their usefulness was over.

Maria says nothing more until we reach the veranda and walk to the ocean side of the house. There the night wind greets us, rushes around us, tugs at our clothes and plays with our hair. The sound of the ocean welcomes us too and she walks across the ten-foot-wide veranda to the waist-high, coral-stone parapet and stares out at the slow procession of waves relentlessly attacking the island's shore.

"They've come a long way," she says when I follow her and stand next to her. Maria moves closer so the side of her body touches the side of mine. "It feels like Miami's a thousand miles away."

I nod and put my arm around her, savor the warm touch of her, the gentle beauty of the night. It feels almost dreamlike—a warm quiet prelude to the excitement we both expect.

A sudden gust of wind buffets us, carrying with it that aroma, that same smell which had surprised me before. The shock of it upsets my equilibrium and I take a step back to catch my balance.

"Are you all right?" asks Maria, hugging me.

Nodding, I struggle to regain my composure. The scent's still only a diffused hint of what it could be, but this time it's strong enough to sear my nostrils and set my heart to racing again. All I can think is, I want more.

Changes inside my body warn me I'm on the verge of shifting shape. I breathe deep, glad to find the smell gone again, yet mournful at its absence. I will myself not to change, but nothing can quench the fire that's overtaken me, the lust that threatens to consume me. It takes all my control not to throw the girl to the veranda's oak-beamed deck and have her now.

She doesn't help by pressing herself against my hardness and murmuring, "I'm glad to see you too."

Feeling like an adolescent caught at school with an erection, I pull back, silently fighting against the forces raging within my body.

She giggles at my reticence, leans forward and kisses me on the mouth.

I return the kiss, all the while fighting for control of my runaway impulses. There's a sweetness to Maria. I like how she carries herself, her smile, the sway to her hips, the ready grin. I would hate to see fear take over her face.

Maria backs away from me, smiles, fidgets with the charm she wears on a thin gold chain around her neck.

I move close, take the gold charm from her fingers and examine it. "A four-leaf clover?" I ask as I turn the thin, delicate piece over, and admire the small, bright emerald inset in the center.

She nods. "My older brother, Jorge, gave it to me for my *Quince*—when I turned fifteen. We're very close."

Only a few centimeters remain between us. The slightest movement by either of us will bring our bodies in contact. Somehow, my holding the charm and with it, the chain around her neck, heightens the intimacy of the moment. I sway forward, brushing her lips with mine.

Maria sighs, pulls back so the charm slips from my hand. "I know what part of the house I want to see next," she says, her voice thick and husky with passion. She holds the gold clover between two fingers, runs it along the chain.

This girl is too full of life and joy to meet an early end, I think, as I lead her around the veranda to the two large, oak doors that open to my room. She deserves the chance to live her life, have lovers and babies, laughter and tears. I know Father will be disappointed, but no matter how he feels, I decide, I won't be the one to take that from her.

3

Maria sheds her clothes as we enter the room, dropping her jacket first, then her tube top, followed by her sneakers and socks and then her jeans—leaving a trail of clothing to the edge of my king-size bed. She turns toward me, naked except for a pair of yellow cotton bikini panties, cocks an eyebrow at my lack of nudity.

"Well?" she says.

"You're still wearing your panties," I say, turning from her, walking away from the open doors, unbuttoning my shirt, pulling it off as I wander around the room, turning on the bedside lamps, opening the windows so the ocean air can caress us as we caress each other.

When I turn toward her again, the panties are gone. I face her, breathe deep at the sight of her naked body, her firm full breasts, the gentle swell of her stomach above the dark tangle of hair between her legs.

Likewise she stands and examines me as I kick off my shoes and pull down my pants. I can smell her wetness from across the room and, erect to the point of near pain, I shed my underwear too.

She drops back on the bed and I join her, both of us touching, grabbing, kissing, until Maria maneuvers herself below me and guides me inside her. It takes all my control to hold back and wait for her. Usually I'm the one to stroke and kiss—to tease and delay until my partner's ready. But this time I'm not always sure who's in command. Gasping and thrusting, we ride each other, Maria leading as often as led, as wild as I've ever experienced.

Her orgasm, when it comes, catches me by surprise, and I hurry to join her. Afterward, both of us hug, tangled in each other's legs, the sea air blowing through the room, cooling our sweaty bodies.

Maria disengages, and looks around the room. "Was this place built by giants?" she asks.

"No." I grin at her question. She certainly has good reason to ask. Both the pair of double doors that open to the outside from my room and the second pair of double doors that open to the interior of the house are ten feet high by ten wide. The bedroom itself measures bigger than most people's living rooms. How can I explain to Maria that the large doorways, the oversize rooms, the wide veranda and wide deep steps have all been built to accommodate a far different creature than any human giant?

"Don Henri built it the way he wanted," I explain and kiss her nose. "Who knows what he had in mind?"

She reaches between my legs. "Well," she says, her voice turning deep and throaty, "some things, sometimes do get big around here."

I allow her to arouse me and, this time, I concentrate on her pleasure. Maria sighs as I move against her, smiles and writhes in tandem with me—follows my lead this time, the slow, languorous rhythm I've chosen to bring us to our eventual, inevitable release.

Her breathing, her heartbeat, her movements, give me signs as to what pleasures her most. When I duplicate a twist and thrust of my hips that I think will elicit a sigh and an enthusiastic response, Maria rewards me with both, as well as a satisfied chuckle.

If I were human, I think, I could fall in love with a woman like this one. I've never had a woman laugh in my arms before, not during sex, and I find it endearing. I pull her closer, cover her face with kisses, even as the tempo of our movements quicken and our chests heave with our loud ragged breaths. We peak together, laughing, gasping for air. Sweat drenched, our bodies collide one last time before we both collapse back onto the sheets.

Remaining inside her, holding her from the rear as we lie spooned together, I nuzzle the back of her neck and kiss it gently.

Maria sighs, pushes back against me. The sea breeze rushes through the open windows, courses over us and she mutters, "Delicious."

Moist from the proximity of the ocean, the wind smells of sea salt. Its humidity envelopes us, leaves our skins sticky with airborne salt.

I cup Maria's breasts with my hands and pull her close to me, listening as her breathing slows, feeling her body relax. She sighs and shifts in my arms, my skin cold where it's no longer shielded by her heat. Another flurry of wind passes over us and I gasp at the foreign scent that invades the room.

"Everything all right?" Maria murmurs.

Cinnamon and cloves—the smell fills my nostrils. My heart races, my nostrils flare, and I force myself to hug her gently, to whisper, "Sure," in her ear. I wait for the aroma to fade away again.

But it doesn't. Each gust of wind seems to make it stronger. I breathe it in, savor it even as it overcomes me. This, I think, must be how a beast in rut feels. I grow hard again, painfully rigid, and Maria shifts position, and says, "Can't we wait awhile before we try again?"

I grunt assent and withdraw from her, but my lust only increases. The first twinges of change roil my body and I gasp when I realize that if the scent doesn't fade soon, I'll lose all control.

I feel as if I'm drowning in cinnamon and cloves. My

back tightens. My shoulders begin to swell. Maria tenses in my arms and I sigh. I can't bear the possibility that she'll see me as I truly am. I don't want to hear her screams, see the inevitable look of revulsion come over her face. And I don't want her to die racked with terror, sobbing and pleading for my mercy.

The change torments my body again. I sense the skin in the middle of my back begin to split, my jaw begin to widen and I hug Maria, one last time. She relaxes in my arms and I nuzzle the nape of her neck again, hold it lightly in my open mouth. She sighs and I embrace her like this for a few more moments . . . then snap my jaws shut.

Maria trembles once, then goes slack. Her blood fills my mouth and a loud sob fills the room. At first I think it's her, but then I realize she died instantly, as I wished. I hear the sob again and this time I know it's me.

My entire life I've wished I'd been born human, but this is the first time I've truly hated my heritage. Cinnamon and cloves consume me. I roll off the bed and surrender to what I am.

Pain and relief, shame and freedom. I try to howl my sadness to the night and find that I roar instead. My skin tightens, then thickens and ripples as it turns color and takes shape. Soon, deep green, armored scales protect my body everywhere but underneath, which is covered with beige scales, twice as thick.

Father has assured me that at eighteen feet from the tip of my nose to the end of my tail, I've grown to full maturity. My wingspan is more than two times that.

I stretch my wings, sigh at the relief of unfolding them. But even though I open them until they reach from wall to wall, I still can't extend them fully. The twelve-foot ceiling prevents me from standing to full height on my rear legs and

I approach the bed on all fours, examine Maria's still body and the blood pooling around it.

Grief overwhelms me and I roar again.

"Peter?" Father mindspeaks.

"Go away!"

"Is it the girl? When are you going to learn not to care about them? You always get too involved. . . ."

"Leave me be, Father. I have things to do. I'll visit you later."

"Peter? They're only humans."

I roar and shut myself off from him. I know Father will be angry over that. It's something I've hardly ever done to him. But this time, I decide he'll just have to cope.

The cinnamon smell returns, intermixes with the scent of fresh blood and I pace the room, alternately consumed with lust and hunger. I approach the still body on my bed, then back away. At last hunger wins out, and closing my eyes, I approach again, nuzzle against the carcass and feed.

Finally, when I'm satiated, I stretch out on the floor next to the bed and allow myself to doze.

The night's still dark when I awake from a troubled sleep full of changing shapes and terrifying images. The air smells deliciously free of any taint of cinnamon and I breathe it in, take great gulps of it, as if to cleanse my lungs of all memories of that strange and wicked scent. I force myself to look toward the bed where Maria lies, her limbs askew, her body rent and torn.

A shudder runs through my body and I look away. Sadness and grief, guilt and shame fill my soul and I will myself to change back to my human form. As a man, at least, I can honor her with my tears.

I sit on the bed next to Maria's despoiled body and sob, tears flowing down my cheeks, streaking my naked blood-stained chest.

Just before dawn, I stop and turn my attention to what must be done.

Father has taught me to despise waste. *"We can live the way we want,"* he's told me many times, *"because we preserve our wealth."*

Even though we now have enormous investments on the mainland, treasury notes, real estate holdings, stocks and bonds, jumbo certificates of deposit—all of them earning more wealth every day, thanks to our human lawyers and advisors and the miracle of compound growth—Father still insists we maintain at least a portion of our riches ourselves.

Tears return to my eyes as I remove Maria's Swiss Army watch, her gold belly-button ring, her gold high school graduation ring, two other rings of questionable value, her two small diamond stud earrings and her gold necklace with the four-leaf clover charm and put them all in a small pile on a nearby night table. Later, I'll take them downstairs to the treasure room and add them to the gold and silver, gems and jewelry my family's been collecting as long as they've existed.

I gather up her clothes, breathe and cherish the scent of her they still carry, and place them in a pile near the door. Then I pick up her small cloth purse and search through it, removing any change, finding a surprising three hundred and eighty-six dollars in bills in her wallet.

The money goes in the top drawer of my dresser—the purse on top of the pile of clothes. I look through her wallet one last time before I drop it on the pile too, gaze at the pictures inside and wonder who the people are in the photographs she carried, whether they will mourn her passage too.

One picture catches my attention especially. Maria, in a bikini, a little younger than now, sitting on the deck of a Hobie catamaran, being embraced by a young man with piercing black eyes and a large, drooping mustache. The man also wears only a bathing suit and the boat's yellow-

and-white, diagonally striped mainsail is behind them. A rush of jealousy hits me and, for a moment, I hate that person. Then I realize how much the man looks like Maria and I think, this must be Jorge. I blush that I could be jealous of a brother's hug.

I drop the wallet and the pictures on top of the pile of clothing. All of it will be reduced to ashes before the end of day.

By now the sun has begun to burn its way into my room. Blinking at its brightness, hating the glare of it on the dead body on my bed, I scoop Maria up and carry her to my door. I shudder at her lifelessness and weep as I take her through the inner doors to the dim interior of the house.

Had she lived, I would have shown her the wide corridor that circles the great spiral staircase which services all the floors of the house. Now I barely glance up as I walk around the corridor to the massive heavy oak doors that open to Father's chamber.

Father's shades are drawn and, no matter the brightness outside, the room remains as dim and murky as the dark middle of the house. He is asleep when I enter, his breathing irregular and shallow. I can make out his form in the shadows of the far corner of the room, a dark shape sprawled on a bed of hay.

I shake my head at the sight of him. There was a time his mere visage could terrify me, but now, he seems to grow a little smaller each time I see him.

In his old age Father has given up shape changing, telling me his natural body is the most efficient way for him to live. And as the years have passed, he's embraced the old ways, refusing to converse out loud, insisting on hay for his bedding, refusing any trace of human craft in his stone-walled, furnitureless room.

"Father?" I mindspeak. *"I've brought you something."*
The shape turns in my direction, coughs and scratches.

Two emerald-green eyes stare at me. *"You shut me off, Peter. There was a time you wouldn't have dared. . . ."*

I return his stare. We both know he's no longer the imposing figure he once was. At best, Father can't be any more than eleven feet long. His color, once as richly green as mine, now has a sickly yellow pallor to it. Age has slowed his movements, buckled and rippled his scales. "I'm sorry, Father," I say.

He hisses, mindspeaks, *"Speak properly to me!"*

"I'm sorry, Father."

"You should be." Father adjusts himself so he's sitting on one haunch, motions for me to approach. *"So, is that what caused you to make such a fuss last night?"*

A flush burns my cheeks and I stare directly at this creature that sired me—that brought me into this world where I could never fit. I growl a warning, "Father!"

He waves one taloned claw, as if to smooth away my pain. *"Who taught you to be so sensitive? Bring her here. Let me see what you have."*

Father clucks with pleasure when I place the body on the hay next to him. *"So young. So fresh . . ."* He inspects the carcass, trying to decide, I know, just where to start his meal.

I look away, busy myself opening windows, bringing light into the room as he starts to feed.

"Don't be so skittish," Father says, chuckling. *"You're the one whose naked body is covered in her blood."*

Shocked, I examine myself, touch the sticky red substance that seems to coat my arms and spot my chest and legs. *"I didn't even think about it. . . ."*

Father chuckles again. *"It's just blood. It washes off."*

I nod, then pace the room as he continues his feast.

When he finishes, he sighs and turns his attention to me. *"Tell me, Peter, why such a fuss last night?"*

"I didn't want her dead, Father. I liked her. I thought,

maybe, I could see her for a while. . . . It gets so lonely sometimes."

"You think I don't know that? I haven't had a wife since your mother's death. You don't see me mooning over some human woman."

"You're old!" I blurt out. Then I say, "Sorry, Father, I'm upset. First the aroma, then Maria's death . . ."

"Ah, the aroma!" Father chooses to overlook my outburst. He coughs and chuckles at the same time. "You said it smelled of cinnamon and cloves?"

I nod.

"Possibly some tinge of musk too?"

"Yes."

"What did it do to you?"

"It drove me crazy," I say. "I wanted sex. I needed to feed. I couldn't control my body. . . ."

Father claps his hands together. "I told you!" he mindspeaks, his thoughts stronger than before, almost joyous. "I knew it and I told you!"

I glare at the irritating old creature. "And just what is it you've told me?"

He laughs, claps his hands again, pauses to eat some more, even though he knows the pause will make me more angry, more anxious.

"Didn't I promise that one day you'd meet a woman of the blood?" he asks finally.

"So?"

He ignores my frown, grins at me in an indulgent way, as if I have no capacity for independent thought. I consider walking from the room.

"Peter," he mindspeaks, "you've found your woman."

"What are you talking about?"

Father shakes his head. "The aroma, Peter. The scent! Why do you think it drove you so crazy?"

He guffaws. "She's in heat, son! Oestrus. Our women

come to term every four months once they reach maturity. Before they mate for the first time, for a few days every quarter they fill the sky with their scent. It travels almost forever."

"But where is she?"

Father shrugs. *"She could be anywhere from within one to fifteen hundred miles of us. You're lucky. I had to go to Europe to find your mother."*

He absentmindedly picks at the remains lying next to him, breaks a rib bone and sucks the marrow from it. I watch it without flinching, without a thought of Maria. My mind's intent now on the memory of that incredible scent and I try to picture the creature that created it. *"How will I find her, Father?"*

He taps the side of his snout with one taloned claw. *"You'll follow your nose, son. You'll learn how natural it is."*

"But, so many miles . . ."

Father laughs and a paroxysm of coughing and rasping breaths overtakes him. I wait for it to pass.

"I promised you'd find a woman, Peter. I didn't promise it would be easy."

4

The idea of a female of my own kind consumes me, occupies my mind, crowds out all other thoughts. I have dozens of questions, all of which Father ignores. *"Later, Peter,"* he tells me as his head nods and his eyelids close. *"Let me rest now. Come to me tonight and we'll talk more."*

His breathing turns rhythmic and I know it's useless to try to rouse him. I look at the bones scattered around him, stripped of all meat, and shake my head at his gluttony. I have no choice but to wait for him to sleep past his languor.

The yips and growls of the dogs outside remind me I've much to do. They've caught the aroma of the kill and are waiting now, not so patiently, for their share. I carry the entrails, and the other body parts Father chose not to eat, out onto the veranda and throw them over the parapet to the hungry pack below. Then I return to my room and busy myself with removing all traces of Maria from the house.

As I strip the bloodstained bedding from my mattress, I take extra breaths, hoping to smell some trace of cinnamon in the air, but the air carries only its usual sea smells. What little wind there is blows light and seems to shift direction every few minutes.

I think about the breezes of the night before, the strong gusts that seemed to have a life of their own and I try to remember if the wind had shifted during the evening too. Surely if I can remember the wind's direction and follow its route backward, it will lead me to her.

Carrying the sheets and Maria's belongings up the spiral staircase to the third floor, I feed them to the fire in the great open hearth. I try to recall where the wind came from during the last evening, but my memory fails me. My attention had been on Maria, not on the bend of the trees' limbs or the direction of the waves. I know that further toward the summer, a southeast wind blows almost every day and night. During the winter, the north wind brings its chilling effect. But in March, the wind could just as easily come from any point of the compass.

I add logs to the blaze, listen to them crack and pop as they catch fire, watch the sheets and Maria's belongings flame, then turn dark and shrivel into ashes.

A weak gust of air blows through the room and I sniff at it expectantly. Nothing.

The wind ruffles the flames in the fireplace and carries away with it a thin trail of smoke as it courses through the remainder of the room, exiting the window opposite the one it entered.

Watching the smoke's passage, I remember the winds blowing through my bedroom the night before, which windows they seemed to favor. I grin and go on with my work, walking to the top of the staircase, grabbing the thick, manila rope wrapped around a large iron cleat bolted to the wall, scooping up the excess line coiled on the floor below it.

A southeast wind! I'm sure of it now, remembering the play of it over our bodies, the windows it entered and exited, and before that the ridges of water rolling northward across the bay. A wind blowing from that direction meant she lived somewhere in the Caribbean or Latin America. I try to picture how exotic she might be.

All of it makes me feel positively adolescent and, for the first time in more years than I care to think, I unwrap the rope from the cleat, grasp it tightly with my right hand and, holding the excess line in my left, jump the railing and launch myself into the open middle of the staircase.

Above me, hanging from a huge hook set in the center of a massive roof beam, an ancient arrangement of wooden blocks and tackle screeches and groans as the rope rushes through it, the line suddenly taut from the heavy burden of my falling body—its motion slowed by the counterweight of the hoist's wooden platform my weight brings up from the bottom floor.

I laugh as the platform rushes past me at the second floor, brace my legs for the rough landing I'm about to make on the first. Judging from the speed of my descent, I must outweigh the platform by at least fifty pounds—a far different disparity than in my younger days, when there was some doubt about which was heavier.

Mother used to hate when I attempted it, insisting Father discipline me. Which he did, a sparkle in his eyes telling me he might like to try it too.

The impact of the landing makes me grunt and I laugh out loud, look up at the wood platform swaying in the air three stories above me. I move out from underneath it and slowly let the line play out until the platform clunks down in front of me. Out of force of habit I tie the line off, even though the rope's slack and the platform's now resting on the bottom floor of the house.

It's quiet here, a place of still air and dark gloom. The light that shines so brightly on the second and third floors seems to wane before it reaches this low. Away from the center of the room everything belongs to the shadows.

I force myself into the dark and run my hands over the rough stone wall until I feel the light switch. Its click echoes in the stillness and, for a moment, when the dim lights come on, the bare bulbs pushing light into all the shadows, I lose touch of the giddiness that has overtaken me and feel silly, a little ashamed, to be standing naked and barefoot in this place, still splattered with her blood.

This floor is the dark underbelly of the house and I know too well the secrets it holds. Here Don Henri built three supply rooms and eight prison cells. Long ago I turned one of the supply rooms into a freezer where we store our meats. Another one holds dry goods and household necessities, while the third serves as a place to store linens and Father's bales of hay.

The cells are another matter. In the old days Don Henri used them to punish his enemies and to hold humans for his future meals.

I prefer to keep the cell doors open. Shut, their iron bars remind me of the terror and suffering that lay behind them. One of the cells serves as my laundry now, another as a tool shop. Five of the other six still function as holding cells for those times that Father or I have found it convenient to keep one or more of our captives alive.

My nose wrinkles at the thought of the winos and beggars that, whenever no other choices present themselves, I occasionally must seize and bring home. *"Those are the ones who'll never be missed,"* Father always insists. But he is never the one who has to cage, feed and clean them until the alcohol and drugs leave their wretched bodies and the regimen of good, healthy meals finally make them fit to eat.

Of course no alcohol or drug recovery program can boast of the cure rate my hospitality generates. I chuckle at the thought. A hundred percent of my guests have given up their addictions and not one of them has ever had the opportunity to backslide.

I pass the sixth and smallest cell. While it appears to be like the others, as Don Henri intended, in truth it's nothing but a passageway to a secret corridor and the secret chambers built under the house.

Beyond the cells I reach the third storeroom. There I load

a wooden barrow with a pitchfork and four bales of hay as well as sheets and pillow cases for my bed. I also bring an empty burlap bag.

The woman returns to my thoughts and I alternately imagine a raven-haired Latin woman or a cocoa-brown island beauty—each with piercing, emerald-green eyes. I wonder what she'll be like as I roll the barrow onto the platform, then step off and operate the winch that raises the hoist to the second floor.

Father has barely changed position since I left. The sight of Maria's bones lying on the hay near him remind me of the night before and I feel a small twinge of regret. I try not to think about her as I gather up the bones and place them in the burlap bag.

I roll the barrow into the room and unload the hay in a different corner of the room, and use the pitchfork to spread it out and fluff it up. Then I turn my attention to the old creature still lost in sleep on the other side of the room. *"Father,"* I mindspeak, *"I've made you a new bed. Come, get up for a minute so I can clean out your old one."*

Father snores, says nothing, moves not a muscle. Since I've no intention of carrying him, I shake him until he finally flutters his eyelids and manages a solitary thought. *"Peter, why must you torment me so?"*

But he lets me help him up and guide him to his new bed before he returns to his dreams once more.

I make no effort to be quiet as I use the fork to scoop up all the old bloodstained hay and load it and the burlap bag onto the wooden barrow. The barrow squeaks as I roll it out of Father's chamber and onto the platform. I grin at the noise. A caravan of gypsies could celebrate a wedding in this room without disturbing Father's rest.

* * *

Once the platform has been hoisted to the third floor, I roll the barrow close to the great hearth and shovel forkfuls of hay over the glowing embers. Fire flares up and consumes the hay almost as quickly as I heave it forward. The brief eruption of heat feels good against my bare skin and I realize the day has turned cool.

I look out the window at the darkening sky and frown. Whitecaps run southward, chased by the angry chill of a north wind. Trees bend before its force. Their leaves may point south to where my love must live, I think, but the north wind that moves them brings me nothing.

It's the kiss of the south wind I yearn for as I turn my back on the window, busy myself returning the barrow, the pitchfork, the burlap bag and the platform to the bottom floor—thinking, how strange that my future, the discovery of my love, could be so dependent on the vagaries of something as simple as the wind.

I watch the *Twelve O'Clock News* to see if there's any mention of Maria's disappearance. I need to know if anyone saw her leave with me, if there's any alert for the boat. I don't expect there will be any, but still, when the newscast ends without any mention of her, I feel my muscles relax. All contacts, such as the evening I had with Maria, involve some risk. Father has said it many times, we are safest when we are invisible. Safe or not, I decide to rid myself of the boat tonight, at the same time as I dispose of Maria's bones.

I wash the floor clean of all traces of blood, put fresh linens on the bed and then I treat myself to a long hot shower. Afterward I lie down, clean and warm under my covers, and allow myself to nap.

The wind howls through my windows and cold rain slashes the island when I awake. I jump from my bed and rush to slam the room's windows and doors shut. "Damn," I mutter, thinking of the open windows on the third floor and in Father's chamber.

I pull on a pair of jeans, a sweatshirt and a pair of sneakers, then run up the staircase to the third floor, shake my head at the cold remnants of the fire in the hearth, the dampness sprayed by the wind throughout the room.

"*Peter!*" Father calls me as I pull the last window shut. "*Come close my windows, the rain's coming in.*"

"*Father, you can close them yourself,*" I say as I look around the room, and make sure everything's secure. Outside, rain drums on the windowpanes.

"*Peter, you opened the windows. You damn well can close them.*"

I grin at Father's intransigence, walk slowly down the stairs to his room.

"*About time,*" he says when I enter. He coughs and wheezes for my benefit, watches as I rush around the room slamming doors, shutting windows. "*Start a fire too,*" he instructs. "*Take the chill out of the air.*"

I stack logs in the fireplace on the exterior wall, grab a few handfuls of hay from Father's bedding to serve as kindling. The fire will soon make the room intolerably hot, but I know Father won't care. Age has made him sensitive to cold and far too fond of heat. I strike a match and watch the hay catch fire, the flames blossom and lick around the logs.

"*Why haven't you told me about our women and the scent they give off?*" I mindspeak Father.

He sighs and turns on his bedding. "*Why make you wait for what might not come? Why have you search for what might not be there?*"

"*But you've always promised that one day I'd meet a woman of our blood. . . .*"

"*And so I've always hoped.*" He sighs again. "*We are so few.*"

I sit on the hay at his side, watch the fire catch and listen to it crack and pop. *"How will I find her, Father? Her scent came on a southeast wind last night. The wind shifted to the north today. She could be almost anywhere below us."*

He takes a deep, rasping breath, coughs and wheezes as he sits up next to me, puts a wizened, taloned hand on my shoulder. *"She's most probably in the Caribbean. The wind will shift again and, if she's untaken, you can follow her scent."*

"Untaken?" I stare at the old creature. It hadn't occurred to me that she could have more than one suitor. *"First you talk as if we're the last ones of our kind, then you speak as if there are hundred of us. . . ."*

"Peter," he says, and shakes his head as he goes on, *"I don't know how many of us are left—whether we're three or three thousand. I doubt she's yet taken. But I want you to know it's a possibility. Which is why, the next time you smell her on the air, you have to go to her."*

"And leave you here alone?"

Father sighs. *"I've lived a very long time. You know that. Your mother was my third wife. I had six sons and three daughters before you—all dead now. Soon it will be time for me to go too."*

"All the more reason for me to stay with you now."

"All the more reason for me to go." Father forces himself to his feet, shambles across the room on all fours and lies by the fire.

"The heat feels good on these old bones," he says. *"I'm tired, Peter. Time has long since ceased being my friend. If you hadn't been born, I would have died when I lost your mother. I've forced my lungs to work, my heart to beat these last few years to make sure you weren't alone. Now that I can be sure there are others of us out there, I can think of letting go."*

"No!" I say out loud.

He nods, ignores my distress. *"Our females come to ma-*

turity in their eighteenth year. After that, until they mate, they cycle every four months. During each cycle but their first, they're usually in heat for three weeks. If this is a young one, as I suspect she is, what you've smelled on the air is the result of her first oestrus and that typically lasts only a few days. I doubt any male will have time to find her in such a short interval."

"Why are you so sure it's the Caribbean?"

Father coughs, stares into the fire as he goes on. *"When the DelaSangres came to the New World, we weren't the only people of the blood to make the trip. Pierre Sang, Jack Blood and Gunter Bloed sailed ships across the Atlantic too. Eventually, Sang settled in Haiti, Blood in Jamaica and Bloed in Curaçao. But all of our ships sailed together for six months each year looting ships and taking prisoners."*

I look at Father, my eyes wide. *"You never told me you sailed with others of our kind."*

He shrugs. *"It was long ago. What better way could there be to maintain our wealth and keep our larder full?*

"We were all privateers. Each of us carried Letters of Marque—Blood's from England, Sang's from France, Bloed's from Holland and mine from Spain. We kept our ships and human crews on the islands south of us. None of the crew ever questioned what became of our captives. They were very good years . . . until the Europeans turned on us and banned privateering. After that, we went our own ways."

"And you think their families are still on those islands?"

"Most probably." Father turns to me. *"She will come to term again in four months, sometime in July. You must be ready to pursue her. If she mates with another, she'll be lost to you forever."*

The fire's heat burns into me and I wonder how the old creature can like it so much. *"What if she won't have me?"* I ask.

He laughs. *"Our women don't work that way. Until they've mated for the first time, when they're in heat they're available to any male that finds them. Whichever one takes her, has her for life."*

"It's that easy?"

Father grins, showing every one of his pointed yellowed teeth. *"Easy?"* He cackles and I blush at his reaction, feeling like a young boy all over again. *"Peter, with our women nothing's easy. Remember, they're the true hunters among us, fearless, impetuous and far too daring."*

He shakes his head. *"Even your mother, who loved gentle pursuits, who cherished her music, books and arts. She was the one who insisted on your being educated like a human. Even she could be unmanageable and headstrong. . . ."* He pauses and coughs. *"If she listened to me, she wouldn't have gone off hunting that night. I told her, with the war going on, the seas were too dangerous. But she insisted on crossing the Florida Straits to hunt over Cuba. On her return she flew too close to a surfaced German submarine. I doubt their gunner realized what she was. The night was too black for him to make out more than a large shadow passing in the dark. But he sprayed the sky with machine-gun fire, striking her with one of the bursts, doing too much damage for her to repair.*

"She tried though, flying until she found a deserted key thirty miles west of Bimini."

I nod, knowing the story, remembering her last few thoughts calling to us so faintly from so many miles, so far away. Father and I had traveled to that island—no more than a glorified sandbar really—and had buried her body there, that night, before there was any possibility of its discovery.

Father senses my thoughts and says, *"I want you to bury me next to her."*

"Of course," I say, experiencing once again the loss of her, wondering how devastating the loss of him will be.

The old creature studies my expression and cackles anew. *"Don't be so morose, Peter. I'm not dying tonight or tomorrow night either. Think of the young bride you're soon to have. Dwell on that and the creation of new life rather than this old creature in front of you. Go now. You've plans to make and things to do. I have memories I want to visit before I sleep again."*

The wind and rain slam against my closed windows when I return to my room. The large exterior oak doors creak and rattle with each gust. I look out the window and see only the dark sky and the white crests of the breaking waves. For a moment, I question whether I want to go out in this. To do otherwise would be to dwell on all the things Father has told me and, just now, I'd rather put my mind elsewhere, worry and plan another day.

I grab my foul-weather gear from the closet, bundle it under one arm. The gold glint of Maria's jewelry catches my attention and I realize I've forgotten to put it away. I scoop that up and drop it in my pocket, then leave my room and bound down the wide steps of the great spiral staircase.

At the bottom, I pick up the burlap bag containing Maria's bones, sling it over one shoulder and walk to the sixth and smallest cell. Inside, it looks like all the rest except that the stone walls remain unmarred. No prisoner has ever had the opportunity to draw or gouge messages on its wall. No captive has ever slept in this room.

I put down the burlap bag and seize the end of the wood cot bolted to the stone floor. It creaks and rasps as I pull up on it, refusing to budge at first, then rising slowly, floor and all, on hinges hidden underneath, speeding up as the lead counterweights hanging below take effect, revealing a narrow staircase leading down into darkness.

Once again slinging the burlap bag over my shoulder, I enter the passageway. The black surrounds me as I descend the stairs. At their end, a dangling rope slaps my face. Once this surprised me but, after all the trips I've made through this dark passageway, it's as familiar as the ocean sounds outside my window. I give it a hard tug and grin at the groan of the moving floor above, the crash as it slams shut.

I proceed forward in the dark, my shoulders brushing against the cool stone walls of the passageway, my hair touching the ceiling. There's no light here and, with only one direction to travel, no need for it. After forty paces I feel the corridor widen, the ceiling rise above me. Running my fingers over the wall to my right, I find the switch and flick it on.

The light illuminates a round chamber, no more than ten paces in circumference, leading to another dark corridor on the other side and flanked by two, steel-plated wood doors, each chained shut and padlocked.

As always I feel uneasy here, knowing that every man who worked on these rooms was slaughtered as soon as they were completed. I turn to the door on my right and dial the lock's combination. Years ago, after Father ceased to visit this floor, I removed the ancient locks Don Henri had installed and replaced them with modern, stainless-steel combination padlocks, both to forgo the need for keys and to save me from any further time wasted on struggling to unlock the aged and rusted devices.

The door swings open and I can't help but gawk at the riches inside, chest after chest brimming with gold and silver jewelry. Boxes containing Rolexs, Cartiers, Omegas and Ebals. Ancient gold and silver ingots stacked knee-high near the far wall. Piles of twenty-dollar bills taken from drug runners who'd suffered a fate far worse from us than they would ever have encountered from the DEA.

Maria's few pieces of jewelry look paltry and cheap alongside the wealth they join. Still I drop all of it in a chest, the gold four-leaf clover resting on the top and proceed on, locking the door, extinguishing the light and entering the other narrow, dark corridor.

Stumbling occasionally over the rough stones lining the floor, I follow the passageway's contours as it curves, then dips, then rises, then ends—another wooden door blocking any further progress. I listen to the wind and the rain outside and I smile, knowing I'll soon be out in it.

It takes only a few moments of fumbling in the dark to pull on the yellow slicker and matching yellow overalls of my foul-weather gear. I throw the ancient bolt on the door, push it open and, leaving Don Henri's escape tunnel, I breathe in the clean cool night's air. I revel in the beauty of the storm as rain beats in my face and lightning illuminates the heavens.

The tunnel opens in the bushes just a few yards from the dock and I pause to add some large rocks to the bones inside the burlap bag, then I sprint to the dock where my Grady White tosses and pitches. Thunder cracks somewhere in the night and I laugh. The seas will be furious and dangerous in their anger. No right-minded person will be out in such weather.

I throw the burlap bag into the cockpit of the Grady White, then make my way to the Chris Craft and release its dock lines, tying its bowline to the Grady White's stern cleat.

Taking my boat's wheel, I fire up the Yamahas and head out the channel, towing the Chris Craft behind me. I gasp when I clear the protection of the island and the full force of the wind hits me. The Grady White's wheel fights my control. Waves crash over the bow. Salt spray and driving rain hammer my face and eyes.

I push the throttle forward even more and concentrate on guiding the boat through the twists and turns of the channel. The Chris Craft follows, fighting its towline, crashing into waves, skittering sideways from their impact.

Taking the last turn of the channel at full speed, turning the wheel hard to the right, I yank the Chris Craft out of the channel, take it over the coral rocks lurking just under the surface. The Grady White quivers when the other boat hits rock, then slows, motors whining, as it pulls the Chris Craft across the coral, ripping and splintering the wooden boat's bottom.

The rain is so dense that I can barely make out the Fowey Rock lighthouse's beacon a few miles away. I pray that the Chris Craft doesn't sink until I'm well past it, out in the deep water where I always dispose of my family's secrets.

Besides, I find I'm enjoying myself, fighting to keep the Grady White under control, steering my way from wave to wave. Fear isn't a possibility. Should the boat founder or I get knocked overboard, I can always change shape and take to the air.

On the edge of the Gulfstream, the waves tower over my boat, threatening to crash down on me. I wait until the Grady White clears the top of one giant wave, then I rush back and cut the Chris Craft's line before we hit the bottom of the trough. The boat disappears behind me, sinking as I guide the Grady White to the top of the next wave.

I repeat the maneuver two waves later, this time throwing the burlap bag containing Maria's bones into the angry sea. I'm too busy to watch it sink and very glad to have my attention required elsewhere.

The run back to the island goes easier. With nothing to tow, the Grady White responds to the lightest touch. Running with the wind behind us reduces its ferocity, lessens the impact of the driving rain and I have time to think of Maria and allow myself to mourn her passing.

Against the reality of her gruesome death, the image of a faraway love's embrace seems even more illusory to me than before. Had Father not confirmed the probability of her existence, I would probably now be assuming that what happened wasn't the result of an airborne scent but rather a moment's madness. It wouldn't be the first time I felt my existence was insane. Certainly no human would think it otherwise.

Near the island, the shock of Father's words sink in and, for the first time in my life, I consider living without him. It makes me ache inside, a hollow empty pain that tears at me and sears my brain. I want to cry out against any thought of it but I know Father's right. For the love of me he's lived longer than he's wanted and, in return, I must let him go without complaint.

I must focus instead on finding the woman, the mate my blood requires. The thought of her brings back the memory of the scent of cinnamon and musk floating in the evening air. My heartbeat quickens and my nostrils flare. To my shame I forget about the undeserved death, so recent, so sad, of an innocent girl.

For the moment I forget Father's words too, his imminent and desired demise. The recollection of the distant female's scent overtakes me and—no matter the rain, the wind, the tousled, frothing seas that batter me—I give in to the fantasies the remembrance brings.

5

Father chooses to die in May. Even though we've discussed his impending death many times, I still gasp when I open his chamber door, the first morning of the month, and find him lying still and open-eyed on his bed of hay.

My nose wrinkles at the stale musty smell his dead body gives off and, for an instant, I feel like running from the room. Instead, I pivot in the doorway, stare into the interior of the house and take a few cleansing breaths.

Just the night before, Father had regaled me with stories from his past, laughing and boasting of the victories he'd won, the enemies he'd defeated. I shake my head as I approach him now. I'd laughed with him, taken a vicarious thrill from his tales, marveled at the strength he seemed to keep summoning to go forward, the sparkle still shining in his emerald-green eyes. Now a dead carcass lies in his place, green scales turning opaque, those bright eyes turned milky and glazed.

I sit on the floor next to his bedding and stare at his remains. I envy humans and their ritual approach to death. If this were a human household, I could wail and gnash my teeth, busy myself calling priests and ambulances, friends and relatives. There would be a funeral to be planned, food and refreshments to order for the well-wishers and afterward, meetings with attorneys and accountants to see what could be salvaged from the estate.

If only, I think, I could busy myself with these things. But

there's no priest for me to turn to, no ritual I can embrace—
even Father's estate has long since been transferred to my
name, his death faked years before and recorded then by our
family's attorneys.

After dark, at least, I'll be able to carry Father's body to
the island where my mother's buried and keep my promise
to lay him down beside his beloved. Until then there's nothing to do but wait and surrender to the pain.

Dark comes late this time of year and I spend the day
wandering the grounds and the veranda, hating the bright
light of day, the white sails billowing far off at sea, the gulls
soaring in the sky, rupturing the quiet of the day with their
raucous caws.

I throw off my clothes as soon as night falls, change
shape in the dark shadows near the walls of the house. Truly
my father's son now, I spread my wings to the evening air
and leap into the sky.

The rushing air embraces me and I flex the great muscles
on my back, push huge quantities of air with each beat of my
wings. Ordinarily the mere act of flying fills me with joy,
but tonight sorrow and anger consume me. Higher, faster, I
spiral over my island. I want—I need to feed, to taste life as
it drains away, and I want to taste it soon. I have no patience
for caution this night. I descend in a long gentle curve as I
search the surrounding waters for prey.

A lone fisherman, foolish enough to anchor his thirteen-
foot Boston Whaler on the ocean side of Sand Key catches
my attention. He shifts his weight with each passing swell,
trying to maintain his balance as he casts his rod, even as I
wheel in the air above him, unseen.

I fold my wings tight to my body and drop, gathering
speed with every foot of my descent, reveling in the roar of
the air rushing around me. Just before I crash into the sea, I
snap my wings out, struggle to keep them extended as I bat-

tle the air to stop my fall, the momentum of my dive jetting me forward now, gliding low enough to feel the waves brush my underbelly, my taloned claws unclenched, ready to grab, to rip, to tear.

He sees me at the last moment—a dark apparition rushing toward him, out of the blackness of the night—and freezes. Good, I think, I want him to see the coming of his death.

A single beat of my wings raises me into position and I strike, my rear talons digging into flesh, jerking my prey from the boat as I glide past. The fisherman is so shocked, he still grasps his rod, the line trailing behind us as I soar skyward.

Other nights I would regret the death of an innocent being, but tonight I feel no guilt, extend no pity. I climb into the sky and, on a whim, release my prey. He screams, finally dropping his rod, flailing the air with his legs and arms as he falls. Laughing, ravenous, I strike him in midair, open his midsection with one stroke of one claw, grab him with another, holding him and feeding even before his life fades away. I consume him entirely in flight, discarding what little remains of him miles out, over the Gulfstream.

Fighting the languor that always comes after feeding, I fly home to gather up my father and carry him to his wife's side.

The island has changed little since Father and I last visited it. Stones, grass and weeds, a few clumps of scrub brush and even fewer scrawny pine trees are all that break the monotony of its sandy existence.

Clutching Father beneath me, I have to fly over the entire length and width of the island four times before I find the pile of stones we placed to mark Mother's grave. It's on the highest point of land—a wind-built dune on the northern quadrant of the island, barely twelve feet higher than the beach.

I land there, gently place Father down and survey Mother's resting place. Grass and weeds have overgrown any sign that a grave had been dug there. Only the stones, carefully piled to mark the grave, remain as testimony to our grief.

A few of them have fallen and I place them back, on top of the pile, and sit and try to remember my mother.

Funny, I think, when I realize all my images of her are of her human shape. I try to remember her in her natural state . . . but nothing comes. Even when we found Mother on this island, she had changed her shape back to human before she died, bleeding and gasping in the sand.

"She wanted to be human," Father told me. *"She preferred to live in that form."*

I wish now she hadn't. Our people keep no paintings, no photographs of ourselves in our natural forms and I have nowhere to turn, to know exactly what one of our women looks like.

Father had laughed at me when I told him of this worry.

"Peter," he said. *"Trust your blood. You'll recognize her as soon as you see her. And believe me"*—he chuckled—*"you'll know just what to do."*

I hope so. My sigh seems louder to me than the ocean sounds filling the island air. Mother had insisted on me being schooled with humans, just as she was, and what did it get me? I'm not even sure how to pursue one of my own women.

I dig the grave without tools, using my strong rear legs and clawed feet to shovel the earth. Then I lay Father's carcass at the bottom of the hole and cover him with dirt. I say no words, sing no prayers. What is buried below is a deserted carcass, skin and bones.

My father once ruled kingdoms. He defeated whole armies singlehandedly. For over a century he commanded a pirate fleet that terrorized the Caribbean. I shake my head at the disturbed soil I've pushed over him, the final resting place of Don Henri DelaSangre, and hope his spirit's gone elsewhere.

Afterward I search for rocks and build a marker for him, just a little higher than my mother's. Then I sit at the foot of their graves, stare at the stone piles, the surrounding land and the restless sea beyond it. Far north, on the horizon, the sky glows faintly from the lights on Bimini Island. Otherwise, there's no sign of man anywhere in sight.

A good thing, I decide. A good place for them both to be buried. Don Henri's last kingdom is perhaps his smallest, but his to rule over in perpetuity.

6

With Father gone, I'm left with no company but the wind, the waves and the island's roving pack of dogs. I go days without eating, wandering from empty room to empty room. The solitude torments me, disrupts my sleep. Father said she wouldn't come to term again until July and I wonder if I can wait that long.

Just to have voices and noises in the house I turn on the television in my room and let it play twenty-four hours a day. I do the same with the FM stereo radio in the great room on the third floor. But rather than allow it to comfort me, I ignore the cacophony and stare into the shadows for hours.

I take to inspecting each room of the house each day, dusting furniture, refolding linens. When nothing's left to be done, I turn my attention to the closets, sobbing when I open the door to Father's and find his and Mother's musty and mildewed clothes. It takes days for me to carry all of it to the third floor and burn it in the open hearth.

More days pass and I finally take myself outside, working for the first time in years in Mother's garden, removing weeds, pruning growth, admiring the exotic herbs she planted—the yellow-green flowers of the Dragon's Tear plant, the deep purple shade of the Death's Rose. If I can't find the girl, I think, I can always crush the purple petals of the rose and brew a tea from it. Father told me the death that comes from it is very peaceful.

The sun's rays and the ocean breezes seem to have a salutary effect on me and, after a day's work outside, my stomach reminds me how long it's been since I've eaten. I've no desire to change shape and fly off on a hunt but, thanks to the dog pack and their constant production of litters, there's always more than enough live meat on the island.

I smile for the first time since Father's death as I stalk the pack, laugh when I single out my prey, a dark brown male which cowers, then runs while the rest of the pack still faces me and growls. It takes only minutes to bring him down. Afterward, I leave his remains for the pack and return to the house to lie down, rest and sleep the first true sleep I've had in weeks.

The morning news wakes me and I'm surprised to realize the month of May has passed. I sit up at once, painfully aware that July will come in a few, short weeks. I have no more time to waste.

Jamaica and Haiti lie too far to the south for a simple evening's flight. I refuse to sit still, waiting until her scent surprises me and only then traveling toward it. I can't risk losing her.

Fortunately, Father kept the maps and charts from his pirate days. As I study the old parchment rolls, I immediately dismiss the possibility her scent might have traveled from an island as far away as Curaçao. She most likely comes from either Haiti or Jamaica.

I weigh the speed of air travel—man's, not mine—against the convenience of boating. Commercial flight will force me to stay in hotels, limit my ability to come and go without notice, change shape as I wish. Anchored offshore in my own boat, I'll be almost as free as on my island.

Logically, I think, I have to start traveling toward her before she comes into heat again. With Father gone, I feel free to leave the island. It will be the first time in my life I don't sleep in my own bed and part of me can't wait to rush away. I realize now that Father gave me a present when he chose to die. For the first time in my life, nothing, no one, holds me to this place.

In the morning, I grin as I steer the Grady White across the bay, anticipating the reaction I'll receive from my attorney and his associate. I haven't called for an appointment nor would I. Jeremy Tindall and Arturo Gomez owe their fortunes and their lives to the beneficence of my family. They will see me when I want and do what I say.

In the Monroe building's lobby, the security guard eyes my sneakers and shorts, sunglasses and tank top. I ignore him. The man's obviously new and unfamiliar with my irregular comings and goings. He tenses when I approach the private elevator to LaMar Associates' penthouse offices, rests his right hand on his polished, black leather holster. I smile at him, let his discomfort build for a few moments, then show him my key before I insert it in the elevator switch's lock.

"Mr. DelaSangre!" Emily, the receptionist, greets me as I exit the elevator. Her eyes don't meet mine and her thin lips struggle to hold her smile. Ordinarily, I appear every Friday afternoon, to check my mail, see if anything's needed from me. This time, five weeks have passed since my last visit.

"Mr. Gomez has been taking your mail," she almost whispers, fluttering her hands, fidgeting with the papers on her desk. "I hope that's okay with you. He, Mr. Gomez, told me you wouldn't mind. It was okay for him to go through it. He said he had your permission."

Her smile broadens when I shrug, and say, "He does."

Emboldened, she stares directly at me, speaks up, "Also, a Mr. Santos has been calling for you . . . a lot. I finally referred him to Mr. Tindall. You might want to ask him about it."

"Santos?" I search my memory, shrug again. "Did he say what he wanted?"

"Only that he was looking for his sister."

"His sister?" I say, remembering now the picture of the girl and her brother in Maria's wallet, wondering how he found me. I hadn't even known the girl's last name. "How the hell did he get my office number?"

The receptionist blanches. "Did I do something wrong? Mr. Tindall said it . . . everything was okay."

"Everything's fine, Emily," I say, though knowing what he'll suggest, I dread hearing what Jeremy has to say. I wish Maria's fool brother had never called. I have little desire to bring any more death into Maria's family, even less to waste much time thinking of them. The girl's death belongs to my past. Today I'd far rather dwell on my future.

"I'll be in my office," I say. "Let Arturo know I want to see him there."

Of all humans, I trust Arturo most. He's the only human I've taught the bends and twists of my island's channel, the only one allowed to visit and leave unharmed.

His ancestor, Xavier Gomez, sailed with Father when he left Spain centuries ago. Xavier's sons and grandsons served on Don Henri's pirate ships. They were the only members of his crew to survive his employ. *"Some dogs will do anything for their masters, no matter how badly they're used,"* Father told me. *"As long as they're fed well. When you find a beast like that, you keep it and use it."*

Gomez's offspring settled on the mainland, not too far from our island, and it became a tradition that one son from each generation worked for our family. At first they just cut wood for us, hauled heavy loads. But as Miami grew, they became useful for other, darker pursuits.

"Peter!" Arturo enters my office, strides across the plush carpet to where I stand by the window, staring out at the bay and the wide sea beyond it. The smell of his Aramis cologne overwhelms me as he grasps my hand, pumps it in greeting, a broad smile on his square, clean-shaven, well-tanned face. "Glad to see you finally decided to grace us with your presence."

I disengage as soon as I can, back up—as much to escape the thick aroma that surrounds him as to put a little more space between us. He continues to grin at me, watches as I fidget with the few pieces of mail on my empty, mahogany desk. In turn, I study his silk tie, the way his custom-made, thousand-dollar suit hugs his thick body, the easy confidence of his movements—as if he owns all that surrounds him.

He knows that he merely runs the company I own. But still, he's far more at home here than I.

"Arturo," I say, "I plan to go away for a while. I need you to watch the island, feed the dogs."

His face clouds up, his barrel chest swells and I know he yearns to tell me of his importance. He's the president of the largest, richest company in the state. Besides massive investments in land developments, banks, office buildings, import and export businesses, resort hotels and banks, we own large shares of every newspaper and television station in the region. Their executives fawn over him, make sure, as he requests, that their editors never allow any stories on my family or our island. How can I expect someone who wields such power to be a house sitter and a caretaker to a pack of dogs?

"You're the only one I can trust," I say. "You're the only one who knows how to navigate the channel. Jeremy will watch after things here. You can live on your boat in my harbor, leave food on the dock for the dogs."

"I thought you were worried about Jeremy," Arturo says. "Remember, you were the one who called and asked me to check up on him."

"And?" I ask.

Gomez shrugs. "So far I only have suspicions. But you know, without me here, Jeremy will rob you blind."

"I know he may try."

The Spaniard shakes his head. "No, he *will* try."

"And if he does, so what?" I ask. "We'll find him out as we have before, take back what is mine and punish him."

"Sometimes I think you underestimate him," Arturo says.

"And sometimes I think you underestimate me too."

"Is that a threat?" I ask, locking eyes with him.

Arturo knows better than to challenge me. "No, just temperament," he says. He runs his manicured fingers through his graying hair, shrugs, grins a grin wide enough to show off all his newly capped, white teeth. "I could use a vacation, I guess. I can keep in touch with the office by cell phone. I already have an accountant secretly going over all the books. I'll have some of my other people watch Jeremy while I'm out." Arturo pauses, straightens his silk tie, grins even more. "How long did you say?"

Jeremy Tindall answers my summons and comes to my office after Arturo leaves. Where Gomez feigned pleasure to see me, Tindall's frown clearly shows he's annoyed to have his day disturbed. "Peter," he says, "you're holding me up from doing your business. I had to leave the mayor and two councilmen sitting in my office—"

"Let them wait," I say, glaring at the tall man—so thin and pale that he looks like a walking cadaver. "If they're unhappy, you can always send Arturo to them with a few more paper bags stuffed with money."

Tindall looks around the room as if he's worried someone's placed a wire. I smile at his show of concern, his never-ending paranoia. As my attorney, Jeremy handles all my legal activities, all my major purchases and sales. As my trusted retainer, Arturo takes care of my and the company's illicit needs, from money laundering and bribery to physical coercion.

Jeremy's perfectly comfortable with availing himself of Arturo's aid, his connections to South Florida's underworld. He uses him frequently to lubricate the process of business, to intimidate those who threaten our interests, but he despises the mention of it.

"We are what we are," Father used to say. *"And we are what we do. The Tindalls just don't like to admit it."*

Father had traveled to Washington as soon as the government took control of Florida from Spain. *"Under disguise, I wandered from lawyer's office to lawyer's office to lawyer's office, asking if the attorneys could help me circumvent the government's laws, bribe officials, help me conceal crimes. At those few offices that didn't ask me to leave, I escalated my requests, alluding to white slavery, even murder. Ethan Tindall was the only one who didn't even blink. He stated his price and I hired him. I told him to move to Florida, to make sure our land grants were honored and to handle our business interests after that."*

Jeremy's face flushes red. "So what's so important?"

The memory of cinnamon and musk comes up in my mind and I'm tempted to tell him about the girl and my need to find her. But no matter how much I want to talk about her with someone, anyone, I control my tongue. *"You can only trust the Tindalls to do what greed and fear dictate,"* Father taught me. *"In all dealings with them, you must remember to be cautious."*

It took Father only a few months to catch Ethan Tindall betraying him. *"The fool stole money from me,"* Father said. *"I was glad to catch him at it early in our relationship. When I confronted him, he, of course, denied it. I grabbed his left arm and bit his hand off at the wrist. I don't believe he ever cheated me again."*

"Your boat," I say to Jeremy. "I need to borrow it."

The man's face glows even redder. "My Grand Banks? You can't be serious."

I nod, not at all surprised by Jeremy's reluctance. Pictures of the forty-two-foot trawler crowd the walls of his office, outnumbering photographs of his family by a ratio of five to one.

"For Christ's sake, Peter, you can afford to buy one of your own."

"No," I say. "I don't have time for that. I want to leave in three days. Have the boat fueled and provisioned for a long cruise. Make sure the GPS is working. I'll need charts and coordinates for the Caribbean."

Jeremy clenches his jaw, and growls, "That's not what you pay me to do."

I ignore him. "Bill my account whatever you think is fair," I say. "I'll come to your house three nights from now. Have the Grand Banks ready."

He stares at the floor.

"Don't worry," I say. "I'll be coming by water—on my Grady White. You can use it while I'm gone."

Red-faced, curling his lip, Jeremy grumbles, "As if I'd be caught dead on a fishing boat."

Tired of his recalcitrance, I snap, "You forget, I *could* arrange that too, any time I want."

The attorney doesn't react to my threat. He says nothing. Neither do I. After years of experience with the man, I know what to expect after a confrontation. He'll change his demeanor, change the subject, act as if nothing has occurred.

After a few moments, his face returns to its usual funereal pallor. He looks up and grins a false smile at me. "Peter, do you know someone by the name of Santos . . . Jorge Santos?"

I frown at the sly slant of Tindall's smile, shake my head. "Emily mentioned his calls. She said you talked to him."

"He's a most insistent young man. Kept asking when

you'll be back, demanding an appointment to meet with you. He said there were some questions about his sister he needs to ask you. He said she's been missing."

Maria again. I hate the reminder. I sigh. "I don't have time for him now. Have Emily call him, tell him I'll be glad to meet with him shortly after I return to town."

"I don't care about the girl. I'm concerned that he's learned that you can be found at this number. You're sure you just don't want me to have Arturo take care of him?"

"I'm sure," I say.

Jeremy cocks his right eyebrow. I know my refusal to harm the man has piqued his curiosity, but I refuse to issue a death warrant just to quiet the man's curiosity. "At least let me ask Arturo to have research done on him," he says. "It wouldn't hurt to know more about this Mr. Santos before you see him."

I pause before I answer. Do I care what Tindall learns about Santos? He'll certainly read whatever report Arturo makes. Finally, I decide nothing harmful can come from it, shrug and say, "Okay, go ahead."

"Good," Jeremy says.

Something in the smugness of his tone annoys me, as if he thinks he's just gained the upper hand. I hate that I can never be sure that he will stay intimidated, despise the self-satisfied grin on his face. "Your car," I say, grinning at the effect I know my request will create.

"My what?"

"Your Mercedes. I need to borrow it for the rest of the day—to go shopping."

Jeremy's face goes red again. "You ever heard of taking a taxi? How am I supposed to get home?"

"You could wait until I bring it back, work late while you wait."

"You know I don't like to work late," he says, spitting out his words.

"Funny, I saw your Mercedes here late a few months ago. If you weren't working, what were you doing?" My eyes go to the missing, smallest digit of his left hand. Only a small stump remains as a reminder of what had once been there, a reminder of the consequences of straining my good will. Father had said every generation of Tindalls would have to learn anew the penalty for disloyalty and Jeremy had received his lesson from me years ago.

He blanches when he sees the direction of my glance, then unconsciously reaches with his right hand to cover the sight of his injury.

"I didn't say I never work late," he mutters. "I must have been behind on something." He reaches into his pocket, produces his keys. "Whenever you're done, just leave the keys with the guard up front. I'm sure Arturo will be glad to take me home."

The memory of Jeremy's expression stays with me, keeps me smiling the rest of the day as I wander through the endless corridors of South Miami's Dadeland Mall, shopping, buying new clothes, looking for a gift to bring her.

After browsing through half a dozen jewelry stores, enduring the self-impressed, haughty tones of their sales staffs—who deign to show me their collections of mediocre, overpriced baubles—I stop by Mayer's Jeweler's. Shaking my head at the display of emerald jewelry in the window, I grin at the piece I like best, a gold four-leaf clover, just like Maria's, with the same brilliant emerald inset in its center, dangling on a gold chain—on sale for four hundred and fifty dollars. Thinking it's foolish to look for anything more here when I can find the same piece, and other jewelry every bit as good, in the ancient chests stored in the depths of my island home, I turn to leave.

The bustle of people around me, the overheard snippets of conversation do much to counteract the emptiness I've felt since Father's death. I'm loathe to return to the loneliness of the island just yet. On the way back to the boat, I stop at Detardo's. It's time, I think, to treat myself to a good meal, allow myself to be surrounded by other beings a little while longer.

"It's been far too long, Mr. DelaSangre," Max Lieber greets me at the door. He fumbles through a stack of papers he keeps next to the menus. "One moment, sir, someone was asking for you not very long ago. . . ."

I arch an eyebrow, look around while he's searching his papers, notice a new poster, a photocopied leaflet really, tacked to the wall by the entrance. A grainy picture of Maria occupies its center. I turn away, stare at anything else.

Max picks up a torn piece of paper, brandishes it over his head. "Ah!" he says. "I knew I still had i. I don't know if you've heard but one of our waitresses, Maria—she waited on you last time you were in, I think . . . anyway, she seems to be missing." He shakes his head. "I told the young man, her brother, I doubted you even remembered her, but he was quite insistent. He said I should give you his number if you came in."

"Certainly," I say, looking as puzzled as I can. "I'm not sure what help I can be." I take it, glance at the number, note it's a local one, fold the paper and put it in my pocket.

"You have to understand, sir, the young man's frantic. He told me the police are no help at all. He's trying to talk to every person who had contact with her before she disappeared,"

"But she just served me a meal. . . ."

"She told him about a customer who dined alone, who had incredible green eyes. When he said that to me, I knew it had to be you she was describing. Maria complained to him that she gave you her number, but you never called. I think she had a crush on you, sir."

"Oh, yes, I think I remember her," I say, concentrating on looking calm, indifferent. "She was a sweet girl, way too young for me, wouldn't you think?"

"That's what I told Jorge."

"I'll be out of town for a while. If you see him again," I say, "let him know I'll see him when I get back."

Max nods, guides me to a table—without saying another word, as if to make up for the torrent of conversation he's just subjected me to—and motions for a waitress to serve me.

She's taller than Maria, thinner, but she smiles at me the same way the other girl did. I look away from her as I order. I want no flirting tonight, no repetition of what happened before.

The folded piece of paper remains an unwanted presence in my pocket. I recall my evening with Maria, and try to catalogue anything I did that could link me to her.

Thanks to Arturo's connections my cell phone calls are routed in such a way as to make them untraceable. Should anyone have seen the Chris Craft, the boat is gone and sunk at sea. And obviously she didn't tell anyone about our last-minute plans.

I sigh and force my mind toward more pleasant things. Only the thought of the girl I seek helps keep my mind from Maria. Still, I bolt down my food and rush out of the restaurant before any more memories can haunt me. I tear the paper to little pieces as soon as I reach the parking lot.

Slash and Scar greet my return, growling and barking in the dark as I let the boat coast to the dock. I find it reassuring to be welcomed by something alive, no matter how hostile, and make a mental note to throw some feed over the wall before I retire for the night.

Now that I know I'm going to leave it shortly, the island no longer seems such a lonely prison. I bring my packages up to my room, then wander out onto the veranda, let the sea breeze worry at me while I admire the summer sky, the silver glow of the moon's reflection stretched out over the water.

I breathe in deep and wish there was a hint of her on the air. But soon, I promise myself. "Soon," I say out loud.

Offshore, only a few boat lights dot the horizon—none shine near the island—and I'm seized by the impulse to do something silly to celebrate my imminent departure, something maybe a little reckless.

Father built the house with defense in mind, placing an arms storeroom on each of the building's four sides. I go to the storeroom on the veranda, between his room and mine. As usual I admire the ancient, massive, iron-sheaved, wooden crossbeam he designed and installed to block access through the room's large, oak door. Better than any modern lock or chain, the bar's set deep into the thick stone wall on either side of the door, with no apparent way of removing it.

I approach the door's right side, place my fingers on a narrow crack running between two large stones and sigh. While shifting from dragon to human form comes as naturally to me as changing shirts, shifting to other shapes requires far more effort. When I was young, Father used to make me practice thinning my limbs, flattening my form. I often complained, I didn't like how it felt.

"We never know what shape chance may require of us," Father always scolded. *"I've escaped from humans more than a few times because their intellect couldn't allow for my ability to squeeze through small spaces."*

Sucking in a breath, I concentrate on reducing the width of my hand and forearm, my cells almost aflame in protest at their compression, my upper arm swollen from backed-up fluids. Gritting my teeth, I push in through the crack, fumble my way until half my forearm is inside the stone and my newly thinned hand reaches open space. I feel for the release lever to the catch, touch it, lose it and find it again. It clicks open as soon as I tug on it.

That done, I withdraw my hand, let it regain its shape. Breathing out, I wonder once again whether I should replace the mechanism with a simpler, key-operated device. But I know as long as Father's device is in place, I'll never need to worry that anyone else can gain access to this room.

I grasp the crossbeam in both hands, slide it to the right— a move only permitted by the catch's release—until another click signals a counterweight has been engaged. Letting go, stepping back, I watch as the crossbeam pivots up, out of the way.

As soon as I throw open the room's door, the dank air within escapes, surrounding me with the burnt sulfur smell of discharged gunpowder intermixed with the odors of rotting wood and mildewed canvas. I recoil from it, stare into the dark room, try to decipher what lurks in the shadows and regret I've never wired the storeroom for electricity and lights. Well aware of the barrels of gunpowder Father kept stored here, I feel around for a torch and, once found, light it outside, on the veranda.

In the torch's wavering, yellow-orange light, I can make out the rusting swords and armor stored on sagging wooden shelves, the ancient pistols and rifles hanging on the walls, the three black cannons pushed back into the interior of the room, surrounded by stacks of cannonballs and sealed lead canisters filled with gunpowder.

It takes over a half hour for me to pull and push one of the cannons out of the room, load it and shove it into place at one of the gun ports cut into the coral parapet. Sweating, smiling, I say, "Father, this is for you," and lower a flaming torch to the touch hole.

A burst of smoke clouds up from the hole and, for a moment, when the cannon doesn't instantly fire, I wonder if the powder's gone bad or if I've done something wrong.

Flame leaps from the cannon's barrel with a roar that pierces the air and seems to reverberate long after it's gone. Far out at sea, a thin white plume of water erupts as the ball strikes.

I laugh and whoop from the sound and sight of it, then feel foolish to have done such a thing. But as I search the water for nearby boat lights, I can't help but grin, knowing that even if the cannon blasts were reported, my family's influence and Arturo's dispensation of cash and favors ensure that the marine patrol will avoid investigating my island no matter what.

When I close up the storeroom, I make sure to leave the cannon outside, in its place, to make it easier to use the next time.

Before sleep, I go down to the treasure room in the bowels of the house and sort through the chests, looking for a gift to bring with me. Even though I put it aside at first, I keep coming back to the delicate gold chain and the gold four-leaf clover attached to it, a small emerald inset in its center.

Finally deciding to ignore its previous ownership, I put it in my pocket and retire for the evening.

Sleep eludes me. I toss and turn, try to focus my mind on the voyage ahead, the woman I seek. Jorge Santos, Maria's brother, keeps intruding into my thoughts. It makes me uneasy to leave Miami, knowing nothing will be resolved with him until I return.

Father, if he were alive, would be annoyed by my softhearted decision to let the Cuban live. He always insisted that I be wary of humans, whether they number one or a hundred. *"They're weak but treacherous,"* he taught. *"To underestimate their power is as bad as arming them. Always be vigilant. Remember, it's always better to eliminate a problem than deal with it later."*

But the man is only a human, as weak and powerless as any of the others. Try as I might I can't imagine any way this one man can do me any harm. Finally I push him from my mind, concentrate on breathing in time to the surge of the waves as they rush at my island's shore.

Fading off, I picture myself gliding through a cinnamon-scented sky, spiraling in slow ascent toward the distant shape of my future love.

7

Three nights later, Jeremy Tindall meets me at the dock behind his twelve-bedroom stucco home in exclusive Gables Estates.

He wrings his hands as I carry my bags to the Grand Banks and fling them onto the boat's polished teak decks. "I wish you would at least take my captain along with you," he says. "It's a big boat for one man."

I shrug. "Don't worry, Jeremy," I say. "Worst thing happens, the boat sinks and I die. If that occurs"—I glance at the house behind him, the surrounding multimillion-dollar estates—"I'm sure you'll be able to afford another boat."

He grimaces, follows me onto the boat, wipes the brass rails where I've touched them. He also insists on reviewing every system on board.

Halfway through, I groan. "By the time we finish all this, the night will be over."

"I'd rather you were leaving in daylight anyway," Jeremy says, motioning for me to follow him below decks and inspect the provisions with him.

In spite of him, I'm under way before eleven. I raise the boat's steady sail as soon as I turn into the channel out of Gables Estates, start grinning when the trawler reaches the Biscayne Channel and begins to motor past the few stilt homes whose owners have been able to withstand the constant storms and the government's attempts at confiscation and demolition.

The ocean swells start to affect the boat and I listen to the drone of the twin diesel engines, adjust my stance to the boat's movement, the dance it's begun with the sea—the roll and tilt, pitch and rise as we pass through each swell.

After the last marker, I turn the wheel south, set the auto-pilot for Key West and allow myself the luxury of going below deck to lie down and rest in Jeremy Tindall's bed. I think of the anguished expression on his face as I pulled away from his dock and smile as I slip, naked, between his very expensive sheets.

A storm overtakes the boat sometime shortly before dawn. The change in the ship's movements, from gentle rolling to pitching and slamming from wave to wave, awakens me. I rush to the bridge, without bothering to dress, take the trawler off autopilot and turn the wheel so the Grand Banks slices through the roughened seas more easily.

I remain at the wheel until the sun rises and the storm fades away. When the sea calms, I reset the autopilot, check my position and study the charts. Originally my intent had been to cruise to Key West, stop there for a few days then head toward the Cayman Islands. But now, studying the maps, I can't shake the desire to get closer to her, as soon as I can.

From the Caymans, Jamaica lies a few hundred miles to the southeast, Haiti another few hundred miles beyond. I have weeks to wait before she comes into term again. I know, even cruising as slow as the trawler does—eight to ten miles per hour—Cayman sits only days away. I reset the coordinates on the autopilot, to bypass Key West, and wonder how I'm going to fill the days and pass the nights.

I go about the boat, opening windows, letting the ocean air wash through the innards of the trawler, hoping the salt smell will lessen the odors of wood polish and Brasso that seem to emanate from the carefully shined surfaces of the cabin.

Something about being alone, off on a journey to find a woman of my blood, begins to work on me and I find myself loathe to get dressed, reluctant to eat anything but fresh meat. I spend hours watching the water, daydreaming about the woman.

As soon as dark comes, I change shape and take to the air. I calculate that Key West now lies behind me but not so far that the waters aren't crowded with pleasure boaters out for an evening's cruise.

Time hardly seems to be an issue so I fly wide, lazy circles around the Grand Banks, admiring the lines of the craft, the way it cuts the water. I memorize the dark shadow shape of it, the placement of its lights, the throbbing rhythm of its engines before I leave it and fly off to hunt.

All my appetites seem increased to me now. Hungry, I search the horizon, hoping to spot easy prey—the shadow of a raft bearing Cuban escapees or the lumbering form of a hand-built wooden Haitian freighter smuggling illegal aliens. I fly high into the sky, sniff at the air, hoping, but knowing it's too soon to catch her scent. I roar from frustration, fold my wings and plummet toward the sea—spreading my wings again at the last moment, cheating death, laughing as I catch the air beneath me and skim above the cresting waves.

The white glow of a mast light, twenty miles in front of my ship, catches my attention. The nearness of fresh prey makes my stomach growl. Saliva fills my mouth. Unwilling to fly any farther to find food, I glide toward it, circle the sailboat from above, study it, and decide on my angle of attack.

A lone man handles the helm, sitting on the stern of the left hull of the ship, his right hand resting casually on top of a gleaming aluminum wheel. The sailboat, a catamaran, has another wheel just like it on the stern of its right hull. From above, the wide boat with its white genoa and white mainsail puffed out, filled with wind, looks like a low-flying cloud gliding over the water.

I hate the thought of disturbing the gentle scene below, and think of Father's admonition to avoid attacking the rich, but my empty stomach aches. The man stands up, as if to go below, and I strike, landing on the boat, pinning him below me as I bite through his neck.

The impact of my landing rocks the catamaran, raises the bow slightly and the now unheld wheel spins, turning the ship into the wind. The sails go slack, then shift and slap and crack before the breeze. I ignore the change in the sailboat's momentum, concentrate on feeding.

"Honey?" A woman's voice calls from below deck. "Jim, is everything all right?"

Hunger has me and I ignore her calls, continue to gorge myself.

She shrieks and I look up from my meal. Frozen in the cabin hatch, her mouth open, her eyes wide, she stares at me while I examine her. Only a short-cropped T-shirt and a pair of bikini panties cover her and I feel my loins stir as I study the curves of her—her body running slightly to fat but still enticing.

She shrieks again, and ducks into the cabin. I resist the urge to assume my human form, to follow her below and take her. I shake my head. I will not do that—ever. I'm a hunter, not a rapist. It's one thing to kill in order to eat and quite another to terrorize a woman for a moment's sexual gratification. I have no desire to inflict any further distress on this woman. I will only do what I must.

But I know there must be a radio below. And I can't risk a distress call being heard. I force myself from my kill, half leap, half fly to the top of the mast and rip the antennae from its mount. Biting through the wire, I toss the now useless instrument into the sea.

Back on deck, I return to my dead prey, ignore the woman's shouts as she tries in vain to reach someone, anyone on her radio. Soon enough, I know, something must be done about her. I can't leave her or her boat for anyone to find. Father has taught me well that the careless hunter can easily become the hunted.

The woman makes it easier by rushing back on deck and pointing a stainless-steel, twelve-gauge, pump shotgun at me. She screams as she fires round after round, almost at point-blank range. The pellets bounce off my scales and I stifle an indulgent grin, wait until the gun's emptied, then leap toward her and end her terror.

Her fat laced meat tastes better than the male's and I sate myself on her carcass, throwing the remains of both overboard when I'm finished. Before I leave, I open the sailboat's seacocks, shake my head at the necessity of having to sink such a fine craft.

I find the Grand Banks before dawn, go below and sleep most of the next day away.

The pattern of my life concerns me as I sleep through each day, hunt each night on the way to Cayman. I never dress, never sit down to the ship's table to eat, never take the ship's wheel unless it's absolutely necessary. Instead, I wander the deck, watch the waves and think of her. Hunger and lust fill my waking hours. To avoid alarming the authorities, I alternate my attacks, one night sweeping away a Bahamian as he walks alone along the shore on Bimini, feeding another night on a Cuban farmer in the fields neighboring Guantanamo—avoiding any more luxury craft but gorging on rafts full of Cuban escapees, plucking men and women at will from the decks of Haitian smuggling boats.

My hunger seems to grow each night. I realize if I continue at this pace that I will eventually put myself at risk, yet I do nothing to modify my behavior.

The memory of cinnamon and musk, the promise of a mate of my own kind overpower any thoughts of caution. The closer I come to her, the more my loins ache, the more sleep eludes me, the more I need to take to the air. Only the night and the hunting its darkness allows provide any relief. Then, at least, while I search for prey I can forget my need for her. Then I can lose myself in the kill. Then, after I gorge myself on fresh meat and blood, I can finally sleep.

When the low island of Grand Cayman finally rises on the horizon, I consider mooring in its busy harbor, but then decide to bypass it for the lesser island of Cayman Brac. Anchoring in an almost deserted cove, I resolve to go no further until I meet the girl.

I continue the pattern of sleeping through the day, hunting after dark. Some nights I see how far I can roam, trying to fly a wide arc between Jamaica and Haiti, attempting always to catch her scent.

Days pass, evenings go by. I sleep. I fly. I hunt. I search. And I sleep again.

When July first comes and goes without any sign of her, I worry that I may have miscalculated. Maybe, I think, I should have concentrated on Curaçao. Maybe I should have waited in Miami.

A storm front comes through and for three horrible days I pace, caged in the cabin of my small ship, my mind filled only with thoughts of her.

The weather clears the next day and I take to the sky the moment the sun sets. The air rushes around me, rain-cleansed, fresh. I allow myself to hope again as I fly far to the south and curve north, then sweep back again.

Nothing.

I gain altitude and repeat the sweep once more. Toward the southern end of the arc something tickles my nostrils—

a hint of an aroma, a possibility of cinnamon. I spiral in the air, breathe in, over and over again.

Nothing once more.

Widening the spiral, I circle down to the water, then rise back into the sky. A whiff of cinnamon and musk attacks my nostrils. Surprised, I roar into the evening air, roar again when I lose track of the scent. I reverse the path of the spiral, desperately sniffing the air, searching, hoping.

My nostrils flare when her scent hits me. Unbearably strong, its effect courses through me the way a drug must affect an addict. My heart races as I continue to follow its trail, my loins ache with want for her. I speed forward into the dark night air, her aroma growing more intense as I fly nearer.

The lights of a city pass underneath me and I realize I've reached land. Jamaica, I think; the time hasn't been long enough to reach Haiti.

Shortly after that the land goes dark below me, barely a light glowing anywhere in sight, only the stars and a half moon to light the countryside.

By now I'm mad with lust, lacking any care or caution, any thought of anything but finding this female, this temptress, and taking her, having her, using her until I'm spent.

The aroma intensifies. I wonder if I can endure it.

Something passes in the air, over and behind me and a delightful sound of laughter, a noise like silver bells ringing, fills my mind.

"Where are you?" I mindspeak.

"Look down," she says, her thoughts touching me, smooth and cool as velvet against skin.

I look below and see a dark shadow skim over the equally dark landscape. Suddenly the shadow turns and the pale, cream-colored underbody of her shows in the moonlight.

My breath escapes me. I realize she's flying upside down

to display herself to me and the pleasure of it is almost unbearable. *"You like?"* she asks. The pealing of silver bells fills my mind again and I fold my wings, plummet toward her.

She turns and swoops out of my way, flies between two hills, then another two—each one a dark mound jutting from the ground, looking like a half-buried giant egg. I follow and she drops out of sight. I descend until the treetops scrape my underbelly, follow her course without catching sight of her. Only her scent remains.

"Where are you?" I call as I regain altitude and spiral in search of her. *"Where are you?"*

No answer. No laughter. Only the sky scented with her aroma. I continue my search, strain my eyes to see into the irregular shadows of the terrain below me, unaware of any other presence nearby.

Something hard, heavy, hits me from above, five thousand feet in the air, wrapping around me, folding my wings. Stunned by the impact, I struggle to regain the use of my wings. I can't understand what holds them in place, why they won't unfold. Frustrated, desperate, I twist and turn and roar as I fall, trying to break free.

A deep roar answers mine and I freeze, finally recognizing my attacker as one of my own kind, his body above me, his wings wrapped over mine, riding me as we plunge toward earth.

"Why?" I ask him.

"For her," he mindspeaks.

"But you're going to die too."

He laughs, tightens his grip as the air whistles past us. *"I think not,"* he says, holding me a few more long moments, then releasing me. He darts away as I struggle to spread my wings.

I just begin to catch the air when the first tree top crashes into me, knocks the breath from my lungs. I gasp for air, curl my body tight, to protect myself as much as possible as I hurtle toward the ground, and put my mind elsewhere—concentrate on the sound of her laughter, the silver bells ringing in my mind and think of the memory of the pale, white flash of her underbody against the black star-studded background of the evening sky.

8

I cry out as I thud into the earth, roar in surprise when it cracks open beneath me like a breaking eggshell, and drops me into a shallow, subterranean pool of water twenty-six feet below.

The silver-bell pealing of her laughter fills my mind and I stare up through the jagged hole my fall just created, at the moonlit sky above. The pale flash of her underbelly passes by a few hundred feet overhead. *"You're in Cockpit Country,"* she says. *"Here the ground is not always as solid as you think."*

"Good thing," I say. Water sloshes around me as I flex my wings, move my arms, my legs and tail. Everything hurts but nothing seems broken. Relieved, I stretch, breathe large gulps of air, will my heart to beat faster, focus internally on speeding oxygenated blood to my injured parts so the cells can draw on its nourishment as they mend. After the first, almost-painful twinge of healing begins, I give way to the rage building within me.

"Who's your friend?" I demand.

"He's a stranger like you. I think he's nearby, waiting for you to take to the sky again."

"Lucky me," I say, still stretching and mending my body parts. *"At least tell me your name."*

"Maybe later," she says, laughing, the sound of it deeper this time, somehow promising to me.

"Later, after what?"

"You'll see." She laughs again—deep rich tones that resonate in my mind as she flies away.

Another shape, darker, larger, flies over the hole. *"Are you finished hiding yet? Are you ready to come out and face your death?"* he asks.

I stand, water dripping from my body. My jaw clenched, I hold back a roar. I am a thinking being, I tell myself, a creature of reason. I force myself not to take to the sky, and ask instead, *"Who are you to appoint yourself my executioner?"*

He flies lower, so I can see the size of him, larger than me, his wingspread reaching at least five feet more. *"I use the name Emil Sang,"* he says, *"If it matters to you."*

"I'm Peter DelaSangre."

"I feel better," he says. *"Now I know who I'm killing."*

"But why?" I ask. *"There are so few of us."*

"There will be even less of us if one of us doesn't get the girl."

"So let's tell her to choose."

"Are you sure you're of the blood?" He laughs. *"None of our women would accept a male who wouldn't fight for her. How can you smell her and turn your back?"*

I nod, think of Father's words. *"Sometimes,"* he told me, *"I think your mother ruined you with too much human nonsense. You have to learn to follow your instincts."*

My nostrils flare and I allow her aroma to work on me. Cinnamon and musk envelope me, fill me, own my soul. If I must kill for the girl, then so be it. I leap into the air, shoot out the hole with a single beat of my wings. Roar my challenge as I regain the sky.

"Surprise won't be so easy again, my friend," I say, circling in the air, looking for the approach of a moving, flying shadow.

"Do you always talk so much?" he says, flying toward me, his talons extended.

We collide in midair and fall together—a whirling jumble of flapping wings, slashing claws, whipping tails. I gasp as he sinks a talon into my right wing, ripping a long gash in its thin membrane. I strike in turn at him, my claw cutting a deep red wound down the length of his neck. The air fills with the sweet, thick aroma of our blood, resounds with the din of our roars.

He disengages, wheels away, dives. I plunge after him, catching his tail, sinking my teeth into its soft meat. His roar changes pitch, almost to a scream, and he pummels my head and neck with his rear claws—slashing skin, tearing muscle, cutting tendons. The pain sears through me, but still I hold on, my jaws clamped tight.

Finally he manages to graze my right eye with one of his talons, ripping the flesh just below it. Partly blinded, I bellow, release him and dive away. With injuries of his own to tend to, Sang wheels off in another direction. Once we've attained some distance from each other, I spread my wings, stopping my fall, then soar upward, wincing at the pain of my injured wing, my eye, my many cuts and bruises.

I concentrate on controlling my blood flow and cell growth, clearing my vision, mending my other wounds. I glide in wide spirals as I heal, husbanding my strength, preparing myself for his next attack. But then the thought occurs—why should I have to wait for him?

I strain my wings as much as possible as I beat skyward, gain altitude until the air becomes hard to breathe, thin beneath my wings.

Far below me, Emil Sang circles, calling, *"Peter! Where are you? Are you hiding from me again?"* I hold back a roar, fold my wings, plummet toward him.

I hit him with the force of a ten-thousand-foot fall. The impact stuns both of us, but I hold my position above him as we drop, pin his wings against his body, sink my teeth into the back of his neck, penetrating his thick scales until I taste his hot blood.

He struggles beneath me, but I only hold him tighter, bite him deeper.

"You know it will take more than your miserable bite to kill me," he says.

"I know," I answer as we speed toward the ground. *"But I think the fall should do it."*

Sang laughs, tries once more to break free. *"And you think you can let go of me in time to save yourself?"*

"No." I drive my claws and teeth even more into his flesh. *"I only hope your body will shield mine from the impact."*

He roars in rage just before we hit.

The deep tone of her laughter is the first thing I notice when I regain consciousness.

"Is he dead?" she asks.

"I thought you said the ground isn't always as solid as it seems."

"Sometimes it is," she says.

I groan, roll off his inert body, force myself to my feet. Sang doesn't move. I kick him and still he lies motionless. *"I think he's dead,"* I say, examining his face, his lifeless eyes—sniffing by his nostrils for any sign of breathing, smelling only the fresh odor of blood seeping from his wounds.

"Did you kill him for me?" she coos, flying close by overhead, cinnamon and musk overpowering me.

Her question irritates me almost as much as the pride I feel welling up within me. I want to say how shameful it is that one of our fellow creatures had to die, but I strut around his body instead, breathe in the scent of her. *"Of course,"* I say.

"Oh." She passes so near the wind from her wings washes over me. *"May I join you?"*

I circle my fallen foe, puff out my chest, spread my wings and roar into the evening sky.

"May I join you?" she asks again.

The scent of cinnamon and musk intensifies and I breathe it in, my heart racing, pounding. This is a time for instinct, I know, not rational, scientific thought. *"Of course you may."*

She lands beside me, approaches until her side touches mine.

"What's your name?" I ask.

She presses against me. *"Aren't you hungry?"* she asks.

The question surprises me. After all my efforts, the long flight, the struggle with Emil Sang, I know I should be ravenous. Only my lust for her has held my hunger in check.

"You want to hunt right now?" I ask, hoping that isn't what she's implying.

"Why hunt when there's a fresh kill right underneath our noses?" She walks forward to my dead foe. *"Besides,"* she says, *"you owe him the honor."*

I regret anew that my parents, especially my father, neglected to teach me so much. *"Women teach traditions, men live them,"* Father said whenever I questioned him. *"It's your mother's fault, wasting all her time teaching you human nonsense. I've taught you what you need to know. You can damn well learn the rest by yourself."*

"Honor?" I mindpseak.

"Yes, honor. You owe him that," the female says.

Hunger finally strikes me. *"Who am I,"* I say, *"to deny him his due?"*

"May I?" she asks.

I nod and she slices Sang's carcass open with a single slash of her talons. Then she tears loose a piece of his flesh with her mouth and offers it to me. Our lips touch as I take it from her and, for a moment, I consider bypassing the meal entirely. Instead, I concentrate on dampening my lust, eating the meat she's so kindly offered. Only after I finish it and begin to eat more, does she start to feed herself.

We feast side by side, no words, no thoughts, our faces touching, our mouths wet with his blood, our lips brushing by each other's as we bite and tear.

My lust builds even more as my hunger abates and I find it difficult to ignore her presence beside me. My breathing turns ragged, my eating slows. She too slows the pace of her feeding. Her breaths also grow louder, more rapid. I press against her, nuzzle her neck and she shivers, stops eating entirely and backs away.

"Where are you going?" I ask.

"You'll find out." She spreads her wings and takes to the air—the deep full tones of her laughter resonating inside my mind.

The sight of her pale-cream underbody flying over me, her womanhood swollen and exposed, makes me suck in a breath before I leap into the air myself.

"Catch me if you can!" she mindspeaks and wheels out of sight.

I hear her laughter, smell her scent all around me, but the irregular terrain, the half-egg-shaped hills, the deep crevasses and ravines in between them give her hundreds of places to hide. I roar in frustration and she calls out, *"Can't you find me?"*

Finally, I catch sight of her entering a deep, long ravine. I swoop in after her, strain to catch her. As I close, I marvel at the beauty, the delicate lines of a female of my kind, thinner, less broad than me, her length four feet shorter than mine, her wingspan six feet less. I wish it were daylight so I could examine her more fully, enjoy the delicate colors of her scales, the flashing brilliance of her emerald-green eyes.

She laughs just as I near her tail, then swerves and shoots skyward, beating her wings as fast and hard as she can.

I laugh too, follow and overtake her, soaring above her, close enough to prevent any further escape.

When she sees her position, she no longer tries to evade me. *"My name's Elizabeth,"* she says, coming closer, turning so she flies upside down, her underbelly almost touching mine.

"And mine is Peter."

I soar slightly lower, let my body brush hers and, when we touch, we both say, *"Oh!"*

We separate for a moment. *"I liked that,"* she says.

Flying closer to her, I know nothing but unbridled lust, insatiable need. I bump against her again, grab, hold and join her in midair, thrust myself inside her.

Sighs explode from both of us and we fold our wings against each other. I ride her, thrust in sympathy with the violent contortions of her body as we plunge toward the earth.

We break free of each other a scant two hundred feet over the trees, spread our wings and soar back into the sky, going higher this time, so we can stay coupled longer the next time we join. Elizabeth and I repeat this three more times. Then, *"Follow me!"* she calls and leads me, aching, wanting, on a twisting journey through ravines and hills until she lights on the lip of a cave, halfway up a hill overlooking a wide valley.

I land behind her, follow her inside the cave to a bed made from branches and soft leaves.

She says nothing, lies on the bed in front of me, watching me, her sweet underbelly exposed.

"I've waited a long time for this," I say, thinking how fortunate I am. I take in her scent, the sweetness of her breath, the rich odor of her body, like the fresh, earthy smell of a forest floor. *"I've come a long way to find you."*

"I'm glad you did, Peter. . . ."

I approach her on all fours. The smell of cinnamon and musk, blended with the thick, wet aroma of her excitement, envelopes me and I breathe it in, every part of my body aflame, aroused.

She lets out a low moan, almost a growl, barely moves as I rush forward, pin her beneath me.

I thrust into her and gasp at the hot, wet hold her body takes of me.

Roaring, thrusting and twisting beneath me, she clamps her teeth on my throat—just below my jaw—rakes my back with her claws, opening and closing her wings, wrapping her tail around mine, pulling when I retreat, pushing when I return, her breath coming in loud gasps.

I bellow and ignore the pain of her bite, her scratches, as I continue to pin her beneath me. When she pulls her head back and opens her mouth to bite me again, I meet her mouth with mine, lock my teeth against hers, breathe her hot breath as she breathes mine—our bodies entwined, entangled, woven together as tightly as a mariner's knot.

When I can't hold back anymore, I pull my head back and roar into the cool night air. Elizabeth bellows, gyrates beneath me and we push each other toward orgasm, writhing, roaring, losing all capacity for thought or control until, at last, our bodies are overwhelmed by a frenzy of wracking, almost painful spasms followed by unbelievable relief.

Afterward we lie apart, let the night air cool us, Elizabeth and I stroking each other with our tails. *"Peter?"* she asks. *"Was it what you expected?"*

I laugh, say, *"More."*

"Good," she says, moving closer.

"Was it what you expected?" I ask.

She pauses before answering and for the first time in my life I worry about a female's reaction to my performance. With human women I always knew I was good and rarely cared. But Elizabeth is oh so different. *"I think it was,"* she says and then laughs at my frown.

"No, it was good . . . wonderful really." Elizabeth hugs me, strokes me. *"But you've had human women before, haven't you?"*

I nod. *"None of them were anything like you."*

"I like hearing that," she purrs. *"But that means you had something to compare it to. I didn't. I only knew what Mum told me and, believe me, she left quite a bit out."* Elizabeth giggles and I laugh with her.

She snuggles against me. *"Peter, really, I'm delighted. . . . I'm thrilled to be with you. I think we'll make each other very happy."*

I say nothing more, but silently thank the fates and Father for my finding her. Content for the first time in my memory, I hold her, listening to her breathing slow, feeling her body grow warmer against me as she falls off into sleep.

A cold wind blows into the cave and Elizabeth shivers and pushes closer to me. I embrace her, pull her toward me, then extend my wings and fold them over us, forming a warm cocoon for us both.

She sighs in her sleep and I grin, slowing my breathing to match hers, giving myself up to sleep just as willingly as, I realize, I've given myself up to her.

9

A flock of green parakeets, screeching and cackling in the trees outside the cave, wake me the next morning. The cool morning air surprises me when I open my wings, then fold them back. Beneath me, Elizabeth mutters, curls herself into a ball and sleeps on. I smile, nuzzle her gently, then get up and stretch.

I can't think of any part of my body that doesn't ache and that's just fine with me. Never in all my couplings with human women have I ever found one with even a hint of Elizabeth's passion. I walk to the mouth of the cave, stare at the mist blanketing the green treetops in the valley, marvel at the way we made love the night before.

All around the valley and beyond, other egg-top-shaped hills jut from the ground. In places where the mist has cleared, I can make out the deep holes in the ground, the ravines and sinkholes in between the hills—everything covered in thick, lush, green vegetation.

Cockpit Country, Elizabeth said. I wonder how she came to it. We've yet to tell each other anything about ourselves and I can't wait to learn about her.

If we were human, I think, this would have been a one-night stand and both of us would wake embarrassed and anxious to leave each other's presence. But somehow, I know with certainty that the sleeping female within this cave now belongs to me, as I do to her—for life.

Elizabeth awakens an hour later to find me sitting near her, admiring her in the light of the morning sun.

"Peter, you'll make me blush," she says as I continue to stare at her, marveling at how much more beautiful I find her than human women—the soft light green of her scales, the delicate arch of her back where it curves to her tail, the delightful, cream color of her underbody, flushed pink around her sex.

"I just think you're lovely."

She laughs—the deep, rich tones of a woman who's sure of herself—turns and displays herself to me. *"Is this what you find so lovely, Peter?"*

I shake my head, start to tell her I find so much more about her that's lovely, but my body betrays me.

"You poor dear," she says, drawing me toward her with her tail. *"Your mind says one thing"*—she touches me between my rear legs—*"and* this *says something entirely different."*

Afterward, we drift back to sleep. Elizabeth wakens me an hour later, pulling and pushing my body. *"I'm hungry,"* she says, *"Come hunting with me."*

"In the daytime? Isn't that too dangerous?"

She laughs, pulls me toward the cave's mouth. *"You forget, this is Cockpit Country. We don't have any roads here, barely any trails. Anyone who travels through has to contend with hill after hill—cliffs and ravines, lakes and rivers, caves and sinkholes, rocks so sharp they can slice through flesh, ground that collapses under foot, underbrush so thick no one can cut through it without a saw. Except for an occasional hunter, some old Maroons and a smattering of ganja farmers, most Jamaicans avoid this area and none of the others dare come this far."*

I follow her out into the morning air, dive with her toward the remaining morning mist and skim through it alongside her. The cool moisture of it counteracts the sun's hot rays beating on me from above and I whoop from the pleasure of it, spiral and dive and zoom skyward, laughing.

Elizabeth lags below me. *"You'll never find prey up there,"* she says.

"I've never flown in daylight before." I swoop down beside her and let out a roar of pleasure. *"I've never felt so free!"*

"Quiet!" She drops lower, her eyes fixed on the terrain passing below.

An almost-perfect circle of water glistens a short distance in front of us and she says, *"Stay here,"* then contracts her wings and dives toward a small clearing on the edge of the lake.

I circle overhead as she crashes into the underbrush at the edge of the clearing, listen to the squeals of the wild boar she pins with her talons, watch the bushes jerk and sway from their struggle. In a few moments all grows calm. *"Come, Peter,"* she calls. *"There's plenty for both of us."*

For some reason the image of a television-sitcom mother, calling her family to breakfast, crosses my mind. I grin at the incongruity of it as I land and help Elizabeth drag the big boar into the clearing.

"Not as good as human meat," she says serving me the first taste of her kill. *"But we'd have to travel to the outskirts, near Accompong or Quick Step, where their farms and ganja fields are . . . and that's best done at night."*

We feed, side by side again, neither speaking, Elizabeth saving special parts for me, rubbing herself against me as we eat. Afterward, she runs toward the lake, leaps into the water and dives out of sight. I follow, dive after her.

When I surface, she's nowhere in view. I swim farther out and dive again. Still I find no sign of her.

I surface again. "Peter!" A voice calls from the shore.

Surprised to hear my name spoken out loud, I stop and turn in the direction of the voice, then gasp at what I see.

A young, naked woman, shorter than I would have expected, her mocha skin still wet and glistening from the lake's water, waves at me from the sandy beach.

I swim toward her, dive and change shape underwater just before shore.

"I thought you might like to see my human shape," Elizabeth says as I approach her. She stares at me, her emerald-green eyes seeming to examine me from head to foot, and her voice goes deep and throaty. "I certainly wanted to see yours."

Her accent surprises me. She looks like a light-skinned Jamaican woman and I expect to hear an island lilt to her words. Instead, her pronunciation is clipped and terse, like upper-class English enunciation.

Droplets of moisture shimmer in the short, dark curls that cover her head. She grins as I inspect her, turns and models so I can take in each delicious aspect, each curve of her thin, lithe form.

"Do you like?" she asks, cupping her small, brown, rounded breasts in her two hands, her dark nipples hard and thick—either from the chill of the wind or the excitement, I hope, building within her. "I could make them larger if you want."

I shake my head, displace her hands with mine, kiss her full, soft lips then pull her warm, wet body close to me, enjoying the disparity in our height, the top of her head nestled under my chin. I lean down a little, whisper, "Do *you* like?" into one of her small, perfectly formed ears as I press myself against her.

Elizabeth nods, wrapping her arms around my neck, pulling me down with her, onto the sunbaked sand.

In human form, I have no need to rely on instinct. I know just what to do and I concentrate on showing her a more gentle way to make love—stroking, touching and teasing each part of her, teaching her to do the same.

* * *

Later, lying in the sand, her head resting on my right arm, one of her legs across mine, she says, "So that's how they do it."

I laugh, gaze toward the sky, watch a pair of black crows fly overhead and say, "Do you think we'll ever stop long enough to have time to just talk—get to know each other?"

She runs a hand over my chest, and speaks softly, "We have time now."

"For starters, how old are you?" I ask.

Elizabeth pulls away a little, makes a small pout with her lips. "You should know that, my just coming into term, your being my first, my only—"

"Bear with me, Elizabeth," I say, sitting up, reaching for her, touching her protruding lower lip with one finger. "My parents sent me to school with humans. I even graduated from the University of Miami. But it seems they neglected to teach me very much about my own people."

"I never went to school. Pa says it would be silly to bother with such things. My mum taught me everything I need to know—how to hunt to feed my family, which herbs to grow and how to use them, how to brew Dragon's Tear wine, even how to read and write a little."

She pauses and looks away from me. "I'll be eighteen in three months. Mum says I came to term earlier than most."

I nod. "My father said you'd probably be young   "

"Is that bad?" Elizabeth frowns, looks down at the sand. "You're supposed to want to be with me from now on."

"Of course I do." I pull her toward me, hug her, kiss her lips, her nose, her cheeks, her forehead. "The question is, do you want to be with someone as old as me?"

She pulls back, and looks at me. "And how old is that?"

"Fifty-seven," I tell her and she laughs.

"That's not very old. My father was a hundred and ten when he finally found my mother. My brother Derek's ten years older than you right now and he hasn't found one of our women yet." She grins. "He'll be as envious of you as my little sister will be of me."

"So you want to be with me?" I ask.

"Of course." She grins as if she thinks me slightly confused. "Is there any other choice?"

The flippant way she talks about us injures my pride. "You don't have to come with me," I snap. "You could wait for someone else to come to be your mate."

"You *are* my mate. You fought for me and took me." Elizabeth shakes her head at me. "Why would I wait for anyone else when your child is already growing inside me?"

10

Elizabeth insists we circle north before we fly back to the cave. *"I want you to see Morgan's Hole, where I grew up,"* she says. She points out a formation of eight hilltops, slightly taller than all the rest in sight. *"That's almost in the middle of Cockpit Country."*

We soar over the egg-shaped hills and look down upon yet another valley, larger than most but still irregular in its vegetation-choked green terrain. *"Why would anyone want to live here?"* I ask.

"You told me your father chose an island to live on, for easy defense. My grandfather, Captain Jack Blood, chose to go inland for the same reason. The valley's almost impenetrable. They call it Morgan's Hole because the old reprobate granted it to my family when he was lieutenant governor.

"My father says the English were so glad to have someone willing to live in an area terrorized by the escaped slaves, the Maroons, they hardly asked for a pound in payment. The Maroons, of course, soon learned to keep their distance from us."

I follow Elizabeth as she flies lower. To me, one hill looks like the other, each valley seems a repetition of the one before. I marvel she can find her way. Without her, I'm sure I'd never find our cave again.

"There!" she says, and I look in the direction of her gaze.

In the far corner of the valley, after a series of cultivated fields, set into the side of a hill, almost hidden by an overhang, obscured by two immense, silk cotton trees growing in front of it, a stone house, similar, but larger than the one my father built, looks out over the valley.

"Are we going to visit your family now?" I ask.

"Oh . . . no . . . not yet," she says, changing course, flying higher.

"But shouldn't they know about us?"

"They already do."

Of course, I think. I should have realized my family wasn't the only one who could mindspeak over long distances. *"And?"* I ask.

"Mum is so excited. . . . She's already planning for the feast."

Once again, I feel as if I've arrived in a completely foreign culture. *"Feast?"*

"Of course," she says. *"That's when you'll meet my family—in a few days, when everything's prepared. You'll like them. Pa can be a little fearsome, but I know he'll like you."* She laughs. *"After all, what choice does he have now?"*

She clears a hill by only a few feet, drops into the next valley beyond and I follow close behind, thinking, this is my child bride, my life companion. Amazingly, she's soon to be the mother of my child. I want all these things, accept them completely, but they've come so fast. For a moment, I envy humans with their dating rituals and courtship, their endless confusion between love and lust, their constant conflict between desire and security.

With us it's almost too simple. Sex and procreation. She becomes fertile, gives off her scent and I have to have her. I have her, she conceives and she's mine. No shy glances across a room, no sharing of histories, not even any conversation.

Neither Elizabeth nor I have uttered the word "love." I wonder how she would react if I did. Had another male arrived before me, or killed me in combat—she would be flying alongside him now with equal devotion.

Part of me wishes she were with me for more reasons than that I was the first to service her. But another part revels in the knowledge—now, no other male of the blood can approach her and hope to win her over, not as long as I live.

In our cave, Elizabeth and I curl up on our bed of branches and leaves. *"I made it as soon as I came in heat,"* she says. *"I'd already found the cave before . . . the last time."*

"I smelled your scent then—all the way up in Miami."

"I cried when no one came. Mum said not to worry, someone was bound to find me eventually."

As the afternoon sun settles and the day begins its slow journey into night, I tell her about my boat ride south and my quest for her.

"Peter, I'm so glad you're the one who found me," she says before we drift into sleep.

I awake, cold and alone, stare out into the darkness beyond the cave. Without such human things as watches or clocks, I have no way of knowing how long I've slept.

"Elizabeth!" I mindspeak.

No reply comes and I get up and pace about the cave. *"Elizabeth, where are you?"*

Her reply comes from far off, faint and strained. *"I'm hunting. I'll return later. Go back to sleep."*

With no light, no book, no television set, I see no other choice. I sigh, settle back into the bed my bride made for me, for us, and think of the logistics of bringing the Grand Banks to Jamaica, worry about Elizabeth's family and the feast and carrying my bride back home . . . until sleep confuses my thoughts and steals me away.

A child's whimper wakes me. I sit up, stare around the cave, wait until my eyes adjust to the dim moonlit night.

The shadow I recognize as Elizabeth, stands near the mouth of the cave, facing me. Two much smaller shadows lie on the cave's floor in front of her. One moves a little and whimpers again.

"What a great night!" she says. *"I flew all the way to Maroon Town and found these two, all by themselves, walking on an old trail. . . . One for each of us. It's such luck, the first night I go hunting to feed my man."*

"Oh, Elizabeth," I say, shaking my head.

She misunderstands the intent of my words, lifts one of the children, a boy, not more than ten years old, kills him with a single slash of her talons, and lays him before me.

I stare at his still small form and sigh.

"Is something wrong?" she asks.

"I don't like to eat their young."

"I don't understand. They're just humans." Elizabeth goes to the other one, another boy, slashes him open too. *"If I'd known, I would have brought you an older one, but I'm hungry now, Peter. I can't eat until you do."*

"Why?" I ask.

She shrugs. *"It's our way."*

I force myself to feed, hating how much I relish the sweet taste of innocent flesh. What I leave, she finishes for me.

Later, she comes to me, lies beside me. *"Don't be mad at me, Peter,"* she says.

"You are what you are," I say to her.

"No, Peter, we are what we are."

True, I think. I wonder if she'll ever understand how I feel. *"You've grown up in one world,"* I say. *"I've grown up in two. Sometimes it's hard for me."*

Elizabeth snuggles closer, places her tail across mine, rubs me with it—slow, rhythmic strokes. *"Soon you can show me your other world. But,"* she says, *"remember, you're in my world now."*

I nod. *"But,"* I say, *"when we return to my world, you'll have to learn to be much more careful. Taking children is just too dangerous. Humans are peculiar. They ignore it when others abuse their own kids, but if one disappears, they go crazy looking for it. If they think a child's been killed, they search heaven and earth for the murderer. Even my father, who loved the taste of the young ones, indulged himself very occasionally."*

"They're just humans, weak and soft," Elizabeth says. *"My Pa never worries about any of them."*

"Maybe so," I say. *"However, there are millions of them and they have guns and cannons and bombs that even we can't withstand. Here it may be safe for you to be brazen. In Miami, it could cost us our lives."*

Frowning, she pulls away from me. *"You're just trying to scare me."*

How little of the world she knows, I think. I look at her, my young dragoness, remembering what she confessed just this afternoon—she's never finished a book, never seen a movie. *"I've never been allowed outside of Cockpit Country,"* she said. *"I've only seen the ocean from high in the air, looking out across the land. It's very blue, I think."*

There will be so much I can show her. Her naïveté strikes me as adorable. I reach toward her. *"Oh, Elizabeth,"* I say. *"I never want to scare you. I just don't want anything to ever harm you."*

Elizabeth graces me with a small smile, sidles back toward me, begins to stroke me again with her tail. I shift alongside her as my body surrenders to the sensuality of its movements. *"Again, Elizabeth?"* I ask. *"Aren't you afraid you'll grow tired of it?"*

She laughs and I smile at the silver-bell sound of it. *"After all, you're already pregnant and I haven't smelled your scent since the first time we joined. . . ."*

"Peter, there's so much you don't know! As far as your questions—yes . . . again. Why not? And no, I'm not afraid of growing tired of it. Mum says it's a gift our people have. One to be used as often as we want."

The room fills with the scent of cinnamon and musk. I roll back from her, face her, my nostrils flaring, my breathing growing rapid. *"Not fair!"* I bark.

"Isn't that what you wanted?" she asks, and laughs again. *"I had no choice before we met. I had to spread my scent. Now it's different. Our women can do that at will, anytime after their first mating. But only for our mates."*

She displays herself to me and I suck in a deep breath at the sight of her. *"Peter,"* she says. *"It doesn't matter that I'm pregnant. It will be eleven months until our child is born. You wouldn't want to spend all that time without me, would you?"*

I shake my head. *"I don't want to spend a day without you,"* I say, approaching her, breathing her scent, wishing the moments to come could be longer, even more intense.

Elizabeth sighs as I lay down beside her and entwine my tail with hers. *"Before we start, Peter, you have to know, this has to be our last time in the cave. I'm sorry. I should have told you sooner. My parents expect me home tomorrow—to help prepare for the feast. It would be good for you to leave after this—to return to your boat tonight, bring it back for me. Mum says my brother will meet you in Falmouth Harbor when you arrive."*

"No," I say, pulling back from her, looking toward the dark interior of the cave. *"How will he find me, know who I am? You come fly with me. We can both meet your brother."*

"He'll find you," she says, reaches for me, strokes my

back. *"You're going to have me for a lifetime, Peter. Surely you can share me for the next few days. . . ."*

I shake my head but allow her to pull me back, to lie down with her on our bed of branches and leaves, lose myself in the feel of her, breathe in the scent that overpowers me, give myself to the joy of belonging to someone who belongs to me.

11

We both leap from the cave's mouth, into the night at the same time. *"I hate to leave you just yet,"* Elizabeth says. She flies by my side for a few minutes longer, then sighs as she breaks away and soars across the valley. I lag behind until I lose all sight of her, climb higher and higher after that—Cockpit Country growing small and dark beneath me, my love hidden somewhere in its gloom.

The half moon stands out in the dark sky like half a gold coin laid down on black velvet. Its yellow glow illuminates the world below me, deepens and lengthens the shadows that rule Cockpit Country at night, follows me as I pass over the lights of Falmouth and Montego Bay, shimmers over the waves after I leave the land behind.

While Cockpit Country, with its crazy mélange of hills and valleys, confuses me, here at sea I know my way. I fold my wings, plummet almost to the ocean's surface, then spread them and glide just over the waves. The fresh salt smell fills my nostrils and I sigh and breathe it in, glad to be away from the heavy aromas of blooming plants and rotting vegetation.

A twinge of guilt strikes me and, for a moment, I wonder why I'm not stricken with grief to have had to leave Elizabeth behind. But it isn't her absence that fills me with joy.

This is far and away the greatest adventure in my life. Already I've crossed a good part of an ocean in my quest to find my love. I've found her, fought for her, killed for her and won her. To have stayed longer in Cockpit Country, hunting and sleeping and making love, would do nothing to bring the adventure closer to its conclusion.

Besides, I think, being far too aware of the protests my muscles make every time I flap my wings, the almost pleasant ache of my overused and congested loins—a few days' rest wouldn't be such a bad thing before I face my young bride again.

I reach the Grand Banks an hour before dawn, thank the fates when I see it riding safe and secure on its anchor line, just as I left it. In my absence, two other boats have anchored nearby, a sailboat and another trawler, and I'm glad to have the cover of the last few minutes of the night when I land on the boat's top deck, change shape, clamber down the steps and rush inside.

Fatigue tugs at me. I force myself to pull out the charts, look up the coordinates for Falmouth, program them into the GPS and the autopilot. My stomach growls and rumbles and I realize how much energy my travel and shape-changing have depleted. I almost sleepwalk as I turn dials, flip switches, cranking up the twin diesels, listening to them roar into life, then settle into a subdued growl. I throw on the generator, the air conditioning, and the once-silent craft now vibrates slightly from the hums and grumbles of its machinery.

The windlass groans as it reels in the anchor line. I stop by the freezer before I go forward to make sure everything's fast, take out a large sirloin and throw it in the microwave.

A man, woken no doubt by the noise of my activity, comes up onto the deck of the sailboat moored a few dozen yards away. As naked as I am, he watches as I secure the anchor on the bow pulpit, then turns his back and urinates over the side. An impulse strikes me to take him, substitute his fresh meat for the steak defrosting in the microwave, but I push the thought away.

I've had more than enough human flesh over the past few weeks. A simple uncomplicated steak strikes me as more of a treat right now.

He turns back and waves. I return the gesture, go inside to the galley, take the barely warm steak out and hold it in one hand, blood dripping on me and the deck as I carry it to the bridge, wolfing down chunks of it. One-handed, still eating, I put the motors in gear and guide the Grand Banks out to sea.

Later, after Cayman Brac has disappeared into the ocean behind me and blue water surrounds me on all sides, I activate the autopilot and head below to the dual luxuries of a hot shower and a soft, clean bed.

Lying under clean sheets, in that frustrating stage before sleep when weariness exists in so much excess that it denies rest, I wonder how Elizabeth will react to all of this.

She knows these things exist. She bragged to me, she saw much of it in the few border towns she was permitted to visit with her brother—the ramshackle buildings and homes in Troy and Warsop astounding to her because of their modern devices. But she's grown up in a home without any of it.

I grin, thinking of how wide her eyes will get when I bring her to the real world, how much there is to teach her, expose her to, feeling like Pygmalion.

Thinking of her makes me miss her and I picture her in my mind, the image shifting between her human shape and her natural one. I wish the boat would go faster, rush me back to Jamaica so I can endure the feast—whatever that may be—and start the long journey home.

Once there, I know, everything will be perfect. It has to be. Elizabeth will have anything she wants. I have the money and power to give it to her.

Just before I drift off, the boat rolling in its sea dance, the motors droning in the background, I remember something Father said . . . and I wish I didn't.

"Remember we once ruled the world," he told me. *"We only lost it because we assumed we would rule it forever. Beware smugness, Peter. Our people have no worse enemy."*

12

I love the way islands rise into view on the open water. My own island, Blood Key, lies out of sight of mainland Miami. Every time I leave Coconut Grove, I have to point the boat in the correct direction without any visual confirmation, the island only revealing itself to me as I travel across the bay, teasing me by first showing a few treetops as thin black smudges above the horizon—then slowly swelling up before me as I speed toward it.

Jamaica first shows itself as a dim glow on the horizon, late into the second night of my cruise. Though I know I may be too far offshore to reach her, I mindspeak, *"Elizabeth!"*

"Peter?" A different voice answers, faint but distinctly male.

I pause before I reply, wondering who, why—worried that something could have happened to her. *"Yes,"* I say.

"This is Derek, Elizabeth's brother. I'm to meet you when you arrive...."

"Is Elizabeth okay?"

"Oh," he says. *"Of course... I thought you knew she can't."*

"Can't what?"

"It's the damned tradition, you know. Bloody pain if you ask me. But Mum and Pa insist on the old ways. God knows I've argued with them. Told them a thing or two quite a few times—if you know what I mean—"

"Derek!" I interrupt, and sigh before I continue. *"What tradition are you talking about?"*

"Elizabeth thinks it's stupid too. She can't understand why you two can't talk or see each other until the feast. I told Pa, you'd already seen everything she has to offer, she's carrying your whelp after all, but he won't go against my mum." His chuckle reaches all the way from Jamaica. *"Not that I blame him."*

"Can you tell her I miss her?"

"Of course . . . She says she can't wait to be with you."

I grin when I hear that.

"Peter?" Derek says. *"How close are you?"*

"I'm not quite sure. I think I'll make it to Falmouth sometime tomorrow afternoon."

"Do me a favor, old man. Could you push on a bit more? Come in at Oyster Bay. You can put up at Sparkling Waters Marina. That way I don't have to drive into Falmouth. I'd rather avoid the place for a little while."

I shrug and say, *"Sure."*

"You'll like the marina better anyway. The water's quite remarkable at night, phosphorescent you know." He pauses but I don't have a sense he expects any comment from me. Rather, it seems, he's following his own train of thought. After a few more moments he continues. *"Good, that settles it! I'll meet you at the dock the morning after tomorrow. I'll tell Mum to expect us before dark."*

Footsteps wake me as Derek Blood strides onto the wooden dock and paces the length of the boat, once, then twice before he hails me. "Peter!" he says. "This *is* your craft, isn't it?"

"Yes!" I call out, sitting up in bed, reaching for a pair of shorts. "I'll be with you in a minute!"

"Fine-looking boat you've got. Wouldn't mind having

one like this myself. . . . No hurry, old man. I'll wait for you on deck."

I find him sitting on a seat on the flybridge, his sneakered feet propped up on the console. Dressed in a striped polo shirt and white shorts, he looks like he's on his way to tennis. Derek flashes a wide smile when he sees me, makes no effort to hide his scrutiny. "Elizabeth described you very well," he says, stands and offers his hand.

It's like shaking hands with a vise. He's at least three inches taller than I am, muscular enough to strain his clothes to the point of bursting. I match the strength of his grip, returning his open stare.

Had I not been expecting him, had I not seen his telltale emerald-green eyes, I'd never guess he's Elizabeth's brother. Blonde-haired, sharp-nosed and thin-lipped, his skin is too white, too untouched by any color, other than a slight red flush on his cheeks, to think him related to her in any possible way.

He sees the confusion on my face and laughs. "Wait till you meet the rest of the family. Elizabeth changed a few years ago, decided she likes looking like a native. Chloe, our younger sister, did the same thing, but chose to be even darker. Mum and Pa, my younger brother, Philip, and I still prefer to look the way our ancestors did."

We both have to squint in the bright early morning sun and Derek looks at his gold Rolex watch and shrugs. "Sorry about the time, old man. I just wanted to make sure we could make it back to Morgan's Hole before dark. Sometimes the roads can get quite dicey."

Derek waits while I go to the marina's office and call Miami. I manage to catch Jeremy Tindall at home, just before he leaves for the office.

"For Christ's sake, Peter," he says. "How much longer do you plan to keep using my damn boat? Is it okay? Where the hell have you taken it?"

"Hello, Jeremy. I'm fine. Just in case you're curious," I say.

"And the boat?"

"The Grand Banks is fine too, not a scratch. Jeremy, listen to me. I need you to arrange some things."

"Like?" he says.

"I'm in Jamaica and I'm getting married."

"To a Jamaican?"

"Sort of," I say. "I need papers for her, citizenship, legal ID, social security, driving license—the works. And a Florida marriage certificate for us too."

Jeremy snaps, "Arturo handles those things."

"Arturo's busy. You know how to arrange it too. Don't screw with me on this, Jeremy. Elizabeth's very important to me."

His voice softens. "Of course, Peter, I'll be glad to help."

He asks for the address of the marina and promises to express a packet of forms for Elizabeth and me to fill out.

"We'll need a current picture of her," he reminds me.

"Will do," I say.

"I think you need to know, your friend Santos is still calling. I had to talk to him again after he became abusive with Emily. He said he's tired of waiting for you. He demanded permission to visit your island. Of course, I told him it was impossible. If he tried we would press charges against him. . . ."

I sigh, wish the man would stop intruding into my life. "Tell him again, I'll see him when I get back. Tell Arturo—if Santos is stupid enough to go to the island—he has my permission to shoot him."

"Tell him yourself," Tindall says. "Arturo told me he wants you to call him on his cell phone. You tell him he can shoot the jerk. I hope Santos gives him the opportunity to do it."

"I hope he doesn't," I say. "I'd rather he just goes off, leaves me alone."

"I've talked to him and I have to say, there's not much chance of him going anywhere until he's sure there's no connection between you and his sister."

"Well, there is none."

"Santos is the one you have to convince, not me." Tindall chuckles. "I don't care what you did. I don't care what he thinks. The only thing I care about right now is my boat. . . ."

"Stop worrying, Jeremy. I'll be giving it back to you soon enough."

"And that would be when?" Tindall asks.

"In a few weeks," I say. "*If* you get all of Elizabeth's paperwork done quickly enough."

Arturo wastes no time on pleasantries. As soon as he hears my voice, he says, "Would you believe one of the accountants tripped him up?"

"Santos?" I ask.

"No, Tindall." Arturo laughs. "I can't believe he could be this stupid."

"And?"

"Jerry Sokowitz brought me the figures on Caribbean Charm, our import company, the one that sells paddle fans and lights to all the big hardware chains."

"Sure, I remember that one. It's been growing nicely. . . ."

"Not anymore. Starting in January, sales started to dive. They're off now over seventy percent. We're losing money hand over fist."

"What does the president say?"

"That's the thing. He quit in January, along with his top three salesmen. They took their customers with them."

"And Jeremy didn't do anything to stop them?"

Arturo laughs again. "Seeing that they went to work for an import company run by Tyler Tindall, his youngest son, I don't know why he would want to."

I sigh into the receiver. Excessive greed always confuses me. Jeremy Tindall already makes more money than most men dream of. Why would he risk diverting any of my business?

"What about Ian?" I ask, hoping somehow that Jeremy's older son, the man I'm grooming to eventually replace him, isn't involved.

"We've had Ian in D.C. at George Washington, taking a special course in tax law. The business is in Jeremy's wife's name and Tyler's. The way that family works, I think there's a good chance Ian knows nothing about it. If he did, they'd have to share with him."

"You know what to do," I say.

"I expect there will be an unexpected disaster," Arturo says. "I doubt the company will survive it."

"When the son is there."

"Of course . . . But you know Jeremy will be furious."

"What he should be is scared."

"I believe he will be that too," Arturo says, then listens as I tell him what to do if Santos dares to come to my island.

My mind's still on Tindall, on Maria and Jorge Santos, when Derek and I leave the marina and start our drive inland. I hope Arturo takes care of Jeremy's son before I return. I want there to be time for it all to sink into his consciousness, time for him to drop his anger and accept the fate he has brought upon himself.

As far as Santos, I thank the fates that I disposed of the Chris Craft already. I go over the events in my mind, make sure again that there's nothing left to link me to Maria.

Derek takes a cue from my silence and says nothing until we pass through the small coastal town of Rock and turn off the paved coastal highway onto a lesser road heading into the interior. His white Land Rover hardly slows on the new surface, handles the rising terrain and loose graveled road as if it were cruising a city street. "This is the easy part," he says.

I move with the bump and sway of the vehicle, watch the countryside, the occasional weather-beaten, unpainted, tin-roofed, wooden house or store—dogs and goats wandering nearby, rusted-out cars and washing machines in front or on the side.

Derek points out items of interest, a green-breasted doctor bird, the bright orange flowers of an enormous African Tulip tree. He's left the windows down and the air conditioning off, allowing the hot morning air to rush around us, surround us with the lush aromas of the foliage we pass.

Fortunately I've followed his lead and dressed in shorts and a polo shirt. With the day's heat building outside, I'm glad of it.

I hadn't been sure what other clothes to bring, for the evening, for the feast and, when questioned, Derek offered no help. "Wear whatever you want," he said, shrugging. "Feasting has nothing to do with how you dress."

Just in case, I've brought along a sports coat, a dress shirt and long pants. Though from Derek's indulgent grin when he saw me carrying them, I assume they won't be needed.

I adjust my shirt collar, pat the right pocket of my shorts, make sure the gold, four-leaf clover necklace I've brought for Elizabeth remains secure where I placed it. Derek continues narrating our journey and I wonder if he's unaware of my nervousness or just politely ignoring it.

Not that he's said a word to help me be at peace. "Derek?" I ask him. "What should I expect tonight, at the feast? I'd like to make sure I don't make a fool of myself."

He laughs, points ahead and says, "Almost to Clarks Town, get ready to turn—"

"About the feast," I say and, without slowing at all, he swerves the Land Rover to the right, onto a road perpendicular to ours. The momentum all but crushes me against the passenger door.

He guffaws as I regain my position. "You can't say, old man, I didn't warn you."

The new road, now before us, consists mostly of tire ruts and pot holes and we bump and lurch along it, slowing as the incline grows steeper and the trees and the bushes grow closer. When the car's motor starts to sound labored, Derek stops, throws the Land Rover into four-wheel drive and proceeds forward.

We break free of the greenery surrounding us and get a quick glimpse of the egg-top-shaped hills of Cockpit Country, the deep cupped holes surrounding them, before the green blanket of the countryside closes in on us again.

"Believe me," Derek says, "if I could, I'd tell you all about tonight. But Mum and Pa were quite explicit. They warned me, there's a tradition to be upheld and if I open my mouth about it . . . They think I talk too much anyway. If I tell you anything, they'll restrict me to Morgan's Hole for a year."

He looks at me. "And I wouldn't like that. You should understand. You're a man. You know what it's like to be without a woman of your kind. All we can do is turn to humans." Derek grins. "That's why I wanted to avoid Falmouth. I mucked up a bit with one of the local women, left a tad of a mess behind me. You know how you get hungry afterward and there's a live meal, ready for you, right in your arms . . ." He pauses and shrugs.

I look away, study the passing trees and bushes, ignore the drone of his words as he goes on about his weekly trips to the coast to find women, sounding more like the world's oldest teenager than a grown male of the blood. Why, I wonder, doesn't he go off on his own, try to find a woman of his own kind?

The greenery clears again and I absentmindedly look down at the ground alongside the road and gasp.

"Welcome to Cockpit Country," Derek says and guffaws. There's a sheer, five-hundred-foot drop just twelve inches from the left side of the Land Rover.

"The ground's all limestone out here," he explains. "Eroded and collapsed by centuries of rain—sinkholes and hills, caverns and caves—all of it camouflaged by trees, waist-high grass and bushes. Wait till we get to the bad road!" He brays laughter again.

My ears pop, the air grows cooler as we climb, our angle so steep at one point that most of what I see out of the front window is blue sky. Then we descend again. My ears pop once more and Derek says, "Barbecue Bottom." We pass a small group of wood shacks, some Jamaican men on the porches, their carefully tilled fields nearby.

They make a point of looking away from us. "Real friendly," I say.

"Don't take it personal, sport," Derek says. "You're with me and I'm not very well liked around this area."

"Oh?"

"These are superstitious people. They believe in all types of evil spirits and odd ghosts. They're most afraid of duppies, night spirits. They think such beings reside deep in Cockpit Country." He smiles. "It's well known around here, I come from that area. . . ."

"And people do disappear in the night around here, don't they?" I say.

Derek laughs, then says, "All the time."

A few miles farther, Derek stops the car, leans back and smiles at me. "Now the real journey begins."

I look around for any sign another road might exist, then

groan when Derek puts the Land Rover in gear and drives off the road and down the shallow sloped side of a bowl-shaped sinkhole. A canopy of green closes over us. Branches and tall grass slap the sides of the car.

"If you look carefully, you can see the footpath," Derek says, slaloming the car around trees, boulders, his eyes fixed before him, a grin stretched across his face. "The Maroons made it centuries ago. You should see me doing this in the dark."

No amount of staring enables me to see the path he's mentioned and pointed to. I shrug and decide I've no choice but to trust in his abilities.

At the bottom, we skirt around a small lake, then ascend the other side. I grow used to the constant climb and fall of our travel, the jolts and lurches we make as we traverse each successive valley, the sheer drops we just avoid every few miles, and I turn my mind back to Elizabeth.

"Why," I ask Derek, "can't Elizabeth and Chloe leave Cockpit Country? You certainly seem free to come and go as you please."

He shakes his head, downshifts and guides the Land Rover around another obstacle. "Elizabeth said you had an outstanding lack of knowledge about our ways. . . . With us, men are not at risk, women are."

"Elizabeth can certainly take care of herself. . . ."

"Not when she's in heat. Then she belongs to the first male who takes her. You should know that."

"I do," I say. "But what has that to do with leaving Cockpit Country, visiting the coast?"

"You saw how hard it was to find a female in heat. God knows, I've been waiting to find one too. Longer than you, I think . . . if Elizabeth's right about your age." Derek sighs. "And you were fortunate to have won the fight for her. So if you knew where an immature female was, wouldn't it be tempting to take her and hold her until she reaches her first oestrus—without any further search, without any risk or challenge—after which she'd be yours for life?"

I nod.

"In the old days such kidnappings were common. But no proud female wants a mate who wins her that way. No parents worth their name would want to see their young daughters taken before their time and matched for life with a male too impatient to wait for her, too lazy to search for her and too cowardly to fight for her.

"That's why we keep our young women close to home," he continues. "The men, they're another matter . . . no one worries about the men."

Derek states the last few words with such venom that I stare at him. "Why do you stay?" I say. "Why not leave Jamaica, search for a bride?"

"My father won't allow it." He barks out a laugh.

I look at the size of him. "How can he stop you?"

"He's killed two sons before me, for disobeying his wishes. Pa prefers that I deal with the outside world for him, bring back whatever riches I can find to add to his coffers."

He looks at me, as if he wants me to think well of his family. "Pa can be difficult, but he's fair. He's promised, I can leave when I pass one hundred. By then my brother will be old enough and experienced enough to take over."

We break out of the greenery once more, crossing a wide trail that Derek tells me leads from the Windsor Caves, six miles below us, to the town of Troy, four miles above. "Bloody damn tourists walk this trail all the time," he mutters, jams on the accelerator and speeds us past it.

Derek stops the Land Rover a few miles later, in a clearing, on a ledge overlooking a wide, deep sinkhole. "Ready to stretch your legs, old man?" he asks as he steps out.

I nod, throw open my door and get out, arch my back as I study the rugged terrain below and above us. "Certainly looks different when you're driving through it rather than flying over it."

"If we were flying, we'd have been home long before this," he says.

"How much longer going this way?"

He stares up at the sun, studies the hills around us. "We're about halfway." Derek goes to the car, releases the catches on a steel, six-gallon jerry jug, holds it in the air and pours water into his mouth. Afterward, he hands it to me.

As I do the same, he asks, "How was it? The scent . . . I mean, her scent, old man. What was it like? What did it do to you?"

A blush burns its way onto my face. "My god," I say. "I smelled it all the way up in Miami. You had to smell it yourself, here."

"You don't get it, old man." Derek shakes his head, goes about the task of replenishing the gas tank from some of the other jerry jugs the car carries. "Of course I smelled it. The air reeked of it. But it couldn't affect me. A family member's scent can't work on close relatives." He shakes his head again. "That would be insane. Didn't your parents teach you anything?"

Derek moans when I tell him about the aphrodisiacal qualities of the aroma, laughs as I describe how out of control it made me. "One day," he says as he gets back in the Land Rover, "I'll leave this bloody small island and find a woman of my own."

"I'm sure you will," I say, getting in too, knowing how hard that task will be, more grateful than ever to have found and won Elizabeth.

The shadows have lengthened, the sun has descended in the western sky by the time we finally come through the narrow pass that leads to Morgan's Hole. The Land Rover skids to a stop next to a small tower of stones piled by the side of the trail, about a half-mile from the house. A similar pile marks the trail only twelve feet ahead of us.

"What?" I ask.

Derek waves off my question, leans out the window and whistles a sharp loud blast. Then he drums on the steering wheel and waits until seven Jamaican men run up carrying long, thick wooden planks.

An older Jamaican, the obvious leader of the men, carefully studies both piles of stones, the placement of the car. Then he motions where the men should lay the planks down. At no time do any of them step any closer than the farthest pile of stones.

Derek watches them. Drives forward as soon as the men secure the planks. He stops just past the pile of stones, waits while the men retrieve the planks and trot off toward the house.

Close up I can see the ragged condition of their clothes, the steel rings around their necks, wrists and ankles.

"Slaves?" I ask.

He grins. "Why not?"

I am their guest, I think. Who am I to insist it's okay to eat them, but not to profit from their labor? I choose only to say, "Father said they're more trouble than they're worth, always plotting to revolt or run away."

"Come," Derek says. He gets out of the Land Rover, walks to the pile of stones behind it, waits until I join him.

"There's a narrow chasm that runs the width of the valley right here." Derek holds out his hand, motions for me to clasp it with mine. "Take a step forward," he says.

I do and the ground groans and crackles beneath me.

Derek yanks me back just before it collapses. "The ground's barely thicker than an eggshell here, with a thousand-foot drop beneath it." He tilts his head in the direction the Jamaicans took. "They know that. They know there are hundreds more pitfalls like this all around us."

He whistles a different note, lower, more challenging and somewhere in the distance behind us, the howls of a dog pack answer him. "They know the dogs are out there too." Derek nods. "They'll stay put. They always do."

We pass well-tended fields, pastures packed with cattle, sheep and goats, tidy rows of wood shacks for the workers, carefully maintained stables and paddocks for the family's horses.

Derek parks in the shade of one of the towering silk cottonwood trees, in the dirt drive in front of the house. Another Land Rover, a beige one, sits under another equally immense silk cottonwood on the other side of the drive. "My spare," he says, tilting his head toward the car.

He honks his horn three times to alert his family to our arrival, then steps out of the Land Rover.

I look at the wide stone steps leading up to their veranda, and realize that this house measures easily twice the size of mine.

"Come on, Peter, you lucky dog!" Derek says, motioning for me to follow him. "The family's waiting for you inside. It wouldn't do to keep Pa and Mum waiting too long you know, old man."

"Coming," I say, breathing deep, forcing myself to move, patting my pocket, making sure the necklace still remains in place, feeling foolish, like a schoolboy before his first date.

"I envy you," Derek says, putting his arm around my neck, whispering as if we had conspired to bring about this evening. "The feast, Peter! If only you had an inkling of what's in store for you."

He laughs at the confusion he sees in my eyes, and says, "Come old man! Pa and Mum grow far too impatient far too quickly."

13

Derek leads the way up the steps to the veranda, rushing in front of me so I have to half run to keep up with him. "I'm always glad to get home," he says over his shoulder. "Too many humans out there. Bloody fools. Things make more sense here."

On the veranda, he stops in front of two massive wooden doors, throws them open and motions for me to enter first. I pause, look into the dim interior, take a deep breath, smell the mustiness inside, try to quiet and slow the thumping of my heart. "Come on, old man." Derek smiles. "It's just my family in there. Chances are, you'll survive meeting them. They might even like you."

"Chances are," I repeat, walking forward, not at all sure of Derek's assessment.

Elizabeth's family stands at the foot of a wide spiral staircase, the room lit only by the diffuse light filtering down from the great room, three stories above, and a series of large, circular iron chandeliers, each one holding at least three dozen burning candles—each fixture hanging from long metal chains anchored to the ceiling's wooden rafters.

The Bloods stare at us as we enter. I stare back, try to adjust my eyes to the room's irregular illumination, the dim light and half-shadows that obscure the family's features and make their pale visages look almost ghostlike. Elizabeth's father, mother and little brother all mirror Derek's pasty complexion and sharp, thin-lipped features. Only Chloe's fine full lips, her rounded Jamaican features and the mahogany hue of her brown skin—contrasted with the white linen shift she wears—allow her to survive the pallor the wan light inflicts on the others.

Elizabeth's parents show no expression, make no movement, their youngest children frozen in place beside them—Chloe next to her mother, Philip alongside his father.

My smile seems fixed on my face. I wonder if I should look as solemn as they, wonder if I could.

Derek introduces us. "My father, Charles Blood," he says. "His wife, Samantha." Each one nods as Derek says their name. Chloe, alone, returns my smile.

Elizabeth's father, tall enough to tower over all of us, thicker than Derek, but not appearing much older, dressed in a black, three-piece, Victorian suit, tugs at the collar of his shirt, and fiddles with the buttons below it. "Bloody stupid thing to walk around weighed down with all this cloth," he announces, and turns to his wife. "Look at them. They're dressed for comfort."

Philip, hardly more than eight, but obviously his father's son, fidgets with his suit too, nods agreement with his father.

Equally formal in an elegant, flowing white gown and equally youthful in appearance, Samantha Blood puts her hand on her husband's arm and says, "Charles, you promised. . . ." She looks at me. "You'll have to excuse my husband. We rarely have company."

Charles Blood shakes his head, steps forward and extends his hand. "You needn't excuse me at all." He squeezes my hand, his grip tighter than Derek's. "You just have to endure me."

He locks eyes with me. For all the warmth that shows in his eyes, they could be true emeralds, cold and hard. I stare back without blinking, my hand held captive by his. "You're related to that old scoundrel, Captain Henry Angry?" he asks.

I'm well aware of the anglicization of my family name and like it no more than Father did. He told me, in the old days the English had called our island Angry Key just as they pronounced Caya Oeste as Key West—even though the Spanish words translated as Bone Key.

"Don Henri *DelaSangre* was my father," I say. "When he was alive, no one dared call him by any other name."

Charles barks out a laugh, slaps my back. "No offense intended, son. My father, Captain Jack Blood, sailed with him. The captain told me many stories. . . . Made me wish I'd been born in those times when our people could do as we wished."

Near us a Jamaican woman busies herself sweeping the stone floor. I glance at her iron collar and say, "It looks like you recreate the old times fairly well around here."

He nods. "Just because the British were fool enough to release their slaves doesn't mean we had to follow suit. Whatever goes on outside Cockpit Country, Morgan Hole is our land. We rule it as we desire."

"Now," Charles says, tightening his grip on my hand, a smile appearing on his face for the first time. "Tell me, Peter, just what did you bring for us?"

He frowns and releases my hand when he sees the blank look on my face. I glance back to Derek, hoping he will explain.

"Sorry, old man." He shrugs. "I thought you had a reason for coming without gifts."

"Gifts?" Wishing again my parents had educated me more on our traditions, I dig in my pocket, bringing out the gold necklace I've brought for Elizabeth and hold it in front of me.

"I brought this for your daughter," I say.

"A trinket?" Charles Blood's face turns bright red as he

stares at my outstretched hand. "You want me to exchange my oldest daughter for a bloody trinket? How dare you, sir!" He turns his back on me and starts to stomp away. Philip follows on his heels.

"Charles . . . for pity's sake, come back right now!" his wife says. She turns to me. "Please excuse my husband's temper. It sometimes gets ahead of his reason."

Elizabeth's father stops ten paces away, and glowers at us.

"Your daughter warned you he was brought up strangely," Samantha Blood says to him, as if I'm not in the room. "I'm sure if Peter had been aware of the custom, he would have brought an appropriate tribute."

For the first time in my life, I find myself empathizing with humans and their in-law problems. I'm tempted to tell them all just what they can do with their customs and their feast. Instead, I take a deep breath, think of Elizabeth and the life we can have on my island far away from these people. "If someone would tell me what the custom is, I'd be glad to try and work things out," I say.

When no one else speaks, Chloe throws an angry glance at her father, another at her mother, and says, "You're supposed to bring your bride's family gifts, expensive ones like gold and gems. I was taught, the more valuable your gifts are, the more obvious it's supposed to be—how much you care for your bride."

"Oh." I nod, picturing the chests of treasure crowding the underground vault at home, thinking how little of it I ever use. "I wouldn't want you to feel I didn't value your daughter," I say to Charles. "If I send you twice Elizabeth's weight in gold, once we return to my home, will that reassure you enough?"

"Righto!" Derek says. Chloe and her mother both beam at my answer.

Charles Blood grins, walks over to me, takes my hand

captive again. "My apologies, son. The anger sometimes gets the best of me. Bloody good gesture that. Your gift is going to go a long way toward replenishing the family's treasure." He frowns at his older son. "Derek could learn from you. All he ever brings home are baubles, cameras, watches and pocket change. I think he lacks the piratical spirit we and our fathers had. He's certainly taken out more gold than he's put in the last few years."

"Sorry about my father," Derek says later, as he guides me to my room. "He likes to muck things up a bit, see who he can scare and who he can't. Honestly"—Derek's voice lowers—"there are times he still can scare me. Wait till you see him in his natural state. He can be most fearsome."

He pauses outside my door. "Mum said to tell you, we're to meet just after sundown, in the great room on the third floor. She'll have one of the servants ring a bell when it's time. Wear your jacket. I think they expect you to."

I pace the floor after Derek leaves and wonder how to pass the next few hours. I feel as if I've gone back in time. Nothing adorns the room's unpainted stone walls. I doubt there's any television, radio, books or magazines in the whole house. What little furniture graces the room—an oversize bed and a chest of drawers next to it—are made of rough-hewn wood.

Two wall sconces holding candles and a candelabra on the chest give testimony to the house's lack of electricity. A pile of hay on the far side of the room looks just as tempting to me as the lumpy, horsehair mattress and worn linens on the bed.

A gust of wind blows a few leaves into the room and I realize the window has no glass, only wood shutters to hold off the outside world. I shake my head, wonder why Derek, at least, doesn't do something to bring his family into the modern world.

Someone knocks on the door and I open it to find an old Jamaican woman, her face averted, carrying a wash basin, a pitcher of hot water, some homemade soap and towels. I allow her to carry it all in, and place it on top of the chest.

After she leaves, I undress and bathe, using a wet towel, standing up next to my bed.

By now I've calmed enough to be aware of the sensations of the place, the dank and musty aroma that seems to permeate every inch of the room, the ongoing murmur of the servants, the distant sobs of captives, held in cells, deep under the house, the faint whiff of their unwashed bodies. I shudder, tell myself it's the chill of the air on my wet skin.

It is full dark outside by the time the bell rings. I listen to the gong reverberate, wait for the sound of doors thrown open and footsteps upon the stairs before I venture from my room. I've no intention of rushing up to the feast, looking like a nervous suitor once again. As far as I'm concerned, Charles Blood has already had as much fun with me as I'll permit.

The bell rings once more and I take measured steps as I ascend the stairs, candlelight flickering around me, shadows blending into the dark.

Another gong rings as I reach the third floor, and I blink at the bright light that fills the room, candles burning everywhere, a fire roaring in the massive hearth that takes up almost one full wall.

I stop and smile at the sight of Elizabeth, waiting alone in the center of the great room—the light glowing around her, shining through the form-fitting, almost gauze-thin, white cotton dress slipped over her body.

My eyes lock on hers and I walk to her, oblivious to the surroundings, ignoring her family gathered nearby. "You look beautiful," I say, taking the necklace out of my pocket and fastening it around her slender neck, breathing in the fresh, clean smell of her, wanting to take her away this instant.

She moves closer to me, fingers the gold, four-leaf clover charm with her right hand, examines it and a wide grin illuminates her face.

"Elizabeth!" Samantha Blood says and my bride's smile disappears.

I turn toward Samantha and glare at her. Elizabeth stares at the floor.

"Sorry, Peter," Samantha says. "There are customs that have to be observed. Bear with us."

"Elizabeth can't communicate with you until you're joined," she says. She motions to Derek, then points to the far corner of the room. I follow her gesture and, for the first time, notice the Jamaicans huddled together, men and women, adults and children, none of them chained, all of them calm and quiet.

Derek walks over to them, culls a young, heavyset man from the group and leads him back. The Jamaican has a few fresh, deep gouges on his face and right arm, but otherwise appears unharmed. His blank expression amazes me. If anything, he looks indifferent to everything around him.

"Dragon's Tear wine," Derek says. "A few drops of it and none of them care a bit about anything. It's most humane, old man. And God's nectar for us when we're in our natural state."

"Enough!" Samantha mindspeaks. *"Peter, do you want to have Elizabeth for your mate?"*

I nod.

She motions for Chloe to bring a large, white porcelain bowl and set it in front of Elizabeth. Then Samantha walks to a long oak banquet table against the wall, and brings back a tall, green ceramic pitcher. Pouring a clear liquid from it, she fills the bowl half full. *"This is Dragon's Tear wine,"* she says and carries the pitcher back to the table.

Samantha returns with each hand clasped shut. She opens her right hand to reveal a small purple rose. *"Do you know what this is, Peter?"*

"Yes," I say, out loud.

She frowns at me, and holds a finger to her lips.

"Yes, it's a Death's Rose. The petals are fatal," I mind-speak.

"They can be," Samantha says. She crumbles a petal into the bowl, mixes it with the Dragon's Tear wine. *"Are you willing to risk death to have Elizabeth as yours?"*

I look toward Elizabeth. She stares into my eyes and nods her head. *"I am,"* I say.

Samantha opens her left hand over the bowl and releases a handful of what looks like dust. *"They call it alchemist's powder. It should fight the poison."*

Derek puts his hands on my shoulders, guides me to stand facing Elizabeth. "It's time to change, old man," he whispers in my ear. "If you drink that stuff as a human it will kill you."

Chloe and Samantha take positions on either side of Elizabeth and begin to unbutton her dress. I take off my jacket, watch as they lift my bride's dress over her head, revealing the lack of underwear beneath. I breathe in at the sight of her naked, human body, tear the rest of my clothes off, drop them at my side. Behind me, I hear the rustle of clothes as Derek and his father and brother follow suit.

I look away as Chloe and Samantha undress, then worrying they'll think me even more peculiar for avoiding the sight of their human nudity, I turn my gaze back, taking in the pale white body of my mother-in-law—thin and muscular, perfectly taut, even her full breasts impervious to the aging effects of gravity. I study the adolescent form of Elizabeth's younger sister, Chloe—a darker, not yet filled-out copy of my bride.

Chloe giggles when she notices my scrutiny and a blush

heats my throat and cheeks. "We aren't human, Peter," Chloe says. "Nudity has no meaning here." She turns slowly, showing off all sides of her young, budding body. "See?"

"Chloe, stop teasing!" Samantha says.

Derek and Philip, both naked now, take places on either side of me. Chloe, fighting a grin, stands to the right of Elizabeth. Charles Blood, looking even more muscular in his nudity, places himself to the left side of the bowl, between Elizabeth and me; Samantha moves to the right.

Chloe waits until the last moment to undo Elizabeth's new necklace, taking it off my bride's slender neck and placing it carefully on top of her folded dress. Elizabeth stares into my eyes as I gaze into hers.

"It is time," Charles says.

Elizabeth begins her transformation—her skin tightening, outlines of scales appearing as her face elongates, her features sharpening and her body growing larger. I follow her lead, turning my thoughts inward, commanding my body, welcoming the almost pain of altered cells, groaning a low growl as I stretch my muscles, my bones, my skin—grateful to leave behind the awkwardness of my human shape, the shame that seems to come with its nudity—glad to embrace the strength and grandeur of my natural state.

All around me others grunt and growl as skin gives way to scales, as hands and feet grow claws, as wings sprout from backs. I realize, if I wasn't completely involved in the process surrounding me, I'd be amazed to be in the midst of so many of my kind—all different sizes, shapes, and ages, from Philip's small, immature frame to Charles's immense, overwhelming bulk.

My heart pounds as I wait for my next instruction. All my life I'd been warned to avoid the Death's Rose, cautioned to not even touch its petals. Now I know I have no choice but to trust that Samantha Blood knows what she's doing. I look

at Elizabeth, take in the brilliance of her eyes, the wide flare
of her nostrils, the cream color of her underbelly and think,
whatever is asked, I'll gladly do.

"Listen to me carefully, son," Charles Blood mindspeaks. *"In a few moments, you and Elizabeth will be offered the opportunity to drink from the bowl before you.
What you drink won't kill you, but it will change both of you
forever. It will bind you to each other in a way neither of you
have ever imagined. . . . Peter, knowing you have to do this,
do you still want Elizabeth?"*

I look into his cold, hard green eyes and nod. *"Of
course,"* I say.

Samantha says to her daughter, *"Elizabeth, knowing you
have to do this, do you still want Peter?"*

She tosses her head back, grins and says, *"Of course!"*

"Both of you please drink at the same time," Samantha
says. *"Make sure you finish it all."*

Elizabeth's jowl brushes the side of mine as we drink, the
clear liquid almost as tasteless as water, slightly bitter from
the Death's Rose and alchemist's powder. At first, I wonder
if all this is just tradition, like the sip of wine at a Jewish
wedding, but then a warmth starts spreading inside me and
a fog starts to settle over my thoughts.

My awareness centers on Elizabeth and me—as if we're
in the middle of a photograph with everything and everyone
else around us out of focus. Somehow I notice when we've
finished the last of the potion and I pull my head up as Elizabeth raises hers. We both stare into each other's eyes and
gasp.

*"Peter! I can see how I look to you—through your eyes!
It makes me dizzy."*

I laugh, staring at her, seeing my dragon face as she stares
at me. *"It makes me dizzy too."*

*"Oh Peter, can you hear every thought I have? What will
you think of me? Do you feel everything I feel too?"*

I nuzzle her and feel her sensation of being nuzzled at the same time. *"Yes . . . I feel what you feel . . . I think. But I only hear what you're thinking as you think it. I don't think I can read your memories. . . ."* I stroke her tail with mine, sigh at the double experience of it. *"Do you feel what I feel too?"*

She sighs, and says, *"Yes, Peter."*

Somewhere, from the haze surrounding us, Samantha Blood's thought penetrates my, our, consciousness. *"Peter? Elizabeth?"*

"Yes," we answer.

"Listen carefully. Death's Rose never completely leaves your system. After tonight, any more potion, just the slightest sip, will turn your blood to poison. Only the correct mixture of Angel Wort and alchemist's powder, taken the right amount of time before drinking the potion, can neutralize it. Otherwise death is certain. You must swear, unless one of you dies and the other remarries, you'll never take the risk of drinking any more potion, ever again."

Elizabeth and I both push away any thoughts of death or separation. We can hear each other's heartbeat, feel the air rush in and out of each other's lungs. We're too vital, too young, too strong for such fears. *"I swear,"* we say.

"I know you're inside each other's minds and souls now," Samantha says. *"But that will fade by the time the morning sun arrives.*

"Remember, this potion can only be taken by you this once. You'll always be changed by having experienced it, always be connected to each other, but you'll never be inside each other as much as this again. Enjoy this night. Enjoy each other."

"Peter," Charles Blood says. *"Elizabeth is now yours. Protect her."*

"Elizabeth," Samantha Blood says. *"Peter is now yours. Make sure he never suffers for lack of sustenance."*

Derek brings over the Jamaican man he's selected, shoves him in front of us, pushes him to his knees.

"Our tradition, Peter, calls for the wife to hunt for her husband and give him the first opportunity to feed on her kill. Elizabeth caught this one in preparation for the feast tonight. Once you feed, you will have signified your acceptance of her as your mate."

I feel Elizabeth's heartbeat quicken. Mine speeds up in sympathy to it. Together we realize the hunger that's been building within us. Elizabeth slashes the man's throat open with one sweep of her right arm and he crumbles to the floor, his blood spilling out, the hot, rich aroma of it filling our nostrils.

Ravenous as I am, we are, I pause, waiting for Elizabeth to feed at the same time. *"No, Peter,"* she says and I feel her form the words just as I hear them. *"You must feed first— please."*

Charles and Samantha grunt approval as I lower my head and bite into Elizabeth's kill, tear off a chunk of meat and devour it. Then Elizabeth joins me, feeding at my side.

We're vaguely aware of the rest of the family choosing others from the group huddled in the corner. Feasting on them, drinking Dragon's Tear wine from the green flagon, laughing, boasting about their hunts. Charles tells stories as he feeds—about Captain Jack and other ancestors. Derek tries to speak, but is being talked over. Human blood is everywhere.

Elizabeth and I take our bites at the same time, press against each other as we eat. As our hunger abates, we become more and more aware of other urges.

"Peter?" she says.

"Elizabeth?" I say at the same time.

We both giggle. *"I know what* you *feel like now,"* I say.

"And I can feel you *like that,"* she says.

"For pity's sake, spare us your drivel and take it to your room!" Charles Blood mindspeaks.

Not quite sure how we get there, unaware of how much time has passed, Elizabeth and I lie side by side on the bed of hay in her room and touch and explore each other, everything felt, everything shared, everything magnified by our duality of feeling.

"Peter, this is how it feels for you?" Elizabeth rubs against me and sucks in a breath as the sensation rips through both of us.

I feel her readiness for me build, just as my hardness intensifies until it becomes almost painful.

"Now!" we say at the same time. Both of us gasp as I enter her.

She resides inside every molecule of my being as I do in hers. We press against each other, move in perfect rhythm to each other's needs, stroke and buck and slow and speed up again in unison, roaring at the same time, growling in tandem, scratching, biting, all thought gone, lungs pumping for air, hearts racing—everything, every sense strained to the point just past ecstasy until we reach one, last great explosion of feelings, senses, movements—together, truly united as one.

Afterward, we lie smiling, her head next to mine—our tails, our legs entwined, our breaths mixed. I allow myself to feel her satisfaction, the pleasant aches that run through her from our exertions. She stretches and arches her back and I feel the lazy pleasure of her movement . . . and something else.

The faintest sign of a heartbeat, a tiny glimpse of an unformed thought.

"Our son, Peter," Elizabeth says. *"Your child growing inside me."*

We doze off together, the cool evening wind blowing

through our window, prompting us to press closer together. Elizabeth's dreams intermix with mine. Images of her valley overlay memories of my island. Her family's faces float in and out with images of my mother and father and her/my memories come and go of oceans, hunts, laughter, love and flying.

Elizabeth nudges me awake shortly before dawn. Already I can sense the distance starting to return between us. I pull her close, as if that act could stop the inevitable separation her mother promised us the morning would bring.

"Peter," Elizabeth says. *"We were dreaming such nice things together and then, then something you dreamed scared me."*

"What was it?"

"I'm not sure . . . I can't quite remember. But it was something . . . someone, who bothered you, threatened us."

"And?" I ask, stroking her.

"I'm not sure. I can't picture any image. I don't know why we felt threatened but I remember you wanted to protect me."

"Of course," I say.

"There was something else but . . . I don't know." She shrugs, turns quiet, snuggles against me and I listen to her breathing slow, let mine slow in tandem with hers.

Just before we both escape into sleep again, she half awakens, turns in my arms and murmurs, *"Peter, who is Jorge Santos?"*

14

"Why don't you just kill him?" Elizabeth says, when she feels me stir next to her in the morning.

Her words jar me from that state of half-sleep, that warm dreamy place our minds occupy when we first resist the necessity of awakening. I stretch and yawn and try to delay answering—Jorge Santos an unwelcome presence in my thoughts.

I would prefer that Elizabeth half doze beside me, but she turns over and says, *"Why don't you?"*

The last vestige of sleep escapes me. I sigh. *"Jorge Santos is simply a human who doesn't know when to stop pestering me. When we get back to Miami, I'll meet with him, answer a few of his stupid questions and send him on his way. That will be the end of it."*

"I don't understand," she says. *"You say he's only a human. Why bother with him at all?"*

Why indeed? I think. One simple phone call to Arturo would ensure the man's rapid disappearance and demise. But what I can't tell Elizabeth is that I possess no appetite to eliminate Maria's brother.

Had the girl just been prey, had Maria been as anonymous to me as the hundreds of others I've killed over the years, I would give her and her brother no thought. But she had laughed in my arms and I had resolved to let her live and then I had failed her. If Jorge Santos is stupid enough to trespass on my property and Arturo kills him—so be it. Otherwise, the least I can do for the girl is to meet with her brother, steer him away from me.

"We'll see what happens," I say. *"If he continues to be an irritant after the meeting—then I'll follow your advice."*

I'm anxious to leave, to be on the way home. I want to walk the corridors of my house again, sleep in my own bed with my new bride beside me. I miss the sea breeze, the ocean's constant song outside my windows. I ache to cruise Biscayne Bay in my Grady White, show Elizabeth the dolphins racing alongside our bow. But when she asks me to stay another day—so she can spend some last moments with her sister and mother—I have no heart to refuse.

Her father finds me on his veranda in the late afternoon, warming myself in the rays of the waning sun. Charles Blood has retained his natural state while I've changed into my human form. The elder dragon towers over me. *"Lost track of your wife already, have you?"* he asks.

"She's upstairs with her sister." I smile, knowing Charles has to be perfectly cognizant of my ability to sense where Elizabeth is at all times. Though the image is, at best, obscure, I picture her upstairs with Chloe, both of them in their human states. Both I guess giggling and whispering, talking of her future.

I'm conscious of Elizabeth's whereabouts and well-being in almost the same way as I know the placement and condition of each of my limbs. This, I think, must be what Elizabeth's mother meant when she said we'd always be connected. We may no longer share the intimacy of our thoughts, but we still share a permanent awareness of each other.

"Actually, I'm glad to find you without her. I wanted to have a word with you before you take her away from us," Charles says.

I cock an eyebrow, wait to hear what he wants to say.

"For some reason, when it comes to our people, you've been given a regrettably inadequate education." He motions with a taloned paw, as if to wave away the statement. *"But that has to do with the past. What's important here is that you understand what you have on your hands."*

"Which would be?" I ask, reminding myself that this is my bride's father, resisting my impulse to turn my back on his lecture.

"Which would be Elizabeth," he says, staring at me with his cold green eyes. *"I know what our young men do and I have no doubt that you're well-experienced with human women. But what you have now is a woman of the blood. She may belong to you, but don't think for one minute that she'll be controlled by you. . . ."*

"Father said our women can be impetuous and head-strong."

Charles laughs. *"Especially your bride. Of all my children, she takes after her mother the most. You can take this from one who's lived with it. There are times it's like bedding with a tiger."* His tone turns stern. *"But it's your responsibility to make sure she doesn't bring harm on herself. I want you to know I expect that from you."*

I nod and promise him that he doesn't have to worry. Yet, after he leaves, I wonder just how I'm supposed to control this supposedly half-wild creature.

The next morning, Derek wakes us by honking his car's horn. By the time I've finished dressing, he's honked three more times. Elizabeth, in her human form, naked, still lounging under the sheets, sighs, and says, "I haven't even finished packing. Please go outside and keep the fool company. Tell him I'll be down soon."

"Soon?" I say, having already learned that, for my bride, soon can be measured in anything from minutes to hours.

She shrugs, gives me an innocent look. "Not too long. I promise."

I find Elizabeth's parents and younger brother, in their natural states, basking in the morning sunlight on the veranda by the front door, waiting to say their good-byes. Chloe in her human form—barefoot and adorable, in cutoff jeans and a skimpy red halter top held up by two thin straps tied behind her neck—sits on the hood of the Land Rover. She waves and jumps off when she sees me.

Derek, also in human form, sitting in the car, the engine running, the windows down, frowns, glances at his watch. "Damn it, old man, it's bad enough I have to run you two all the way to the coast. Do you have to keep me waiting like a common taxi? The least you could do is let me leave in time to make it home before dark."

"Don't pay any attention to him," Chloe says, running up to me. She kisses me on the cheek, straining on the tips of her toes to reach. "Derek's just jealous that Elizabeth's getting to leave before he can."

"Elizabeth said she'll be down soon," I say.

"I've heard that before," Derek says.

Chloe giggles, and grabs my hand. "Come to the stables with me while you wait. I'll show you my horse."

I let her tug me along.

"Do you see many movies?" she asks. "TV shows? What books do you like?"

My answers just invite more questions. Smiling at her interrogation, I find myself wishing we could bring this girl home with us. Of all the members of Elizabeth's family, my bride included, this girl seems to have the most curiosity, the most willingness to experience human things.

"I named him Atticus," Chloe says at the stable as she leads a small white horse out of its stall. She giggles. "Pa asked why. I told him I named him after someone gentle and Pa said, 'But you never knew anyone by that name.' You

see, Pa doesn't like me to read very much. I didn't have the
heart to tell him I named him after the lawyer in *To Kill a
Mockingbird*.

"You read it, didn't you?" Chloe says.

I nod and she rewards me with a wide grin, then leaps on
the horse, riding him bareback, nudging him forward with
her bare brown feet, walking him beside me as we head back
to the house.

As we approach, Elizabeth, now downstairs, waves from
the veranda. I wave back, grinning at the sight of my bride
in her human form standing in the midst of three dragons,
each one, even her younger brother, towering over her. But
then I notice the single leather suitcase and small, wooden
box placed on the floor beside her.

"Is that all she's bringing?" I ask.

"That's all she has," Chloe says. "Here at Morgan's Hole,
we don't have much need for large wardrobes."

"And the box?"

"Seeds and herbs. Mum wanted her to bring them so she
can start her own garden."

I nod, thinking of my mother's garden back on Blood
Key, thinking how good it will be to see someone care for it
again.

Once we're in the car and on the way, I tell Elizabeth, "I
think we'll get you some new things as soon as we get to
Montego Bay."

Chloe insists on riding her horse alongside our car. She
keeps pace with us, leaning forward on her horse, urging
him to go faster, moving in unison with him as if she were
melded into his back. She waves her farewell only after we
reach the pass out of Morgan's Hole.

Elizabeth waves back. "I'll miss her," she says, frowning.
She turns her attention to the passing scenery and says noth-

ing more, quite clearly lost in her thoughts. Derek also makes the trip in silence.

Just before he leaves us at the marina at Oyster Bay, Derek presses a piece of paper into my hand. "Claypool and Sons—our agents in Kingston, old man," he says. "Pa said to remind you that is where to send the gold you promised." He drives away without a word to his sister.

My impulse is to prepare to leave immediately. Only the knowledge that Elizabeth lacks the proper papers stops me from rushing us away.

I rent a convertible the next morning, take Elizabeth north to Montego Bay. The stores and crowds of tourists leave her wide-eyed and openmouthed and I find myself smiling at her behavior, taking vicarious pleasure from her reactions to a world that's fresh and new to her. "Wait until you see Miami," I tell her.

Elizabeth darts into every store we pass, tries on almost everything she can. By early afternoon she's bought enough new clothes to fill two more suitcases. When I insist we stop shopping and seek out a photographer—to arrange for ID pictures of Elizabeth to be expressed to Jeremy Tindall's office in Miami--she pouts, but finally humors me.

"This way," I explain, "by the time we leave Jamaica, you'll be an American citizen."

She's less tolerant afterward, when we stop at a bookstore and I spend a half-hour selecting five paperback books. "What do you want those for?" she asks.

"I like to read them."

Elizabeth shakes her head. "I tried to read one once but it bored me. Chloe gets Derek to buy them for her. Pa doesn't like it. . . . He says, 'Why bother? They're just stupid stories about humans.' I think he's right."

Back at the boat that night, she shakes her head again, when I tell her I don't want her to go hunting. "In a few days," I say. "After Tindall sends your papers back and we put to sea. Then we can hunt every night, feed as much as you want."

"But I'm hungry now. . . ."

"And we have meat in the freezer. This isn't Cockpit Country. There are lights here. People have powerful guns. You have to be more careful around civilization."

Elizabeth sulks but accepts a defrosted steak, nibbles at it, leaves it half finished. "I'm going to bed," she says, and goes to the cabin without waiting for me to accompany her.

I join her later, lie down beside her, pull her toward me. She wiggles away and I accept her rejection.

Later that night I awake to find the bed empty beside me. I sense that she's miles away, on a hunt, and think of her father's words. Once again I wonder—if she won't listen to me, how can I hope to protect her?

Elizabeth seems content to hunt and feed at night, sleep through most of each day. I refuse to accompany her, continue to ask her to stop until we're away from land. She ignores me but, as a good mate, returns with her prey each evening to share with me.

Some nights she carries her fresh kill to the boat; other nights she lures men home and slays them below deck, in the salon. "Human men are so easy," she says. "They'll follow me anywhere, do anything I ask if they think it will lead to sex."

While I frown at her, scold her for the risks she's taking, I neither turn down the fresh meat she brings me nor the lovemaking she offers after we feed.

I watch her sometimes as she sleeps, marvel at her innocent countenance, wonder at her seeming contentment. Even when Elizabeth awakens, late in the afternoon, she moves about the boat with the same fluid motion, the same air of absolute indifference to her surroundings cats possess. She rarely bothers engaging me in conversation.

"Don't you want to know more about me?" I ask her one night before we surrender to sleep. "Isn't there more about you, you want to tell me?"

She shakes her head and sighs. "Why do you always want to talk about everything? We have plenty of time for all that, Peter. Why not just enjoy each day we spend here? They don't have to be anything more than they are."

But the hours go by too slowly for me. I pace the deck, worry about each new person who approaches the docks. I call Jeremy Tindall the next morning, demanding to know where the papers are.

"For Christ's sake, Peter," Tindall snarls. "My youngest son Tyler was just burned to death. The business he built is nothing but cinders. I think you *know* that. My wife is a wreck. And you're bugging me about some stupid damn papers?"

Thank God for Arturo and his efficiency. "Too bad you couldn't have helped him find a safer business," I say, choosing my words, speaking without inflection. "Hopefully you'll be more careful about yourself and the rest of your family. Hopefully you'll remember your commitments . . . including your promise to rush the papers to me."

"Relax," Tindall says. "The Santos report you ordered is already here. All of Elizabeth's papers are being rushed. You should have both soon. And Peter, I doubt that my wife, my other two sons or I will be looking to engage in any risky behavior. I surely hope nothing else happens. . . ."

"I doubt anything will," I say and hang up.

15

To my relief, a courier finally delivers a packet from Miami on the morning of our sixth day on the boat. I open it in the marina office, take out two manila envelopes—one labeled ELIZABETH DELASANGRE, the other marked JORGE SANTOS— feel the heft of each and grin. I know I have no need to check the contents of either. No matter how much Tindall balks or complains, he does what's necessary as quickly and completely as possible—especially when he's threatened.

Envelopes in hand, I rush back to the Grand Banks. I'm tempted to open the Santos file immediately but, instead, I store it in the chart drawer by the lower helm and go below to wake my bride. Once we're at sea, I think, there will be plenty of time to read up on the man.

Elizabeth groans when I gently stroke her awake. "Bother me later," she says and burrows below her covers.

"Look." I throw the manila envelope labeled ELIZABETH DELASANGRE on the bed next to her. "The courier finally came. We can leave."

She sits up, opens the envelope. "How soon?" she asks, sitting cross-legged on the bed, naked, her small round breasts swaying slightly as she sorts through the official documents, examining the birth certificate, passport, Social Security card, Coral Gables High School diploma, Florida's driver's license and voter's registration card that all bear her name.

As usual I'm delighted with her appearance whether

she's in human form or dragon. I sit next to her, cup one breast in my hand, consider lying with her. But, I know, once underway, there will be more than enough time for that.

Elizabeth stares at me when I take my hand away, shocked, I think, that I could ever resist her. "Later," I say, my mind on home, planning the steps necessary to getting underway, letting myself fully smile for the first time in days. "We're leaving now."

Her pillow hits my back as I leave the cabin.

Ordinarily Elizabeth takes her time getting up, going about the business of washing and dressing in preparation for the day. But today I barely have time to reach the flybridge and start the motors before she joins me.

Wearing only a skimpy, bright blue bikini, her hair wildly in disarray, she smiles at me. "So let's get going," she says.

But Elizabeth offers no help. She yawns, looks away when I attempt to tell her about the motors and instruments. "Just teach me how to drive the boat," she says. "I don't care how it works."

She only comes close to me when I turn my attention from her to the gauges and dials on the console in front of me. "Is it later yet?" she says, pressing against me.

I shake my head, trying to keep my mind off the soft warmth of her body, the sweet smell of her, while I make sure the engines warm up properly, the systems all work.

Taking the wheel, I tell Elizabeth to jump off the Grand Banks, instruct her on how to disconnect the shore power and uncleat the dock lines. She glares at me, waits until I say, "Please."

Even then, she moves so slowly I'm tempted to do it myself. But I find I can't keep from admiring the catlike way she moves, grinning at her less-than-nautical efforts. When she finally finishes, I throw the boat in gear.

Elizabeth hops back on the boat as soon as it starts to

move. Obviously aware of my gaze, she moves slowly on the bow deck, coiling and stowing the lines where I say, bending and twisting more than necessary, moving in such a way that her breasts seem to be on the verge of escaping the bikini's flimsy cups—the sweat from her exertions glistening on her mocha flesh, spotting the bikini, making it cling all the more where the skin is wet.

I stare, thinking of how salty she must taste.

Elizabeth looks back, laughs, cries out, "Peter!" and points behind me, "Watch out for that pole!"

My face flushed, I throw the motors out of reverse, push the throttles forward just enough to stop our rearward movement, complete our turn without striking the channel marker.

"Captain," she says, hands on her hips, "you really should keep your eyes on where we're going."

"You're not making it easy for me, you know," I say.

"Oh," she says, all innocence, toying with her bikini top, suddenly yanking it up, flashing me a quick glimpse of her firm mocha breasts, her dark brown nipples, then covering them. "I thought you weren't interested anymore."

I begin to frown at her but, somehow, I end up smiling. "I never said I wasn't interested."

"That's how you acted," Elizabeth says. She turns her back on me, looks forward as we glide past the other boats still tied to their docks.

I know she's punishing me for my earlier neglect, but still I almost gasp when she shouts, "You'll never get anything like this!"

Shocked, hurt, I begin to reply, then realize she's reacting to the leering gaze of an older, potbellied man, sitting on the stern of a catamaran at the end of the dock, an unlit cigar clamped in his mouth. His elderly wife, sitting beside him— a woman whose entire body seems to sag inside her one-piece, black bathing suit—follows the movement of our boat, shaking her head in disgust, not at her husband but at my wife.

Elizabeth pulls off her top, waves it at her, then as we pass, yanks her bottoms off too. The cigar falls from the man's mouth.

"Eat your heart out!" I yell, gunning my motors, creating a wake behind us that I know will still rock them long after we're out of sight.

On the deck Elizabeth spins and whoops, throws her bikini into the air. Then she faces forward and, spreading her arms and legs, lets the wind—created by our speed—caress her naked skin, and dry the sweat from her body. She stays that way, oblivious to the stares of any passing boaters, until we exit the harbor. When she finally turns and looks in my direction, I motion for her to come join me on the flybridge.

"You aren't mad, are you?" she calls out.

I look at her and shake my head. "How could I be?"

Elizabeth grins, rushes to the bridge. She hugs me, kisses me on the cheek and whispers, "I want you."

"Not yet," I say, working the wheel, guiding the boat through the worst of the ocean's swells near the shore.

She presses her naked body against my side, her skin cool from the wind—her nipples rock hard. I try to ignore her, tend to my piloting, but she rubs against me, kissing my neck, tugging at my clothes.

"Elizabeth!" I object.

She laughs, continues to tease me and I suck in a breath, and force myself to pay attention to the boat traffic around us, the movements of the waves. But the farther Jamaica falls behind us, the less able I am to concentrate, the more conscious I am of Elizabeth's presence beside me. Far before the ocean swallows the last remnant of the island's image, I give in, set the autopilot, tear off my clothes and turn all my attention to my bride.

"It's about time," Elizabeth says, disengaging from me,

walking slowly to the bench seat at the rear of the flybridge. Perfectly aware that my eyes follow each movement of hers, she lies on the bench facing me. "Come, Peter," she says. "You've already made me wait far too long."

Staring in the daylight at her naked body, I whisper, "Now I guess you'll want me to make up for having you wait."

"I wish you would, Peter. . . ."

Later neither of us bothers to dress. We lie holding each other, listening to the rumble of the engines, letting the sea wind wash over us, smelling the salt air, being lulled to sleep by the rolling rhythm of our passage.

Neither of us wakes until after dark. Without a word or a thought between us we change shape and take to the evening sky to hunt, to kill and to feed. Later we make love again on the rear deck of the flybridge and then give in to sleep, waking after dawn to find the sunlight burning down on us, searing our scales. We change to our human forms, go below deck to continue our slumbers and the next night we repeat the pattern, preying on the crews and living cargo of dilapidated smuggling boats, attacking the countrysides of poor islands, creating a host of new folk tales I'm sure will terrify many uneducated island children for years to come.

Time turns elastic. I lose track of the days, forget to check on our location. The books I bought go unread. Jorge Santos's file remains untouched in the drawer next to the lower wheel. Elizabeth and I sleep through the days. We hardly talk, share nothing of our thoughts and histories. Sometimes I worry, we only seem to care about the next hunt, the feeding that follows and the lovemaking after that.

Late one afternoon, before we've changed to our natural forms, before the sky has grown dark enough to allow us to hunt, Elizabeth comes to me, her eyes glistening from the tears she's holding back. "I tried to talk to Chloe just now—we've been mindspeaking each day. . . . I couldn't reach her."

I nod, check the GPS, then wrap my arms around her—surprised at how tender her tears make me feel, pleased to have her come to me for comfort. "We're near Cuba," I say. "Too far for mindspeaking. Even we have limits. You'll have to write her from now on."

"It won't be the same." She pouts.

"No, it won't," I say. Elizabeth pulls away and I wish I knew what to say to her to ease her sadness.

Later we change and hunt, make love and sleep. We do the same the day after that. The Grand Banks and the ocean that surround it have become our only universe. I wonder what will lie beyond it.

16

Lightning or thunder or Elizabeth's laughter—I'm not sure which—awakens me just before another dawn. I sit up, still in my natural state, the remnants of our kill—a young, attractive couple who maintained a small farm on the Cuban coast—lying nearby. Rain slashes across the deck, soaks me. The wind chills me as waves rush at us and the bow rises, then crashes down. The stern does the same, the props whining when they break free of the water, and I hear Elizabeth laugh again.

A lightning bolt streaks across the sky, its momentary brilliance freezing a snapshot of the frenzied sea leaping all around us and illuminating the wet, naked, human form of my bride at the wheel of the ship.

"Elizabeth?" I mindspeak.

"When the storm woke me, I turned off the autopilot and took the helm." She adjusts the wheel a quarter turn to the left, to keep the bow facing the waves. *"I've never seen anything like this. Isn't it wonderful?"*

The Grand Banks shudders, almost stops as a massive wave crashes over its bow. *"You can go below. Use the lower wheel, in the cabin,"* I say.

"Why would I want to?"

I shrug, throw the carcasses off the boat and revert to human form too. As soon as I do, I start to shiver. Elizabeth hardly notices when I approach and kiss her wet, cold cheek.

"I'm going below to get some foul-weather gear. Do you want me to bring you any?"

She shakes her head, laughs and whoops as we crash through another roller.

Below, inside the cabin, the pitching and rolling seem even more intense. I have to concentrate on maintaining my balance as I dry off and pull on a sweatshirt and jeans. I try to think how many days it's been since I was dressed, and give up the attempt after a few moments.

The lower wheel turns, the boat changes position and I picture Elizabeth, naked and laughing, at the wheel above. I grin and shake my head. I've never met anyone as free as my bride. I'm amazed how seductive her wildness has been. My memories of our voyage from Jamaica almost frighten me—that I could succumb to such a careless, untamed life.

I think of Elizabeth's question the night before. *"When you met me, you thought you were going to teach me more about how to live as a human, didn't you?"*

"Yes," I said.

"Well, I think you didn't expect one thing." She chuckled.

"Which was?"

"That maybe, I'd teach you more about how to be a dragon instead."

A massive jolt knocks me off my feet, throws me across the cabin. The boat wallows and turns. The lower wheel spins freely. *"Peter!"* Elizabeth mindspeaks. I sense at once she's no longer on the boat. *"Peter!"* she calls and I feel her drifting farther behind me each moment that passes.

I stand, rush for the wheel, reach it just as another breaker hits the Grand Banks on its beam, the boat half rolling on its side before it rights. *"Elizabeth, are you hurt?"* I ask as I tug on the wheel, steer the boat, bow first, into the waves.

"No . . . I don't think so," she says. *"I'm not sure how any of it happened. The waves are huge. One swept me off the flybridge. . . . Peter, I can't see the boat!"*

Thankful that Jeremy had opted for the extra expense of dual controls, I reset the autopilot from the comfort and safety of the lower bridge and then let go of the wheel. *"Don't worry. We can always find the boat."*

"We?"

"After all the trouble I went through to find you, do you think I'd risk losing you now?" I mindspeak, stripping off my warm clothes. *"I'm coming for you. Change to your natural state. You'll be stronger that way."*

"Yes, Peter," she says.

I arch an eyebrow when I realize she hasn't argued with me. Another wave rocks the Grand Banks and I wait for the boat to reach the bottom of the next trough before I rush out the door, slam it behind me and leap from the deck.

Wind tears at me, rain blinds me as I change shape in midair and attempt to fly toward my bride. But I can't overpower the storm. Rather than wear myself out in a futile attempt to conquer the wind, I choose to drop into the water.

"Peter!"

"I'm coming, Elizabeth. Can you sense where I am?"

"It's so far."

I know both of us are too strong to be in much danger, but I'm not sure Elizabeth realizes it. *"Don't worry,"* I tell her. *"The water's warm. You'll be fine."*

"I'll feel better when you reach me."

A wave swells in front of me. Diving beneath it, I sense what direction I have to take to reach my bride and concentrate on moving through the water with the least effort, using my tail and wings to propel me forward, one strong coordinated stroke at a time.

"I'm swimming toward you now," I say *"Swim toward me. You can do it. Go below the water. The waves are less difficult to fight that way. . . ."*

"Yes, Peter."

The distance between us slowly diminishes as we force

our way through the water. I swim until my lungs burn, surface long enough to take a few gasps of air, dive and repeat
the pattern again and again until I lose any sense of how
much time has passed, how many waves I've encountered.
When I surface yet another time and yet another wave
crashes over me, I sigh, tread water and look around. All I
can see are gray skies and breaker after breaker. Diving
again, I swim on, wondering how I'll ever reach my bride in
such a turbulent sea.

Finally, it's Elizabeth who brings me to her. *"Peter, I can
feel how near you are. Can you sense me too?"* she mindspeaks.

I stop, tread water, concentrate on detecting my bride's
presence. *"Yes, I can!"* I mindspeak and race toward her as
she speeds in my direction.

We meet on the surface, rising with a wave, the wind
howling at us as we embrace. I wrap Elizabeth in my wings,
both of us floating, nuzzling our cheeks against each other.

"Don't be mad at me, Peter," she says.

"Why would I?"

*"I didn't pay enough attention. If this happened at home,
Pa would be furious. He hates carelessness. He always punishes us, even Mum, when we make stupid mistakes."*

"I'm not your father," I say, pulling her closer, glad to
have her safe. *"You've done nothing wrong. It was just a bad
squall."*

We float in the water for hours, neither of us speaking,
keeping each other afloat until the storm wears itself out.
When the winds finally die down, we take to the air and
search for our craft. Toward dusk, Elizabeth spots it, fifty
miles from where we had floated, making its way north as if
nothing had hindered its passage.

Exhausted, we land on the flybridge. Laughing with relief to have something solid beneath our feet, we change into

our human forms and rush below. Hunger and cold stop us from collapsing into sleep. Elizabeth gets towels while I check the GPS and read our location.

"Two more days and we'll be home," I tell her as I defrost some steaks in the microwave. We towel each other dry, gorge on the food and afterward, lie in bed, pressed close, warming each other under the covers.

"Peter?" Elizabeth says.

Eyes shut, I nod, wait to hear what she wants to say.

"Do you love me?"

The question makes me open my eyes. I look at Elizabeth, see the concern on her face and resist the impulse to dismiss her question with kisses. Silly, I think, that a relationship as intense as ours has never had any spoken declaration of affection. "Of course I do," I say. "It's just that what we have has been so much more than that. . . ."

"Chloe talks about falling in love all the time," Elizabeth says. "She reads about it in all her books. She says it's a feeling that consumes every part of you. But Mum says that's nonsense, love is for humans. She says our people work differently."

I take Elizabeth's hands in mine, stare into her face. "But I do love you. I'll always want to be with you."

She sighs. "I always want to be with you too. You know that. Neither of us has a choice with that. But today, when you reached me in the water . . . I felt something more. It's like you touched a place inside me where no one's reached before . . . only . . ."

"Only what?" I ask.

"I'm just not sure if that's love or not." Elizabeth shrugs. "I don't know what it's supposed to feel like. And I don't want you to be upset that I'm confused. . . ."

I want her to say she loves me but, even wishing that, I'm not positive I know much more about true love than she. I know our people can love. When Mother died, I watched my father suffer. He wailed and roared and lashed out at everything around him—so much so that I hid from him for days. I wonder if I could care that deeply about anyone. Would Elizabeth's death drive me to such total despair? I'm only sure of our connection to each other, the invisible bond between us so strong that it's almost palpable. For now, that's more than enough for me. "I'm not upset. I know what we have," I say.

"Good." She squeezes my hands in hers. "I'd hate it if you didn't understand."

Later she takes my hand, guides it to the warmth between her legs. "Do you think maybe, you could make love to me tonight, like we were humans, madly in love?"

I grin at her. "I think I can do that."

Elizabeth surprises me with her willingness to forgo any further hunting. She no longer complains when I defrost steaks for us. The closer we get to Miami, the more compliant she becomes. She agrees to don clothing, promises to stay close to me, not to change or fly off until I tell her it's safe.

"This is your country," she says. "Until I get used to it, I'll trust that you know best."

She delights me by finally starting to tell me about her life, growing up in Morgan Hole. "Mum made it as good as she could," she says. "Pa mostly ignored Chloe and me. He paid most of his attention to Derek and then to Philip, after he was born. Derek thought he was too old to have much to do with any of us. It was Mum who took us swimming, horseback riding, flew with us as soon as we could take to the air. She taught us everything—how to make Dragon's Tear wine, how to mix potions. She showed us how to read and write, had us help her in the garden, took us hunting with her. Most especially, as soon as we could understand, Mum taught us to avoid angering Pa.

"We were all afraid of him. Even when we were little he'd occasionally strike us hard enough to draw blood. Most of the time though, he'd take whoever displeased him, lock them in one of the cells under the house and leave them there for a day or two without food or water."

I shake my head, say, "That must have been terrible."

"No," Elizabeth says. "It wasn't so bad. We could always mindspeak to each other. When any of us were punished, the others would sneak down with food and drink. We'd giggle and make a picnic of it. And I wasn't in trouble very often anyway—not after Chloe got older."

"Chloe?" I ask, thinking of her cute younger sister, the smile the little teenager always had on her face, wondering how much of a discipline problem she could be.

"She likes human things too much," Elizabeth says. "Chloe's always reading or painting. She prefers to stay in her human form, goes out of her way to talk to the servants. Pa hates it all, but no matter how much he punishes her, she keeps on doing what she wants."

"Why do you think she likes human things so much?" I ask.

"You're a funny one to ask that question," Elizabeth says. "Why do you?"

"You know I was raised with it," I say. But when Elizabeth continues to look at me, as if she's waiting for more of an explanation, I shrug and continue. "After my mother died, Father told me her family had been accidentally killed in a cannon barrage, in France, during World War One, when she was a baby. An orphanage took her in and raised her. She didn't even know what she was until she came to term. Father found her then and took her for his bride.

"He said, of his three wives, she was his favorite. Father loved how different she was. He tolerated her passion for human art and literature, but argued when she insisted I learn human ways too, that I go to school with them. He worried she would make me too gentle. She said, knowing human things and human behavior would make me more powerful. In the end, Father acquiesced. But I suspect his agreement had more to do with his love for Mother than his respect for her arguments. I think it's a mark of his devotion that, after she died, he continued to send me to school."

"That makes sense." Elizabeth nods. "For Chloe, it was one of the servants. Mum was sick for a few months after she gave birth to my sister. She allowed this one servant, Lila, to take care of Chloe. The two of them grew very close. Even though Mum frowns at it, Chloe still makes sure to spend some time with Lila every day."

"Well I don't think it's hurt her," I say.

"Of course you don't." Elizabeth smiles in a way that slightly parts her lips, as she usually does before sex or when she wants me to do something. "I just hope," she says coming closer, putting her arms around my neck, "you don't wonder whether you got the wrong sister."

Our last night at sea, Elizabeth insists on staying above deck. I sit with her on the flybridge, watching with her for signs of land. The evening ocean has calmed so much that its waters are as flat as any lake and the Grand Banks glides along with only a gentle tip and roll to its movements—the hiss of the water, as it's displaced beneath us, commingled with the purr of our twin diesels. The mild rocking of the boat, the quiet lullaby of the passing waters finally overtake me and I fall into a deep sleep.

Elizabeth stays up, wakes me when she sees lights on the horizon. "The whole sky is glowing over there," she says.

She hugs me when I nod and say, "We're almost home."

The sun begins to break into the sky shortly before we reach the Fowey Rock lighthouse. I turn off the autopilot and take the helm as we approach it, the dark lines of its skeletal structure looking in the early light like a child's construction toy rising from the sea. Elizabeth stares at it, turns toward the lights of Miami—their glow bleaching out from the coming dawn—then gazes back at the dark, light-streaked clouds floating in a sky that first turns gold, then blue on the horizon as the sun rises. "It's all so beautiful," she says.

Her eyes widen as we enter Biscayne Bay and cruise by the first of the stilt homes that line the Biscayne channel, Miami's skyline still too far in front of us to be fully visible. But Key Biscayne, just a few miles to our right, sits close enough to dazzle Elizabeth with its upscale homes and towering, white-concrete condominiums. "Is that Miami?" she asks.

I shake my head, point to the dozens of high-rise buildings slowly rising into sight, far across the water.

"Oh," she says.

A pang of homesickness hits me when I glance to the south and see the green treetops of Soldier Key and the dark smudges on the water beyond it that I know will soon grow to show both Wayward Key and Blood Key. "See the islands?" I ask Elizabeth.

"Is that yours . . . ours?" She points to Soldier Key.

I shake my head. "Look farther south, the second one past it. That's your new home."

She stares, squints her eyes, then shrugs. "I can't tell," she says. "It's too far."

I examine the sandbars barely showing on either side of the channel, realize the tide has a while to go before it reaches its lowest point, leaving us plenty of time to reach the island. I grin and say, "You'll see it soon enough."

17

The dogs hear us first. They start barking and yelping while we're still wending our way through the channel—the boat under just enough power to maintain forward momentum— my bride on the bow, peering into the water, shouting, "Watch out!", guiding me away from any threatening rocks.

By the time we reach Caya DelaSangre's small harbor, Elizabeth's shouted warnings of underwater dangers, the mutter of our motors and the howls of the dog pack have brought Arturo Gomez—bearded, barefoot, long haired, shirtless and tanner than ever—to the deck of his sleek, thirty-five-foot SeaRay cabin cruiser, a black automatic pistol in his right hand.

He uncocks the gun and shoves it into his cutoff shorts' right front pocket when he sees me. The weight of the pistol pulls the cutoffs down a little, accentuating the swell of his protruding stomach. I shake my head and smile when he takes notice of Elizabeth's red halter top and tight khaki shorts and sucks in his gut as he grins and nods toward her. It's hard for me to think that the scruffy vagabond in front of me is the same man as the dapper, always meticulously dressed president of LaMar Associates.

As I'd suspected, Arturo's anchored in the middle of the harbor to keep his distance from the dogs. There's barely enough room alongside his boat for the Grand Banks to pass. To reach the dock, I have to steer uncomfortably close to the SeaRay.

"Nice girl," Arturo calls out as he walks along the side of his boat, watching our movement, obviously prepared to jump forward and fend us off if it appears we're going to run into him.

"Nice beard," I say as we glide past.

He rubs the thick growth on his face and flashes one of his wide smiles. "You damn well gave me enough time to grow it."

"Didn't you say you could use a vacation?"

"A vacation, yes." Arturo laughs. "But I've been gone from the office so long I'm afraid they're going to think I either died or retired. Do you realize it's August already?"

I shake my head, and marvel how time has become so unimportant to me. "What day is it?" I ask.

"Tuesday, the second."

"Peter!" Elizabeth warns from the bow. I look forward, see we're moving too quickly, back off the throttles and turn my attention to bringing us close to the dock without striking it. She maintains her position, a coiled line in her hands, waiting patiently for the opportunity to jump off the boat and secure its lines. As we close, Slash and Scar and a half dozen other growling dogs watch us from the dock, legs splayed, teeth bared, hackles raised.

"Are you sure she's going to be okay?" Arturo asks from the safety of his boat.

Elizabeth turns and stares at him as if he were a dead, rotting fish, spoiling the air with its odor. She purses her lips and whistles one sharp loud blast and laughs as the dogs scurry off the dock and rush out of sight. I laugh with her, amused to see the red flush rise on Arturo's face.

After Elizabeth cleats our lines, I cut the motors and sit back to stare at the dock, the nearby trees, the coral walls of my home. The sea breeze quickly washes away the last remnants of the Grand Banks's diesel fumes and I breathe in the familiar aromas of salt air and fresh green vegetation that welcome me home. I half expect to hear Father mindspeak to me, feel the loss of him once again, and wish he were here to meet my bride.

Arturo rows his dinghy over and joins us on the dock. "Good to see you," he says, shaking my hand and slapping my back. Turning his attention to Elizabeth, he asks, "Is this the bride?" He holds out his hand to shake hers, grins and says, "She's beautiful. Congratulations!"

Elizabeth looks past him, ignoring his gesture. *"Can we go inside now?"* she mindspeaks. *"I want to see the house."*

Arturo waits, sweating, squinting from the hot sun's glare, his smile now strained, his hand still extended.

"Please, Elizabeth, take his hand. The man is useful to me. He'll be gone soon enough."

Elizabeth sighs, offers forward a limp hand, gives a thin smile as Arturo grasps it lightly and quickly disengages. *"Now Peter?"* she asks.

I force a smile. "Why don't you go below and put your things together? We need to unload the boat. I'll come down in a few minutes to help you."

She glares at me, mindspeaks, *"He's just a human. Why not have him do it?"* Then she clambers onto the boat.

"I hope I'm not interrupting," Arturo says.

"Not at all," I say. I fight the impulse to apologize for my spoiled bride. "Thanks, by the way, for your help with that Caribbean Charm thing."

The Latin grins. "No problem. My guys tell me the fire was one of the biggest the county's ever seen. It started during the day, killed everyone in the executive offices. Caribbean Charm's been shipping merchandise like crazy ever since."

"Good." I nod, thank him for watching the house and ask him to call Jeremy Tindall, tell him that I'll be returning his boat later in the day.

"Not that Jeremy has any desire to hear from me these

days," he says, stares at the Grand Banks and grins. "I'd wash the decks if I were you. Jeremy will have a fit if you return it in this condition. He'll be complaining for weeks."

"Doesn't he usually?"

Arturo laughs and nods. "God, it'll be good to get back to work," he says. "I even miss Jeremy. Though I doubt he wants to see either of us very much." Then he looks at me. "What did you think of our boy?"

I knit my eyebrows at his question.

"Santos. What did you think of the report? Tindall faxed a copy to me."

"I haven't read it yet," I say, remembering the manila envelope I stowed in the drawer next to the lower wheel. "I haven't had time."

"No time?" Arturo says. "How busy could you have been? What were you doing, rowing back?"

Banter may be one thing, but too much familiarity is another. I give him a blank stare.

Arturo's grin disappears. He knows better than to continue in the same vein. "Well," he says, "I wish you would read it soon. The guy's a pain. He even hired some ultralight pilot to fly over the island. Damned plane buzzed me four days in a row. He's still driving Emily crazy too. He calls and asks for you every day."

I nod, frown that I have to pay attention to this annoyance so close to my homecoming.

"There's no reason you have to meet with this guy, you know," Arturo says.

I wave my hand, as if to push away his suggestion and the violence it implies. I've already promised myself to try to avoid bringing any more death to Maria's family. Besides, I wonder at the man's persistence. "I want to see what this man is like," I say. "Just tell Emily to arrange a meeting this Friday morning at ten."

* * *

Below deck, Elizabeth sits in the salon, greets me with silence, her arms folded across her chest. Through the passageway I can see our belongings piled haphazardly on top of the bed.

"He's gone," I say.

She shrugs, says nothing.

"Nice job of packing," I say, going to the drawer next to the lower helm, taking the manila envelope out of it.

"At home we have servants do such things."

"Here we don't." I go into the bedroom, start separating the pile, folding and organizing the clothes.

"We should."

"Father gave up slaves before the Civil War."

"Who does all your cleaning? Who maintains the house?"

"I do."

"I don't see why you would want to," Elizabeth says. She joins me next to the bed, stares at the clothes, picks up a pair of shorts, folds it slowly. "I'm not used to having to do these things. I don't think I'll be very good at it."

"It's okay," I say. "I am."

After Elizabeth asks three more times, I finally agree to leave our belongings on the ship and take her to the house. "We can bring everything in later," she says.

She grins as we walk down the dock, her smile widening when I unlock the iron gate and throw the switch to turn on the generators. "We have power?" she asks.

"And lights and air conditioning, TVs and stereo . . ." I say, smiling when she runs ahead of me, watching her climb the wide coral steps leading to the veranda, two at a time.

Elizabeth waits for me on the veranda, leaning on the parapet next to the cannon, staring at the ocean. When I join her, she says, "I'm going to love it here! Show me all of it, every room. Please."

I take her to my room first, throw open the double doors and wince ● the heat and dampness, the smell of must. I open the windows and the doors to the interior and rush from room to room, opening doors and windows, letting the fresh sea air cleanse and cool the house. Elizabeth follows me, helps me open everything. Along the way she touches the windows and the doors, sits on the beds, turns the light switches on and off, runs her hands over the smooth stone walls of the interior.

"This house is much smaller than Morgan's Hole," she says. "But it's much nicer, I think."

On the third floor, in the great room, she wanders from one side to the other, taking in the panorama from each window, asking me to tell her the names of the islands she sees and point out the mainland in the distance. The sea breeze courses through the room, cooling it and comforting us, making us forget the August heat outside.

"Is it always so comfortable inside?" she asks.

"Mostly," I tell her. "But in the winter we sometimes need the fires to keep us warm."

"It's cold every night at Morgan's Hole," she says.

She walks to the wall, touches the old cutlass that has hung there as long as I can remember.

"My father's," I say. "From his pirate days."

Elizabeth nods, studies the oil paintings hanging on the walls nearby, asks me about them too. "French impressionists," I say, looking at the landscapes and portraits my mother brought with her from France and insisted on displaying throughout the house. One shows a nude young woman posed on a couch.

I point to it. "That's my mother. She lived with an artist in Paris and posed for him before Father found her. Father only told me about it just before he died. He said, after she became his bride, he brought her back to the city and bought her whatever she wished, including all the paintings she wanted. She insisted that, no matter the cost, he had to buy this one."

"And you, Peter," Elizabeth says, her voice turning coquettish as she goes from picture to picture, "can you afford to buy your bride whatever she wants?"

"You'll see," I say.

By the time we walk down the spiral staircase to the bottom floor, Elizabeth's pace has slowed, her lips have settled into a partial smile, a show of polite, if indifferent approval. She gives the cells we pass only a cursory glance and hesitates when I enter the smallest one. "Peter, I've seen cells before. . . ."

Her eyes widen when I pull the cot up and the passageway opens.

"Where are we going?" she asks as we descend into the darkness.

I say nothing, avoid turning on the lights at the bottom until the treasure room's open. Elizabeth allows me to guide her into the small cold room, and I stand behind her and flick the switch once she's in place.

"Oh my," she says, her hands to her face, her emerald-green eyes wide as she glances from chest to chest. "My father would do anything for this."

"As I promised—he'll have some of the gold."

She picks up a handful of jewelry, holds it to the light, then turns to me. "We don't have to be too generous, do we, Peter?"

Outside, to my surprise, the garden thrills her even more than the treasure room. "Dragon's Tear," she says, examining the plants, pulling weeds as she looks. "Death's Rose. Angel Wort. Why didn't you tell me you had all of these?"

I shrug. "It was my mother's garden. Father and I mostly ignored it."

Elizabeth puts her hands on her hips. "With all this and the seeds that Mum gave me, we'll have a proper garden in no time. There's already enough Dragon's Tear here for a good few quarts of wine. I'll have some made within a few weeks."

"And then?" I ask.

She gives me a sly grin. "And then I'll teach you a few things."

I don't even think of the Santos file until late in the day, after we've returned Jeremy Tindall's boat and cruised home in my Grady White.

Tired and weary of maintaining her human form, Elizabeth insists on reverting to her natural shape before she takes a nap. *"I don't know why you like the human form so much,"* she says after she changes. *"I always feel better like this."*

"And I'm used to the other."

She helps me make a bed of hay for her on the far side of my room, lies down and motions for me to join her. I take in the soft green hue of her scales, the gentle curve of her tail, her delicate beige underbody and almost accept her invitation. But I refuse to revert to the thoughtless pattern of life that I've lived the last few weeks. After dark, there will be more than enough time for me to take my bride for her first hunt in the waters near my homeland, ample opportunity to let her taste fresh meat once more. For now I have other things I must do. Setting foot on my island, wandering the halls of my home has reminded me of my responsibilities.

"You're powerful enough to do what you want and take whatever you wish in your life," Father taught me. *"But so what? We live to build a future and only die when we have*

*no future left. Each of us has to find something more—a rea-
son to our lives. In the end, the best of it is always about our
families."*

I lean over and kiss her scaled left cheek—running my
hand over her underbody as she adjusts herself, thinking of
the child growing within her, feeling the need to protect each
of them. "I'll wake you later," I say, then leave the room and
climb the spiral staircase to the third floor where Jorge Santos's file remains unread on the oak table in the great room.

Picking up the manila folder, I carry it over toward the
windows facing the bay. I glance out at the water—squinting at the last rays the late-afternoon sun gives off as it rides
lower in the sky, preparing to set over the mainland. I notice
a large, white, cigarette-style speedboat floating just a few
hundred yards off my island's shore.

I wonder why it's stopped. . . .

The impact spins me away from the window. Falling, the
manila folder flying from my hand, I finally hear the crack
of the rifle, the splintering of the middle window's glass,
followed by the throaty roar of the speedboat's engines as
they come to life, the drone they make as the boat races
away. Pain sears through me and, *"DAMN!"* I yell, realizing
a bullet has torn through my chest, just above the right corner of my heart, ripping flesh, muscle, ligaments—shattering a small part of my right shoulder blade.

"Peter?" Elizabeth mindspeaks.

"I've been shot." I breathe deep, turn my mind inward,
concentrate on narrowing blood vessels, slowing my heart,
limiting blood loss.

Roaring, my dragoness bursts into the room, rushes to the
shattered window. *"Was it a boat? A white one?"*

I grimace. *"Later,"* I say. *"Help me move away from all
the damned glass."*

"But I still can see them!"

"That boat can do at least sixty miles an hour. You'll never catch it."

"I might."

"And then you'll be seen and then we'll both be dead. Help me!"

After Elizabeth carries me to the oak table and lays me on it, she changes to her human shape. She picks glass shards from my hair, my clothes, my skin, while I go through the process of healing, guiding my cells to rebuild, working the bullet to the surface where Elizabeth can pluck it out.

The sun has set by the time I'm able to sit up—the room dark, my bride sitting near me. "Who did it?" she asks.

I shrug. "Who knows we've returned?" I say, getting up, walking to the wall switch, flicking on the lights.

"Arturo does," Elizabeth says.

"And Emily and Jeremy and anyone else any of them told, including our friend, Mr. Santos." I take a broom from the cupboard and begin sweeping up the glass fragments.

Elizabeth gets up to help and I motion her back. "You'll cut your feet," I say, reminding her of her now-human vulnerability.

"What are we going to do about it?"

"Not much right now. I'll call Arturo, have him run a check on white speedboats, but there are probably hundreds of them, like the one they used, within cruising distance. If he's the one, or Jeremy, my call will at least alert them to the fact that I'm not so easily eliminated. After that, I guess the main plan is to avoid standing near windows whenever boats are near . . . until someone shows their hand and we can get things resolved."

Elizabeth frowns. "You named four humans. If each of them were dead—I doubt we'd have to worry about any windows. . . ."

I shake my head. "My father said, 'Know your enemies

before you try to destroy them.' I won't kill people who are useful to me without knowing they acted against me."

"But Santos? He's nothing but a bother. . . ."

Tired of Elizabeth's questions, furious that someone would have the nerve to attack me in my home, I glare at my bride, spit my words at her. "But I don't *know* enough yet." Elizabeth grimaces and looks away.

"Damn it, Elizabeth! What good will it do us to kill the wrong people? I promise you, whoever caused this will die. We *will* find who it was." I sit and upend the envelope. A handful of newspaper photograph clippings flutter out, followed by a few sheets of paper stapled together.

I study each picture, then pass them to Elizabeth.

The first shows a woman holding the hands of a young boy and a younger girl as they attend a funeral. In the next, Jorge Santos, no older than eighteen, is pictured handcuffed, being guided into a squad car by two policemen. Santos is pictured alone in the third, older this time, grinning, standing in front of his Hobie Cat accepting a trophy. In the fourth, a group of men pose, dressed like Civil War soldiers with Santos brandishing an antique rifle in their midst. And the last presents a different image, another gathering, but everyone dressed this time in eighteenth-century military garb, Santos lighting the touch hole, firing a cannon in front of an old fort.

I've no doubt the children in the first clipping are Maria and Jorge. Even the old black-and-white picture shows their shared resemblance, especially around their eyes and mouths. The woman, their mother I assume, has the same features. She and the boy look in pain. The little girl seems merely confused. I shake my head and sigh, no longer quite so angry, realizing the further anguish I've brought them all.

I turn my attention to the report. Typed double-spaced on plain paper it bears no letterhead, no salutation, no indication for whom it's intended or who has created it. Not that I would expect Arturo Gomez or Jeremy Tindall to want those things. I pass each page on to Elizabeth after I finish it.

CONFIDENTIAL REPORT
SUBJECT—JORGE SANTOS
TYPE: COMPLETE
DATE: 7/15/98

Full Name: Jorge Miguel Lario Santos
Address: 1213 Drexel Avenue, Apt. 13B, Miami Beach 32128
Phone: (305) 555-7312 Fax: NA E-mail: NA
Age: 27 Height: 5'10" Weight: 165 lbs. Eyes: Brn Hair: Blk
Birthdate: 11/16/71 Race/Heritage: Cuban
Education: Coral Gables High School (graduated 1988)
　　　　　 Miami Dade Community College (one year)
Occupation: Bartender
Employer: Joe's Stone Crabs (1993–present)
Military Service: None
Family: Father, Emilio (killed 1978 in raid on Cuba)
　　　　 Mother, Hortensia (never remarried)
　　　　 Sister, Maria (reported missing in March of '98)
Relationship(s): Casey Morton (eight months)
Organizations: Hobie Fleet 36, Alcoholics Anonymous, Narcotics Anonymous, Tucker's Brigade
Hobbies/Interests: Sailing (Hobie Catamarans), Black powder shooting, Reenactor (Volunteer cannoneer at Castillo de San Marcos in St. Augustine)

Note: This report was compiled through both document searches and personal interviews. While we are relatively sure of the precision of our findings, due to the short period of time we had to accumulate the information and the understandable secrecy we had to maintain during the investigation, we can't guarantee all of our conclusions to be 100% accurate.

History: Jorge Santos, the son of Cuban exiles, was born and raised in Miami. When he was 7, his father, Emilio, died while participating (it's unclear whether he was killed in action or captured and executed) in an exile raid on Cuba. His mother, Hortensia, subsequently raised Jorge and his sister, Maria, by herself, supporting the family by working as a bookkeeper at Joe's Stone Crab restaurant on Miami Beach (where she is still employed).

Santos was an unremarkable student, graduating in the middle of his class without earning any special recognition or getting into anything more than normal adolescent trouble. People who knew him at the time report his only memorable trait was his outstanding devotion to his mother and his sister (possibly brought on by the early loss of his father).

In college (Miami Dade Community College) he discovered drugs and was arrested on campus for possession of marijuana (which he was smoking at the time of his arrest). Ejected from college (he would have failed anyway), let off with a warning by the judge, Santos spent the next two years living at home, going from job to job from party to party, graduating from pot to cocaine, barbiturates and Quaaludes.

Finally, confronted by both his sister and his mother, Santos agreed to clean up his act. He began to attend Narcotics Anonymous and looked for steady work. His mother, acting on his behalf, arranged for a job at Joe's, one of the premier restaurants in South Florida. Ironically, they trained him as a bartender.

Making good money for the first time in his life, Santos moved into his own apartment on Miami Beach. (According to his 1987 tax return he declared an income in excess of $38,000 for the year. He probably made much more than that in undeclared tips—all of this income earned in only 7 months, since Joe's traditionally closes their doors from mid-May until mid-October.)

Because of the long vacations each year, he was able to actively pursue his other interests. Santos bought his own sailboat (a 16-foot Hobie catamaran) and sailed and raced it, winning his class in the Miami to Key Largo race three years in a row. He also joined Tucker's Brigade, a group of men who like to dress up in period garb and reenact historical battles, where he learned how to load and shoot replicas of antique, black-powder rifles and pistols.

His interest in reenactments eventually led him to St. Augustine where he became enamored with the big guns at the old Spanish fortress of Castillo de San Marcos. Volunteering to become one of the cannoneers, he spent each summer (from June through August, from 1994 to 1997) in St. Augustine.

Possibly because of the irregular lifestyle his work required, he developed an alcohol problem, entering AA in 1995 and subsequently suffering periodic lapses (the most recent a two-week binge in March of this year). Only his mother's relationship with the owners of Joe's and the tragic disappearance of his sister prevented his dismissal on this last occasion.

He met his current girlfriend, Casey Morton (age 26, a graduate of University of Miami and a staff writer for the business section of the *Miami Herald*) at an AA meeting in December. Because Morton's an Anglo and a recovering alcoholic, Santos's mother disapproves of the relationship, which has been tumultuous at best.

The disappearance of Santos's sister, Maria, seems to have sobered Santos and drawn Morton and him closer. It also seems to have given his life a focus for the first time. Since his mother called him looking for her daughter, Santos has devoted all of his leisure time to looking for her or, as he loudly says he suspects, her killer. In this pursuit, Morton has been invaluable, both by using the *Herald*'s archives, using her own contacts at the newspaper and her coworkers' contacts with the police to further their investigation.

Santos personally found Maria's car in the parking lot at the Dinner Key docks and has subsequently interviewed every wino and derelict who may have been in the vicinity that night, as well as every apartment owner or hotel guest whose windows overlooked the area.

Two winos, Sam Pratt and Harry Watkins, have told him (and subsequently told the police) that late that night they saw a tall, blond man meet a young woman on the docks and take her away in a wooden speedboat. Watkins described it as a classic, like the one they used in the Fonda movie, *On Golden Pond.*

(Both men decided, after our operatives interviewed them, that they would be better off leaving town.)

Santos and Morton have visited every marina and dock in South Florida looking for such boats. They've found none whose owners might have been involved with Maria's disappearance.

That is not to say that Santos and Morton have no suspects. Shortly after Maria's disappearance, Santos asked the police to take a close look at Peter DelaSangre. He informed them that his sister had expressed a romantic interest in Mr. DelaSangre and that DelaSangre met the description given by Watkins and Pratt. Adding to that the knowledge (thanks to Miss Morton) that Mr. DelaSangre lived on an island and, therefore, would have to use boats for transportation, Santos insisted he was the most logical suspect.

Due to Mr. DelaSangre's standing in the community (not to mention his political clout), the police refused to target him without any further evidence. Likewise the *Herald* and all the other media refused to carry any stories about the police's refusal to investigate him. Furthermore, *Herald* management has assured us that Miss Morton has been cautioned to cease using newspaper assets to help further their quest.

The lack of support has done little to dampen Santos's zeal to bring his sister's abductor to justice. He's been very open in expressing his doubts that the system will do anything to support him. His intent is to administer justice himself.

Toward this end, at a gun show in April, both he and Morton took and passed a concealed weapons course and applied for concealed weapon permits. Records show they purchased a nine millimeter Glock semiautomatic pistol, a two-shot forty-five caliber Remington derringer and a thirty-eight caliber Smith and Wesson snub-nosed revolver.

Sources, who've observed them practicing at Tamiami Gun Shop's indoor target range, report that Santos wears the Glock on an ankle holster on his right leg and the Remington on an ankle holster on his left leg. Miss Morton carries her S&W in her purse. Both are passably decent shots.

Peter DelaSangre has become something of a fixation for both of them, Miss Morton gathering information on him from any source she can (unearthing, by the way, DelaSangre's connection with LaMar Associates) and Santos calling LaMar Associates on a daily basis thereafter, seeking an interview with Mr. DelaSangre. Santos also has made attempts to spy on Blood Key, Mr. DelaSangre's island.

After we received complaints that an ultralight seaplane buzzed the island four days in a row, we investigated and found that Santos had paid Tony Ribini, of Tony's Seaplanes on the Rickenbacker Causeway, to overfly the island with him onboard as passenger. Ribini said Santos had expressed disappointment that overhanging trees had prevented him from seeing the entire harbor. Mr. Ribini also agreed (after conversation with our operatives) it would be unwise, should he be asked again, for him to participate in any more such intrusive overflights.

We would caution Mr. DelaSangre that these people represent to him, at minimum, a threat of serious annoyance (including possible legal harassment) and, at worst, a threat of major, possibly deadly, harm. If he continues to insist on meeting with them, he should be advised to take utmost care (up to, and including armed bodyguards) in his dealings with them.

After I finish, I put down the report and pick up the clippings again. It's hard for me to see much danger in Santos's face. I see too much of Maria in him. I shake my head and grin. The man has passion. I respect that. Maria deserves nothing less.

"Why are you smiling?" Elizabeth asks. "The man wants you dead. He may already have tried."

"If he did, he failed," I say, thinking how angry Santos would be if he knew how little I fear him. "Read the report again. This man wants to look me in the eyes before he kills me. I doubt he was on the boat. I hope he wasn't. I want to see how it plays out with him . . . how he chooses to confront me. But"—I shrug—"if he was the shooter, he'll die. Remember, with one word, I can have him and his girlfriend destroyed any time I want."

"If it wasn't him, who was it?"

"In due time we'll find out," I say. "In due time, whoever it was will die."

I return to the clippings, study Santos's face and wonder what he'll say to me Friday morning. I find myself looking forward to meeting this man.

As comfortable as power and wealth are to possess, I've found they make life far too easy and far too predictable. Most humans can either be bought or intimidated, but not Santos, I think. Leaning back in my chair, I continue to study his pictures and luxuriate in the pleasure of not knowing what to expect of him.

18

Though I suggest otherwise, Elizabeth insists on accompanying me to my meeting with Santos. She promises to wake early, to be ready to leave whenever I wish. The night before, after we hunt across the Gulfstream over the back roads of Bimini, she emphasizes her intent by changing to her human form and lying beside me in my king-size bed.

I welcome her company. Each night since we've arrived, we've retired to our separate beds after lovemaking, my dragoness remaining in her natural state, preferring to sprawl and doze in her bed of hay while, across the room, I choose to sleep under sheets, on a mattress, in my human form. I've missed the intimacy of the slumbers we shared on our voyage home but I must confess, I've been as unwilling as she to give up my preferences.

When I wake in the morning to the heat of her breath on the back of my neck and the weight of her legs tangled with mine, I smile. When Father lived I still spent many hours each day alone, time enough to know the bleak despair of loneliness. Elizabeth's presence on the island has changed all that. Even when she remains asleep in our chambers as I go about my chores elsewhere in the house, I feel her presence and the knowledge of her nearness warms me, keeps me content. As irritating as she can be, as headstrong as she is, she makes my life complete and I love her for that.

But I care little for the small struggles our relationship brings each day. Elizabeth never wakens easily before the afternoon. Promise or not, this day is no different. When I turn, take her in my arms and whisper, "Elizabeth, it's time to get up," she shrugs my arms off and turns away.

"Later," she mumbles.

"The appointment is at ten." I spit my words as I disengage from her and scowl as I get up. "I plan to be early, with you or without you."

Elizabeth doesn't answer until I give up waiting for her. Only then, after I've turned my back on her, laid out my clothes for the day and begun to put on my pants, does she sit up. "Of course it will be with me," she says, hurls her pillow at me and laughs when it hits her mark. "And I expect you to show me around Miami after the meeting ends."

While Elizabeth dresses, I search my drawers for Derek Blood's slip of paper with Claypool and Son's address on it. She comes to the dresser just as I find it. I show it to her. "I promised your father a gift of gold. As long as we're going to the office anyway, I thought I'd bring it along, have Arturo send it out to your family's agents. If you want to write to Chloe or any of your family, this would be a good time to do it. I could send it in the same shipment."

My bride shakes her head, reaches for the gold necklace she left the night before on top of the dresser. "I'm no good at it," she says putting on the necklace. "Why don't you write something for me?"

I shrug, say, "Sure."

Elizabeth flashes a smile, pirouettes in front of me so I can admire her new yellow silk dress. I make a show of examining her, but, as much as I want to smile, I can't keep from frowning at the gold, four-leaf clover charm dangling from her necklace, the emerald inset in its center.

"What?" Elizabeth says.

"I'd prefer you didn't wear that today," I say pointing to her necklace.

She touches it with her hand. "But I always wear it. You gave it to me."

"Santos will notice it. I took it from his sister."

Elizabeth scowls. "It's mine now. Who cares what he notices?"

"I do," I say. "We're having this meeting with him to see if we can ease his suspicions, not raise them. You can wear something else for one day."

"No," she says. "Not for a human . . ."

"Elizabeth . . ." I sigh.

"I'll tuck it in for you," she says, lifting the chain, dropping the charm inside her bodice so all that shows of the necklace is a glint of the gold chain. "But I won't take it off for him."

"Fine," I say. "Just as long as he doesn't see it." I turn my attention from her, take a moment to write a quick note to her family telling them that all is well and then go downstairs to the treasure room.

It takes a few minutes for me to decide between the gold coins in the treasure chests or the heavy gold bars stacked near the wall. Deciding Charles Blood would be most pleased to receive some of Father's ancient gold ingots, I heft one and grin at its weight. Just four bars would be far more than twice my bride's weight. Five, I think, wrapping the bars in burlap, should keep the old monster happy.

But not Elizabeth. She frowns when I carry the bars to the boat, and asks, "Why so much?"

"We can afford it, Elizabeth. It's for *your* family."

"It's for my father," she says. "Trust me, none of the rest of my family will benefit from it at all."

A uniformed guard, armed, one hand on his holstered pistol, opens the door to the Monroe building's lobby when we approach. Inside, three other armed-and-uniformed guards—each one anxiously examining the burlap bundle in my arms, cautiously touching his pistol grip—watch us enter. I grin at the increased security, look toward the video cameras located near the ceiling in each corner of the room and nod, sure that Arturo is watching.

One of the armed men escorts us to the private elevator that will take us to LaMar Associates' executive offices. After we enter it, he stands guard in front of the open doors and waits for them to close. Arturo meets us when we arrive, yet another security guard standing behind him.

Clean-shaven once again, clothed in one of his tailored suits, clearly anxious to look in command of the situation, Arturo motions for us to leave the elevator as if the concept of stepping off wouldn't occur to us.

"Don't you think you're overdoing this?" I ask.

He shakes his head. "Didn't someone shoot at you the other day?"

I nod and turn to Elizabeth. "Arturo's worried about our being assassinated."

Arturo frowns when she opens her eyes wide in mock alarm. "They may very well be armed," he says to my bride. "You read the report, didn't you? This Santos fellow is no friend of your husband's."

"Welcoming him into an armed camp will hardly make him less hostile," I say. "I would prefer you have the guards position themselves in a less conspicuous way. The man is coming to have a conversation with me. I doubt he'll start our meeting by unloading his pistol into me."

"And if you're wrong?"

I grin at him. "Then Elizabeth will become a very young and very rich widow."

The Latin turns his attention to the burlap package in my arms. "And that is?" he asks.

"A gift for my father-in-law. I need you to send it to his agents in Kingston. I have their address in my pocket."

Arturo nods, pulls back a corner of the fabric, enough to

catch the dull shine of a gold ingot, and whistles. Perfectly aware of the weight of what I'm carrying, he makes no attempt to relieve me of my burden. "You better put this in the back of my office closet. I'll take care of it after the meeting with Santos," he says.

Jeremy Tindall comes in to greet us once we arrive at my office. He scowls as he pumps my hand, and growls, "Ever since the fire and Tyler's death, my wife can't stop crying; my other two sons are scared of every shadow. . . ."

I shrug. "Shadows don't kill people, mistakes do. Just like someone made a mistake shooting at me."

Tindall blushes scarlet. His voice turns shrill. "And my boat's a mess! You could have been more careful. Stains on the deck, on the flybridge—I've scrubbed everything, everywhere . . . four times already and still I keep finding spots I've missed. I had to tear out the damned carpeting in the salon and order it replaced. What in God's name did you two do on my boat?" Then, before I can answer, he shakes his head, says, "No, don't tell me."

He turns to Elizabeth, offers his hand, frowns as he says, "Congratulations. You've married a real piece of work."

My bride nods, briefly accepts his grasp, then turns away and walks to the window. She stares out at the parking lot across the street and the bay beyond, the morning light coming through the glass, enveloping her, turning her yellow silk dress almost diaphanous—silhouetting her trim body beneath the translucent cloth.

For the first time I notice the slight curve of her normally flat, lower abdomen, the new, barely perceptible, increased swell to her breasts. I go to her, hug her from behind, put my hands on her stomach. *"Our son's beginning to let his presence be known,"* I mindspeak.

She turns, faces me. *"If it displeases you, I can change my shape. . . ."*

"No." I kiss her forehead. *"It pleases me very much."*

Jeremy clears his throat and says, "Arturo and I think we should sit in on your meeting. We may be able to be of help."

"Whatever," I say.

"Is there anything you need us to do?" he asks.

"No." I shake my head. "I just plan to answer his questions. Then, afterward, I think I'll take Elizabeth around town. Buy her a few things."

Elizabeth notices Santos first. "Look." She points out the window toward Monty's parking lot across the street. I follow the direction of her gesture, watch as an old green MGB sports car, its top down, pulls into a spot. A dark-haired man and a thin, blond woman get out. "He looks like the man in the clippings," she says.

"I think you're right."

Arturo calls downstairs, makes sure that one of the guards will escort the couple up. Then he begins to rearrange the chairs in my office. "Of course you'll sit behind your desk and Elizabeth can sit to your right," he says, placing a chair for her on that side of my desk. "Jeremy can sit on your left. We'll have Santos and his woman sit in front of your desk. I'll sit across the room behind them. Just in case . . ." He reaches into his jacket's right front pocket, pulls out a small, chrome, automatic pistol, cocks it and replaces it.

I frown at him and he shrugs, saying, "If it's needed."

Our receptionist, Emily, obviously nervous, her face flushed, her hands fluttering, leads Jorge Santos and Casey Morton into my office, stays just long enough to announce them, then rushes off.

Seated behind my desk, everyone else in their chairs as Arturo indicated, I let Jorge Santos and his woman stand by the doorway for a few moments while I examine him. Santos makes my rudeness more acceptable by taking the same opportunity to stare at me.

He seems a bit thicker, a little older than his pictures. As I expected he would, he's come to the meeting dressed informally, in jeans and a yellow T-shirt. But Casey Morton surprises me by wearing an austere, navy-blue business dress, carrying an equally plain, small, round, blue leather purse. Even in her flat shoes she stands at least three inches taller than Santos. With her blond hair chopped into an almost boyish cut, her figure trim and athletic, verging on bony, she hardly looks like the type of woman I'd expect him to choose. I had imagined her shorter, more curvaceous, less severe.

"She'd have to put on some weight before I'd consider making a meal of her," Elizabeth mindspeaks.

I grin and nod. Then I stand and motion the couple to their seats, introducing them to Arturo, Jeremy and my bride. Once Santos has taken his seat, I sit facing him, the sunlight streaming through the window behind me so he has to squint when he looks at me. I make no offer to lower the shades, knowing Arturo would be scandalized if I did anything to lessen the man's discomfort.

"Well, Mr. Santos, I gather you've been anxious to speak with me," I say.

He looks from me to Elizabeth, to Jeremy, swivels around to glance at Arturo behind him. "With you, yes. But I didn't expect your whole office."

I smile at his bluntness. "Mr. Tindall is my attorney. Mr. Gomez is my close business associate. They've expressed concern that you don't wish me well and have requested they be allowed to sit in to make sure my statements aren't misrepresented. As for Elizabeth"—I nod my head toward Casey Morton—"surely if I have no objection to your girlfriend being in attendance, you'll have no objection to my wife doing the same."

"I just thought we would talk, you and me . . ." Santos looks at Elizabeth. "Of course, I don't mind if she's here. But them . . ."

"*They* are in my confidence. I'm afraid I must insist on their presence."

Santos shrugs. "They don't matter very much," he says, almost to himself and Morton.

She nods agreement, and says, "Go ahead."

He looks at Elizabeth again, knits his eyebrows and asks, "Did Maria know you were married?"

"Mr. Santos, your sister waited on me just once—at Detardo's Steakhouse. I wasn't married at the time, but had I been, I doubt it would have been discussed. Whatever conversation we had couldn't have encompassed more than fifty words. We certainly didn't address anything of a personal nature. After my meal, she did give me her phone number and she did ask me to call her. But I never bothered to."

"You have to understand my sister is . . . was very important to me," Santos says, lowering his voice, looking down as he speaks. "After my father died—when my mother was too busy grieving, we took care of each other. We never stopped. I could always tell her anything. I could always count on her support. She could always count on me too. When she disappeared, it was like somebody stole a part of my heart. . . ."

Casey Morton leans forward, stares at me, her pale blue eyes hard. "Two men said they saw a tall, blond man meet Maria on the dock. She left in his boat. No one has seen her since."

"And how many tall, blond men are there in South Florida? How many more vacation here?" I ask, then turn my attention to Santos. "I understand your grief. From the small interaction I had with your sister, she seemed to be a sweet person. But I have to tell you I resent the implication of your questions."

"Mr. DelaSangre, where were you on the night of March eighteenth?" Casey Morton asks.

"At home, on my island."

She glares at me. "Do you have any proof?"

I feel a flush rise on my face, and wonder why her questioning bothers me. It's not her place, I decide. The matter of Maria belongs between Jorge and me. "First," I say, returning her cold stare, "I agreed to meet with Mr. Santos and answer his questions. I agreed to nothing with you. You are here as a guest and an observer. I suggest you let Mr. Santos handle his own questions from now on. Otherwise, this meeting will be at its end.

"Second"—I look at Santos, lock eyes with him—"I'm under the impression you've been quite active in investigating me. If you have and if you've been in the slightest bit competent, then you know I prefer to live a fairly secluded lifestyle. I spent almost all my nights at home last year, alone. And no, I can't prove that."

Santos nods, ignores Morton's stiff posture, her red face and tight lips, and leans toward me as if we have a game of chess going and he's about to move another piece. "Have you ever owned a classic wood runabout? A Chris Craft or one like it?"

I lean forward too, smile at him. He forces a grin in return, both of us acting like old friends, deep in discussion. "Once again, I have to refer you to your own investigation. Haven't you checked what boats I have registered?"

Santos nods.

"And what did you find?" I ask.

"A Grady White," Santos says.

I lean back in my chair, swivel so I can look out the window to the bay. "Mr. Santos, do you boat?"

"I sail."

"Do you know where my island is out there? How far off-shore it is?"

He nods.

"Have you ever been caught out there in a storm?"

"Of course I have," Santos says.

"Then you know how wicked it can get. Do you think I would care to use anything as unseaworthy as a runabout when I own a wide-beamed, deep-V hulled boat with twin, two hundred Yamahas that was built to handle the worst the ocean can throw at it?"

"Some people use different boats for different purposes."

I turn back. "And I use mine for transportation."

Santos shrugs. "You could still have more boats than you've registered."

"I could, but I don't. Mr. Santos, your sister may have been abducted by a tall, blond man in a wooden runabout, but she wasn't taken by me."

Shaking her head, Casey Morton shoots up from her chair, her small blue bag spilling from her lap, the purse landing by Elizabeth's feet. The blonde slaps both hands, palms down, on the desk, and spits out, "Then why the hell have you been so tough to get hold of?" She glares at me. "Where the hell have you been for all these months?"

Jeremy Tindall cuts into the conversation. "Miss, who do you think you are? Sit down. The man told you to stay quiet. Do you have a hearing problem or comprehension difficulties?"

She turns toward him, the veins in her neck visibly throbbing. Before she can answer, Santos places his hand on her forearm and says, "Casey, honey, relax, sit down, let me handle this."

"It's a fair question to ask," he says to me as Morton sits.

I shrug, watch my bride from the corner of my eye as she bends over, and picks up the blonde's purse, Elizabeth's charm falling out of the dress top as she does so. *"Careful!"* I mindspeak. But it dangles for only an instant before she tucks it back in with one hand while she hands the purse to Morton with the other.

Santos shows no reaction, gives me no sign that he noticed. He continues speaking, his voice and expression the same as before. "Max Lieber told me he saw you months ago at Detardo's and gave you my phone number then. You never called."

"No, I didn't." I look at Santos and his woman and marvel at the difference between them. His questions are polite, his tone noncombative, while she almost vibrates in her chair. Her breath exudes the acid tinge of the bile building in her stomach. "I had a marriage and a honeymoon to think of," I say. "I think you'll understand my desire to focus on those things first."

Santos nods and examines Elizabeth. "Sure, if Maria was only a waitress you met once. I guess I can understand. But, if you don't mind my asking . . ." He points to Elizabeth. "Just how old is she?"

Elizabeth glowers at him. *"Why don't we just be done with these two?"* she mindspeaks. *"I don't understand your patience."*

"Just a few minutes more, then they'll be gone."

I turn my attention to Santos. "I'm not sure what this has to do with this conversation, but Elizabeth's twenty-one. She's also, as you may notice, a little miffed to be listening to someone suggest her husband had an interest in someone else shortly before he married her. Which, once again—I must insist you believe this—I did not."

"You told Lieber, Maria was far too young for you."

"I didn't want to say anything unkind." I look at Santos and see the resemblance to Maria in his eyes and mouth. I wish I could tell him how much I had wanted not to harm his sister. But, instead, I go on. "Nor do I want to be rude to you.

I had no interest in your sister for a number of reasons which I prefer not to list, not the least of which were my plans to marry the woman I love."

Jorge Santos nods, looks at his girlfriend, then looks at Elizabeth. "My apologies if this is difficult," he says to her. "I'm almost done.

"I'm not sure what I expected to find out today," Santos says. "Mr. DelaSangre, I know you're rich. Obviously, you're a powerful man. The police certainly don't want to take you on. Your two protectors here can't come cheap. But I have a missing sister to worry about and so far, you're the only possibility I've found."

I stand up and offer my hand. "I hope you realize how improbable a possibility I am."

He stands and shakes my hand, a good firm grasp. "Well, at least I don't feel any more sure today than before I came. . . . Maybe . . ." He pauses, tightening his grip on my hand. "Do you think it would be possible for me to come out to your island and scout around a little—just to get rid of any remaining doubts?"

"Certainly not!" Jeremy Tindall says. "Mr. DelaSangre has been more than gracious enough already. As his attorney, I recommended against this meeting in the first place. . . ."

"Enough, Jeremy." I disengage from Santos's grasp. "You must understand how much I value my privacy. I'm sure your research has shown you how reclusive my family has always been. We are very wealthy and that always keeps us in danger. We've found that seclusion protects us best. For these reasons I must refuse your request."

Jorge Santos smiles at me, nods his head in a slight bow toward Elizabeth, everyone standing now. "And you must understand, because of your refusal I can't throw out the possibility of your involvement in Maria's disappearance."

"We all do what we must," I say, walking from behind the desk. "I just hope one day you'll come to believe me."

Santos nods. "The eyes . . ." he says, looking from Elizabeth's face to mine. "Maria raved about your emerald-green eyes. Her's are the same color."

"They run in my family. Elizabeth's a distant cousin."

"Oh," Santos says, examining Elizabeth again, focusing this time on her lower neck. "I think I saw something before. May I?" he says, reaching toward the thin, gold chain she's worn since our wedding day, grabbing it, pulling up, untucking the gold charm, examining it.

"Do I have to tolerate this?" Elizabeth backs away, her movement jerking the charm from his hand.

"No!" I say, moving forward, shoving him back. "You forget. That's my wife you're bothering." I push him again. "Leave her alone!"

Santos says nothing. He allows the momentum of my second shove to knock him off his feet, drop him to his left knee. Crouched, glaring at me, he pulls up his right pants' leg, yanks his Glock automatic from the ankle holster underneath and points it at me. "Where did she get that necklace?" he growls.

Casey Morton throws open her purse, rummages through it for her pistol. Before she can produce it, Arturo presses his chrome automatic to her temple.

"What the fuck do you all think you're doing?" Jeremy asks. "This is a meeting, not a Goddamned gang war."

Santos glares at me, continues to point his pistol.

"Peter?" Elizabeth mindspeaks.

"Don't worry. We can survive far worse than this gun," I reassure her, smiling, glad I'd gone shopping at Dadeland Mall in June. Pleased to have a safe answer to his inquiry.

"Stop looking so damned smug and answer my fucking question!" Santos stands, approaches me with his arm outstretched, bringing the Glock within a foot of my head.

"Back off!" Arturo says, grabbing Morton with his free arm, pinning her arms, pointing his pistol at Santos.

Santos shakes his head. "I'll put down the gun when he answers me."

"That's hardly the way to ask me a question," I say, "but in the interest of peace I don't mind telling you—I found it in the Dadeland Mall, at Mayer's, back in June. They had it in their window. It cost me four hundred fifty dollars plus tax. I paid cash. If you give me a couple of days, I think I can search through my stuff at home and find the receipt."

"You're bluffing," Santos says. He continues to aim the gun at me. "I gave Maria a chain like that on her *Quince* . . . with the same clover charm, the same emerald in its center." He shakes his head. "This is too much of a coincidence."

"Call them now." I point to the telephone on my desk. "Ask them if they carry anything like that."

I follow him to my desk, allowing him to keep his pistol targeted on me while he dials and talks to a sales clerk at Mayer's. Finally he says, "Thank you," and hangs up. Then he lowers his pistol.

"Put yours down too," I tell Arturo. He frowns at me but does as he's told. Casey Morton rushes over to stand next to Santos. He ignores her, keeps his eyes on me.

"They don't stock them anymore," Santos says. "But she said they sold quite a few pieces like I described over the past few years. She said she thought some of the other stores might still have a few. I think I might owe you an apology."

"I believe you do."

"I still want to see the receipt."

"I'll have Arturo bring it to you, but I won't let you keep it."

Santos nods.

Jeremy comes over, stands directly in front of the Cuban. "Mr. Santos, you know you could be arrested for this firearms display today," he says, pointing his long, bony finger at him. "Someone shot at Mr. DelaSangre earlier this week. Fortunately they missed. After your little demonstration today, I would say you're the most likely suspect. I think the police would agree. I strongly suggest you keep your distance from the DelaSangres and this office from now on. If you don't, we'll have you in court, or worse, do you understand?"

Santos looks at me. "For a shooting victim you look real healthy. Trust me, if I was the shooter, you'd be a corpse." The Cuban pauses, stares at Jeremy. "Tindall's your name, isn't it?"

Jeremy nods.

"Then Mr. Tindall, watch out who you fuck with." He pushes Jeremy out of his way, takes Casey Morton's hand and walks to the door with her. He stops there, looks back at Elizabeth and me.

"I don't know," he says, shakes his head. "I have this feeling about you two."

"Feeling or not, you're wrong. I wish you well, Mr. Santos."

"Why do I doubt that?" he says, forcing a grin, his tone false friendly. "Look, you don't have to sound so damned formal. I just held a gun to your head. I think Miss Manners would say that means we've achieved some degree of intimacy. Call me Jorge."

"And you can call me Peter," I say, my tone and smile equally insincere until I spit out my final words to him. "But I think from now on, you should consider that the warning you gave to Jeremy cuts both ways."

Jorge nods, says, "Message received and understood," and leaves.

Once enough time has lapsed for the couple to have walked down the corridor and caught the elevator, Tindall lets out a breath and says, "Good riddance."

"He isn't gone for good, Jeremy," I say. "I'd bet on it."

"He could be," Arturo says.

"No," I shake my head. "I don't want him hurt."

"Sorry," I mindspeak to Elizabeth. *"But I need to take back your necklace for a little while."*

She frowns, shakes her head. *"Why are you bothering with all this?"* Elizabeth asks. *"He's nothing."*

"Elizabeth, please, humor me. I enjoyed myself this morning," I say, reaching for the chain. *"It isn't often that I deal with humans who are willing to oppose me. I just want to see how this all plays out."*

She glares at me, backs away. *"Then humor me too. It's been a long time since I've tasted young flesh. I want to hunt tonight. I want us to find young prey."*

I sigh, wonder if Mother had been this difficult for my father. I have no desire to go on such a hunt, but I see no other way to win my bride's cooperation. When I nod, she grins, steps closer, permits me to undo her necklace.

Handing the necklace to Arturo, I say, "I want you to get me a receipt for this from Mayer's, dated back to June."

"How?" he asks.

"I have no idea." I shrug. "Just get it and arrange to show it to Santos. And bring back Elizabeth's necklace soon. I like how it looks on her neck."

Elizabeth moves closer to me, so our bodies touch, then strokes her now bare neck with her right hand. *"I like that you took it from his dead sister,"* she mindspeaks. Then my bride says aloud, for Arturo and Tindall to hear, "I like how it looks too."

19

When I was much younger, I once asked my father why our people, who had the ability to shift our bodies into other shapes, were so locked in to our male and female identities. Couldn't we eliminate the need for opposing sexes and give ourselves a form capable of bringing its offspring into the world by its own solitary endeavors?

Father chuckled before he replied. *"I suppose it could be possible, but it would be a dull world,"* he said. *"We already have so much power. We take what we want, feed when we wish. We have little reason to fear other beings. If we didn't have to confront the uncertainty and aggravation of romance, the constant ebb and flow of our relationships, how could we possibly avoid boredom?"*

Life with Elizabeth is anything but dull. She rarely wakes before noon. But once she arises, she amazes me by managing to be in constant motion, sometimes gardening, other times roaming around the island or the house, borrowing the boat to race across the water, insisting on hunting each evening, demanding we make love afterward before we sleep.

Keeping her entertained remains a constant challenge. "Watching humans on TV only makes me hungry," she says. Elizabeth cares little for the books I read or the recordings of Mozart, Handel and Bach that I play. She dismisses all of it as "Human foolishness." But human-made goods, especially clothes, fascinate her and she asks me almost every day to take her to the mainland to go shopping.

Still busy getting the island in shape after my long absence, I try to channel her energy in more practical ways but, except for her garden, she remains aloof from all household chores. When I request her help in any type of housekeeping she sniffs, shakes her head and dismisses it by saying, "That's slave work," and punishes me with her silence.

By the time Arturo visits the island to return Elizabeth's necklace, almost a week after our confrontation with Jorge Santos, I welcome his presence. The Latin beams as he steps onto my dock and I greet him as if he were a long-missed, cherished friend. Elizabeth—also glad for the break in our solitary lifestyle, I suppose—joins us at the dock and acknowledges Gomez's presence with a smile before she takes the gold chain from his hands and fastens it around her neck. She stays by my side and listens as we begin to discuss Santos.

"All the man did was shrug when I showed him the receipt from Mayer's," Arturo tells me, handing me the receipt I told him to acquire. "I doubt he's convinced of anything."

"All the more reason for your associates to keep a watch on him and his girlfriend," I say.

Arturo grins. "They already are. The day after our meeting, Casey Morgan tried to sell her editor a story on your family and its businesses." He chuckles. "As soon as I heard about it, I called and had a long talk with the man. He turned her down. A few days later, he called to tell me he had her transferred to their Fort Lauderdale office, to write for the local news section up there."

"What about Santos?" Elizabeth asks. "Can't we arrange the same sort of thing for him?"

"It's not as easy," Arturo says. "He's a bartender at Joe's. I have enough influence to get a table there when I want. But

I certainly can't get him transferred. We have to wait to see what he does and act when he gives us the right opportunity."

"And the white speedboat?" I ask.

"My people told me one was reported stolen from the Miami Beach Marina a few days before the shooting. It turned up, abandoned, in Eleuthra."

"And?"

Arturo holds up his hands and shrugs. "And that's all they know. I'd like to say it was Santos but this looks like it was contracted. I don't think he has the resources."

I nod agreement. "Under any circumstance, I don't think he'd want to let anyone else do it."

"True," Arturo says. "Which means we probably have another problem."

"I think so too." I smile, then say in half-jest, "You better get more of your people looking into it before I start to think it's you."

Arturo doesn't smile back.

Elizabeth's busy arguing with me about cars, neither of us thinking about the shooting or Santos, when we arrive at the dock at Monty's the next afternoon. "If we're so rich," she asks as we wait by the restaurant's valet stand for a taxi, "why don't we own our own cars?"

I shake my head, thinking of the dozens of times my father had lectured me about lack of necessity for car ownership and the waste of owning one. "We live on an island," I say. "We need to own a boat. But for the few times a month we come to land, it makes far more sense to hire a taxi."

Elizabeth grins. "We're rich," she says. "We don't have to make sense."

She looks off, frowns as I begin to explain if we used a taxi every single day for two years, it would still be cheaper than any car we'd choose to buy. She doesn't answer when I finish and I ask, "Are you listening?"

"Peter, look in the public parking lot across the street," she mindspeaks.

I follow her gaze, see nothing but cars. "What?" I say.

"In the row by the water, next to the tall palm tree."

The green MGB, parked in position to observe both our boat slip and Monty's parking lot, means nothing to me until the driver sitting behind the wheel grins and waves. Not wishing to let him think he can intimidate me, I smile and wave back to Jorge Santos.

Elizabeth continues to pester me about cars. I finally give in when we pass by a red Corvette in Monty's parking lot and she stops and says, "I'm not moving until you promise to buy me one of these."

To Arturo's dismay, I purchase a silver Mercedes sedan for me too. He frowns, and says, "I don't see why you need any car let alone two."

"With Elizabeth, it's easier to give her what she wants than to argue about it," I say. "Besides you should have seen her face when we bought the Corvette."

Arturo shakes his head. "All you two do is shop. You're spending more money faster than Don Henri ever did." But he arranges for the cars to be kept and maintained in Monty's private parking lot, just next to the valet stand.

At Elizabeth's insistence we begin to come to shore more often—both for her to shop and to drive her car around town. Not a day passes that we don't arrive to find Santos's green MGB parked in the free lot near the docks, the man watching our comings and goings.

Finally, I complain about it to Arturo. "You should have told me sooner," he says.

The next morning, as soon as Jorge Santos pulls into Monty's lot, two Miami police cars cut him off. Arturo has trouble stopping laughing as he tells me about it. "I watched from my office window," he says. "The cops yanked him out of the car, made him breathe in their machine—even though he was completely sober—and then arrested him for driving under the influence." He stops to laugh again. "They threw him in the drunk tank. They promised me they won't let him arrange for bail for at least a couple of more days."

The next day Elizabeth and I come to shore for another day of shopping, this time at the ritzy stores at Bal Harbour Shoppes. We arrive back at the docks in the afternoon. Relieved to see no sign of the green MGB, I say, "Look, our friend's still missing. I wonder when they'll let him out?"

"Never, I hope," Elizabeth snarls.

She takes the helm of the Grady White, turns the key in the ignition while I stow her packages from Gucci, Saks and Lord and Taylor in the cabin. The Yamahas cough to life without the slightest hesitation.

I undo the dock lines, settle into the companion seat next to my bride. By now, when it comes to handling boats, I trust Elizabeth as much as I do myself. Relying on her to pilot us home, I close my eyes and prepare to allow the fresh air and the rolling motion of the boat to lull me into an afternoon nap.

"Peter!" she says, about halfway across the bay, the brittle tone of her voice jolting me awake.

"What?"

"Something's wrong. The boat's not handling properly."

Still groggy, I check, listening to the Yamahas' drone. "The motors sound okay."

"But we're slowing . . . the steering feels strange. . . ."

I take over the wheel, turn it slightly to the right. After a slight pause, the boat reacts to my touch, heeling more than I would have expected from such a slight move. We hit a small wave and plow through it, the boat shuddering, rather than cleanly slicing the water. I push the throttles forward and the engines rev but, instead of leaping forward, the Grady White only slowly increases its speed.

"You're right," I say, cutting back on the throttles. "We're riding lower in the water than we should." The boat settles into the water, wallows as we slow, the bow dropping lower than the rest. I check the depth finder, find it reads eighteen feet.

Opening the cabin hatch, I shake my head when I find what I expect to see. Water everywhere—seat cushions, Elizabeth's packages floating, ruined. "We're taking on water," I say. "Something's leaking, somewhere."

"What do we do?" my bride asks.

"Worse comes to worse, we'll take a long swim. Still I'd rather not sink in the deepest section of the bay." I take the wheel, throw the throttles forward, my anger growing at the boat's sluggish response, the water rushing back as we speed forward, weighing down the stern, slowing our movement. I turn us toward shore, hope we arrive at the dock before we sink low enough to stall the engines.

I have Elizabeth call Arturo on my cell phone, arrange to have him speed out to meet us on the water, somewhere before we reach shore.

By the time the yellow Seatow boat approaches us, we're already close enough to make out the large green marker of the marina's main channel. The Grady White has sunk low enough that saltwater reaches up to our ankles in the cockpit. Arturo, still in his suit, stands next to the rescue boat's helmsman, waves with one hand while he dials a cell phone with the other.

Our phone rings and Elizabeth answers, listens. "They want you to cut the engines and let them come aside and pick us up," she says.

She frowns when I shake my head. "They say we're too low in the water to keep going. . . ."

I push the throttles further forward, aim the Grady White for the channel to Monty's a few hundred yards to the north. "Tell them to follow us. If we sink, they can pick us up."

We make it as far as the pine-covered spoil islands on the perimeter of the marina before I'm willing to concede defeat. "Brace yourself!" I tell Elizabeth and steer the craft toward the sandy shore of the northernmost island, shuddering at the yowl of the Yamahas as they collide with the bottom and tilt back from the impact, wincing at the scream of sand tearing at the hull bottom—even before we reach the beach—furious that my boat has to be treated this way. The Grady White slams to a stop, its bow dug into the sand, water rushing forward from the cockpit, then sloshing back.

I cut the engines and silence overtakes us, interrupted only by the whisper of the seawind through the pine trees and the growl of the Seatow's engines as it approaches us.

"Are you all right?" Arturo yells.

"No," I say. "After you get us to shore, you damn well better get someone to bring my boat in and I damn well better be told, damn soon, what the hell happened to my boat!"

Arturo brings the Grady White back to my island two days later. I meet him at the dock. "I thought I'd save you the bother," he says, and nods his head toward the twenty-five-foot Wellcraft tied nearby. "I'll take the rental back for you."

I say nothing, even though I'm glad to have my own boat again, glad not to have to endure a lesser craft.

"I don't know what they were thinking," he says.

Cocking an eyebrow, I ask, "Who?"

He shrugs. "We don't know yet but whoever it was certainly didn't wish you well. They reversed both your bilge pumps and opened the seacock to your head. If a plastic bag hadn't been sucked up by the intake and blocked the seacock, you would have sunk far before shore."

"Saved by litter," I say, and can't help grinning.

Arturo grins too, then turns solemn. "It could just as easily have been a bomb."

"Santos?" I ask.

"I don't think so. He just made bail yesterday. We both know where he was before that."

"Then who?"

"My people are checking."

"Your people are always checking," I growl.

Arturo sighs. "Be patient, Peter. These things take time. Just be careful in the meantime. Check your boat and cars before you use them. I'll have my people watch them but, until we get this resolved, you have to take care too."

To my relief, my bride agrees to cut back on her landside shopping trips. Our life as a couple settles into a comfortable pattern. Elizabeth turns her attention to her garden, which prospers under her renewed and constant ministry. Within weeks, new plants—many of them strange, brightly colored ones I've never seen—begin to crowd the formerly empty earth. The Dragon's Tear and other herbs become so numerous that she has to harvest her first crop.

Most of the time I go about the necessary chores to keep up the maintenance of our household while Elizabeth divides her free time between the garden and the kitchen, planting and weeding in the former, processing herbs and potions in the latter. Sometimes I work in the garden alongside my bride, brushing against her, both of us smiling, enjoying the intimacy of quietly sharing the same tasks. She never mentions Jorge Santos's name and, while he remains in my thoughts, neither do I.

"I've just brewed my first pitcher of Dragon's Tear wine," Elizabeth tells me a few evenings after her first harvest, just before we're to venture forth for our nightly hunt,

both of us already in our natural forms. *"Here,"* she says, placing a blue ceramic pitcher and two large crystal mugs on the oak table in the great room. She pours the clear liquid into the mugs. *"Let's try it."*

I recognize the pitcher as one of my mother's and wonder if she used it for the same purpose. I pick up my mug, sniff the colorless liquid, then swirl it. It gives off no smell. Looks like simple tapwater. *"Should we, before we go out?"* I ask.

Elizabeth nods. *"Just remember, never drink this in your human form."*

"Why?"

"In that form you have no defense against its power. It will stun you the same way it stupefies them," she says, and waits for me to drink first.

I have a hard time believing it can affect anyone. The wine looks harmless, tastes as featureless as it appears. I drink two large swallows and then glance at Elizabeth. *"It tastes like water, maybe a little thicker, a little greasy. . . ."*

She laughs, drains her mug with one long, sustained swallow. *"Finish yours and then tell me what you think,"* she says.

I shrug and follow her example. The warmth follows a moment later, radiating from my insides, tingling its way to my extremities. For a moment I feel dizzy. I have to readjust my stance, brace on my tail, to remain upright.

"Isn't it wonderful?" Elizabeth asks, moving closer, rubbing against me with her body, her tail.

My senses explode wherever she touches. I feel nothing like on my wedding night when Dragon's Tear wine, mixed with Death's Rose and alchemist powders, enabled us to merge our minds, but I find myself unable to stop grinning and unwilling to defer any of my appetites.

We begin to make love in the great room, let our passion take us from its floor to the sky outside, soaring upward until we consummate our union in the midst of a long dive toward the sea. Then we fly, side by side, in search of prey, the Dragon's Tear wine still warming our insides, making us hungry. I guide us offshore, thinking to take us to the island of Bimini, only sixty miles away.

Elizabeth, who has long complained about my insistence on our hunting over the waters, preferably far from home, asks again, *"Why fly so long for food when there's so much prey nearby?"*

"Father always insisted we do most of our hunting far away from our island," I say. *"Even if we weren't spotted, too many missing people would make the humans too suspicious, too wary. Cuba and the Bahamas lie close enough and their people remain primitive enough to dismiss our acts with their superstitions."*

But Elizabeth turns back toward land. *"I'm hungry,"* she says. *"It won't do any harm to feed close to home this one night."*

"I don't like the homeless ones. It takes months holding them in the cells, feeding them, to make them edible," I say.

"Isn't there somewhere out of the way? Where we can find what we want now?"

Warm and content, my hunger a pleasant rumble in my stomach, I sigh, wishing she didn't have to puncture my mood. But either the wine or her enthusiasm makes me reckless. I guide us south, so we can approach the agricultural area west of Homestead from the Everglades.

By the time I decide on a white, two-story farmhouse, acres away from any other dwelling, I'm as ravenous as my bride. We burst through their windows, go from room to room, slashing, killing. I feed on the father, while Elizabeth feeds on the three small children and the mother.

We dispose of their remains over the ocean before we return home. Later, lying in each other's embrace on the hay in my room, the wine still coursing in our veins, we make love again.

News reports flash the missing family's pictures on the TV the next day and for days afterward. I have to turn away each time they show the children.

20

When the middle of October arrives without our receiving a single new report on Jorge Santos's activities or any information on the shooter or the boat saboteurs' identities, I call Arturo.

"We have a problem," he says. "I didn't want to call you until I had some solutions."

"Do you?"

"Not yet. But my friends in the islands did find the two Bahamians who handled the shooting. The fools were flashing a lot of money at all the bars on Andros. On a poor island like that they were bound to be noticed. After some persuasion from my people, they admitted they had received a contract from an Italian gentleman in New York, Ralph Escalante."

"With the Gambini family?" I say.

Arturo says, "Yeah . . . gave them ten thousand dollars down, promised them ten more on completion. Someone he knows wants you dead in a big way. . . ."

"I would think that's fairly obvious," I say.

"Anyway, you know there's no way we can intimidate Escalante. Fortunately, some of our Italian friends are friendly with him. They were able to find out that he was acting as an agent for some Chinese guy in Los Angeles."

"Has anyone talked to him?"

Arturo sighs. "No. No one's seen him for weeks. The word is, he may have gone back to China."

"It doesn't make any sense," I say. "Why would someone from China care about me?"

"I was hoping you'd tell me. And there's more too. . . . When Santos got out of jail, I wondered how he could make bail so quickly. The judge is a friend of ours, he set it for far more than Santos's family could afford. I had my people check into it. The lawyer that posted bail for him was acting on the behalf of an attorney in California. Neither of them knew the name of the principal who put up the money and issued the instructions. . . . And Santos didn't know any of them."

"I just don't get it," I say. "If Santos has so much help, then why hasn't he tried anything since he got out of jail? He's not the type to give up."

"Maybe he is," Arturo says. "He hasn't bothered anyone about you since his arrest. My operatives say his restaurant, Joe's, just opened for the season. He has to work again, five nights a week. He may be too tired to do much more on his days off than sail or hang out with the Morton woman."

"In the meantime your people need to find the Chinese guy," I say. "Ask him some questions."

The Latin says, "I've already given those instructions."

As the days pass, Santos remains on my mind. What plan can the man have that he's waiting to spring? It bothers me to remain passive, waiting to see what may happen. As usual, Elizabeth's counsel is short and direct. "My father would never let a human take up so much of his thoughts," she says. "Kill him."

"No," I say. "Not yet. I don't see any need for it. But I do think I'd be more comfortable if I saw him again. I need to get a sense of how he's feeling, get a look into his eyes."

Elizabeth stares at me. "I think you're worried he's given up. Whatever game you think the two of you have, you don't want it to end."

I look away from her emerald-green eyes. "Maybe," I say, shrugging. "I don't know."

We arrive on Miami Beach early, but not early enough for Joe's. Even though it's just six-thirty and a weeknight, cars pack the parking lot. I let the valet take the Mercedes and escort Elizabeth into the Mediterranean–style building, newly redone to blend in with all the other new and remodeled buildings taking advantage of the resurgent popularity of South Beach.

Inside the cavernous room, a line of people wait to talk to an indifferent maître d'. *"It's too crowded, too noisy,"* Elizabeth mindspeaks.

I nod. At every table people dine or wait for food, tuxedo-clad waiters bustling around them, carrying large trays laden with beige-and-orange stone crab claws, the restaurant's specialty. Other patrons crowd the lobby and the bar, waiting for tables that might not become available for an hour or more.

It takes me fifteen minutes to get close enough to talk to the maître d'. He barely reacts when I say my name, but after I say, "Arturo Gomez said I should tell you we're good friends of his," he looks up and smiles, reassures me it will be only a few minutes and suggests we wait in the bar.

Three bartenders, each wearing red brocade vests, rush around the U-shaped, mahogany bar. At first I worry that Santos has the night off, but then I see him pouring a scotch for a red-faced man at the far end of the bar. I force our way through the waiting crowd, push toward him and have the fortune to find a seat for Elizabeth at the bar and a space for me to stand next to her.

Santos freezes, then frowns when he first notices us. Another bartender comes over to see what we want, but he interrupts. "I know them. I'll take care of them."

"Mr. and Mrs. DelaSangre," he says as if we were old

friends, his hard eyes belying his wide smile. "What brings you here?"

"Dinner." I grin too. "I thought you said we should be less formal, Jorge."

"Yes." He nods, places both of his hands on the bright wood surface of the bar. "I did. But that was awhile ago, Peter. I guess I forgot."

"It has been quite a while. . . ."

He nods again. "Too long," he says. "But, you know how it is, Peter, work and other things get in the way. Then again . . ." He looks at me. "You don't have to work, do you?"

"No," I say.

"But I bet you know how to play real hard, don't you? I bet guys you play don't win very often. But enough of that . . ." Santos motions toward the bottles behind him. "I have a job to do here. What would you like tonight?"

"Just Evian for both of us," I say. "We don't drink."

"Really?" he says. "Me neither. I gave it up after Maria disappeared. Funny thing though, the police arrested me a few months ago. . . ." He shakes his head. "Peter, they charged me with DUI even though I was cold sober. I can't imagine why they'd do something like that. Can you?"

I shrug. "Sometimes stuff happens."

Jorge narrows his eyes, growls, "You're a profound guy, aren't you?"

Before I can answer, the maître d' calls my name.

"You must know someone big," Jorge says, bantering again. "Barely anyone gets a table that fast. I bet someone with that much drag could get someone transferred from their job. You think so, Peter?" He motions us away. "Go ahead, don't worry. You don't have to wait. I'll send your drinks over to you."

"Happy?" Elizabeth asks me once we're seated at our table.

I am, but I'm not sure I want to admit to enjoying my exchange with Santos. Elizabeth would hardly understand my curiosity about the man. I hardly do myself. But, whether it's because I liked his sister and I see something of her in him, or just that he tickles my curiosity—I find myself wishing I could know him better. "Well," I say, "I think it's obvious he still plans some sort of response to our last meeting."

"Especially after you've gone out of your way to tease him."

A waiter brings a tray bearing two filled glasses. He places one in front of Elizabeth, the other in front of me. "Jorge said to tell you, it's with his compliments," he says.

I nod, pick up my glass, catch a strong whiff of alcohol before I take my first sip. "Is this Evian?" I ask.

The waiter grins. "Jorge said you'd kid with me. It's Ketl One vodka, just like you like."

"We don't drink. . . ." I shake my head, hold the glass out to him.

"Jorge said you'd say that." The waiter ignores my outstretched hand, chuckles as if we're sharing a joke. "He told me, if you said that, I should tell you, 'You might want to think about starting real soon.'"

21

The next Tuesday, I wake to find the morning air changed, shed of the last remnants of summer's warmth. I breathe in deep, savor the crisp, clean smell of fall—the lightness that the air takes on when it casts off most of its humidity. It invigorates me, makes lingering in bed impossible and I rush upstairs to the great room and throw the windows open so the north wind can fill the room with autumn's first chill. Smiling, wishing Elizabeth had wakened with me, I stand by the windows facing north, toward Miami, and let the cool air wash over me.

My smile fades when I notice the sail far to the north—the tiny yellow-and-white triangle bobbing on the bay's blue waters, too far away to make out the shape of the boat. At first it seems not to move, but slowly, inexorably, it travels in the direction of my island. I shrug, try to ignore it, but find it impossible not to watch its progress, not to wonder why it's sailing toward me.

Finally I force myself to walk away from the window. I can't think of any reason this one boat should catch my attention. I know the most westward channel in the bay lies a half mile to the east of Caya DelaSangre. I realize that, a quarter mile offshore on the ocean side, the water remains deep enough, even at low tide, for almost any pleasure boat to pass. Certainly, I think, no day goes by without at least a few boats cruising near my island. Still, this craft bothers me.

Frowning at my uneasiness, I return to the window every few minutes to check on its progress. Within an hour I can make out the cut of the boat's sails, the small triangular jib and the larger main sail—both made of alternating, diagonal strips of yellow and white sailcloth.

"It may be Santos," I tell Elizabeth when she wakes and joins me in the great room, the Hobie cat now large enough for us to make out its twin hulls and the "H" insignia in its main sail.

She shrugs, says, "You taunted him. You must have wanted this," and goes downstairs to work in her garden.

I maintain my vigil as the sailboat approaches, then passes by on the bay side, close enough for me to see Santos alone on the boat's canvas deck, the man wearing only cutoffs and a sleeveless sweatshirt, his gaze fixed on my island. Walking from window to window, I follow his progress, admiring the way he handles his boat.

The man circles the island, finally letting his sails go slack, the boat stalling, bobbing in place while he reaches into a small blue bag lying on the canvas next to him and takes out a pair of binoculars. On his knees, constantly shifting his balance to counter the pitching of his stalled boat, Santos scans the island.

I back away from the window when he turns the glasses in my direction but still, before he sails off into the open bay, he waves, as if he's sure I'm watching.

He repeats his visit the next day, disappears for almost a week, then visits us again, this time with the Morton woman on board. It becomes a pattern, a few times each week for him to sail around us—sometimes alone, sometimes with the woman. At each circumnavigation of the island he sails closer, always staring at the land, studying the house.

October passes, then November. During that time my pregnant bride's body progresses from slightly rounded to moderately swollen. Elizabeth complains about her human form, insists on buying new clothes each week. She gives up driving her Corvette and switches to the more comfortable seating of my Mercedes. Our lovemaking, once a daily affair, diminishes to random, occasional couplings. Elizabeth spends less time in her garden, asks less often to go to the mainland and, when we do go, complains that bumping across the bay jostles her too much.

Food, always important to her, becomes her primary interest. While we continue to hunt and feed each evening, it no longer suffices for her. I begin to defrost steaks each afternoon. Elizabeth accepts them without uttering a single complaint.

No matter the weather, Santos manages to continue to visit the waters around us at least once each week. Elizabeth ignores his presence completely. When I point out his boat to her, she says, "It's in your power to stop him."

It is. Arturo wants to eliminate him, requests I let him do it each time we speak. Unable to get my permission for that, he offers to have the Marine Patrol harass him or to arrange for the police to arrest him again for DUI. "I finally had the opportunity to talk to the manager at Joe's," he tells me. "The man assured me that for the right sum of money, Santos will be fired any time we request it. And one of the governor's aides has promised me the state will be glad to offer him a ranger's job at the Castillo San Marcos in Saint Augustine in the event he needs a new job. If you want"—Arturo grins, obviously proud of his ability to manipulate events—"we can get the *Herald* to transfer Casey Morton to their Jacksonville office too."

I refuse all of it. "He's harmless," I tell Arturo. And I repeat to Elizabeth, "Nothing's happened since October. If the man could do anything, he would have done it by now. If he wants to serve his dead sister by sailing around my island a few times each week, so be it."

* * *

Still, whenever his boat arrives, I stop whatever activity occupies me and turn my attention to his movements. Some days, when the wind and water collude to provide safe passage for him, I envy his time on the boat. I've sailed Hobie Cats myself and know the pleasure of skimming across the water before a stiff breeze.

On the days that the weather turns bad, the wind punishing Santos with its gusts and shifts, the waves leaping around him, threatening to engulf him, I wonder at his perseverance, wonder if I would be so constant, so willing to risk injury for a lost cause.

"I admire him," I say to Elizabeth when she refuses to look at the catamaran cruising off the island's shore.

"Why give the fool any recognition?" She shakes her head. "What he does accomplishes nothing. One day he'll realize that and go away."

She harumphs and walks from me when I say, "At least he'll be able to tell himself, he tried his best for his sister."

22

Elizabeth's appetite amazes me. By mid-December, she takes to consuming her human prey each evening, as well as two twenty-four-ounce steaks upon awakening and another two each afternoon. She catches and eats so many of our younger dogs that I have to ask her to stop, lest our pack declines so much it no longer represents a threat to outsiders.

"The child must be fed," she says. "I have to maintain our strength."

I nod and take my swollen bride in my arms, smile when she accepts and returns my embrace, holding me longer than she used to. Pregnancy has softened her, made her more needful of my affection. I find I like her wanting more from me than sex and food. We often spend hours sitting side by side in the great room, watching the waters outside, silently enjoying the warmth of each other's company. Other days we walk on the island's beaches, holding hands, discussing our future.

Elizabeth provides no argument about the child's first name. "Henri," she says, "is a fine name, a strong name. Could we give him my father's name too?"

"Of course." I smile at the weight of such a name—Henri Charles DelaSangre—for such a small, yet-unborn presence. I wish he could be born sooner. I possess no doubt that Elizabeth will be a good mother. Already she has begun to prepare a birthing chamber in one of the other bedrooms, helping me scrub down the walls and floors, reminding me again and again that we'll need fresh hay when her time nears.

I no longer wonder about our relationship. *"If you demand perfection from your mate,"* Father taught me, *"then you must learn to expect loneliness in your life."*

As much as I would like Elizabeth to share more of my likes and dislikes, I find myself cherishing the time we spend together. She may not care for books, but she seems to enjoy sitting at my side while I read them. She may not love music, but she tolerates my listening to the stereo. We both smile at each other's presence, both reach out to touch each other whenever we're near and, I think, if it never gets any better, it still can be more than enough for me.

Even Santos no longer seems to bother her. When his boat comes into view, she no longer leaves my side. We discuss the water conditions and his sailing technique. "After the baby's born, I'd like to learn to sail a boat like that," she says. "Will you buy me one?"

"Sure," I tell her.

The first true winds of winter arrive a few days before Christmas. For the first time since summer, the sun fails to warm the midday air. Outside, the wind beats against our closed windows, moans when it can't force its admittance. I take one look at the gray skies, the frenzied, frigid waves leaping on the bay and call the office, tell Emily to cancel my weekly meeting with Gomez and Tindall. Then I build a fire in the great room for Elizabeth and me. "This is Florida," I say. "It's not supposed to get this cold."

Elizabeth grins, shakes her head at my discomfort. "The weatherman says it's only sixty degrees. At home it grows colder than this every night," she says. "You're acting as if a blizzard has attacked us when we both know it will be warm again in a few days."

I leave her laughing in the great room while I go below

to light a fire in our bedroom. Elizabeth mindspeaks to me a few minutes later. *"He's here again."*

"Santos?" I say. *"In this weather?"*

Elizabeth joins me at the window, watches with me as the sailboat fights its way through the water, one hull rising and lowering with each wind gust, the boat almost going airborne as it races from wave to wave. "He's crazy," I say.

"They're both crazy," Elizabeth says and I nod when she points out Casey Morton standing, busy working the jib lines, helping keep the boat from flipping by leaning out away from the Hobie, supported only by her feet against the trampoline and a wire suspended from the top of the mast, connected to a canvas sling beneath her rear.

"It's called being out on a trapeze," I say to Elizabeth, pointing to the other wire that supports Santos in the same way.

In their full black wetsuits, they look to me like two shadows sailing. "No life jackets," I say, shaking my head. But I have to admire his control, the Hobie leaping and bucking, slicing the tops off waves as it overtakes them.

Santos amazes me by turning and zigzagging north, battling the vicious north wind until he finally reaches the channel between my island and Wayward Key. The boat turns toward the channel, slows for a moment, wallows in the rough sea, then shoots forward. Santos and Morton lean back, away from the boat as the windward hull rises, Morton shifting position, her left foot slipping.

She shouts, reaches for Santos, her body pivoting away from the Hobie, only her right foot remaining in contact with the trampoline. He grabs for her with his right hand, his fingertips touching hers.

A gust of wind hits the sails and the boat speeds ahead, burying both bows into the wave to its front. The Hobie stops as if it's hit a wall, the stern rising, Morton flailing her arms as the momentum launches her in an arc controlled by the trapeze line attached to the mast. Santos follows, their forward momentum and the wind beneath the trampoline combining to somersault the boat, the man and the woman colliding as they wrap around the mast, their heads crashing together—mast wires tearing their skin, the boat settling over them, floating, bottom up.

I breathe in deep, watch the disabled boat drift forward, and shake my head.

"Aren't you going to save them?" Elizabeth asks.

"No," I say. "They're under the boat. They'll drown before I can reach them." I turn, look at her. "Anyway, I thought you'd be relieved to see them out of the way."

She shrugs, and continues to watch.

A head emerges from the water. I stifle a celebratory shout. Instead, I calmly say to Elizabeth, "I think it's Santos."

The man holds on to the capsized catamaran, fumbles with the lines attached to him and, once they're free, dives under the boat. A few moments later he surfaces, pulling Morton with him. He has to almost throw half her body onto the overturned boat before she tries to hold on, slipping a little as he undoes her lines, staying in place only with his help. When he lets go of her for a second, to get a better grip on the boat himself, she slips away, and sinks into the water.

I almost moan when she does, hoping that Santos has enough sense to stay with the boat, thinking it better that one of them, at least, survives.

Santos shouts at her, but the current whips Morton away. He pauses a moment before leaving the safety of the boat, pushes off when she surfaces, treading water, twenty feet from him.

Neither has a life jacket and I know the current will carry them into the ocean within minutes. Do I have enough time to rescue them? I look at Elizabeth, try to calculate how angry a rescue attempt would make her.

"I think you should save them," she says.

I stare at her, my mouth open until I regain my voice. "Why?" I ask, not about to admit my own desires in this.

"Go now! Bring them back here. I'll explain later."

The Yamahas thunder to life the moment I turn the ignition key on the Grady White. I throw off the dock lines and speed out the harbor, smashing into waves as soon as I leave the island's protection. The cold wind lashes me, salt spray soaks my clothes as I negotiate the channel, twisting and turning, the boat battering its way through the swells.

"Elizabeth!" I mindspeak when I reach the open bay and turn north. *"Can you still see them?"*

"He reached her. . . ." she says. *"He's been trying to swim holding her. Their boat floated past him a minute or two ago. . . . He's trying to catch up to it, but I think it's moving too fast."*

I push the throttles forward, fight the wheel as the boat takes a glancing blow from one roller, then goes airborne over another. *"How far are they from the ocean?"* The Grady White leans on one side as I turn into the Wayward channel, salt spray coating the windshield, turning it opaque, nothing in view around me but churning water.

"Not far at all."

"Where are they?" I cut back on the gas, slow the boat, and search the waters in front of me.

"To your right . . . about fifty yards. Look toward the corner of our island, just offshore."

I turn the boat in the direction Elizabeth says, stare at the waves, catch a glimpse of a black wetsuit, a flash of yellow hair. *"I see them!"* I say, keeping my eyes on them, speeding up, going past them, then returning, so the current will bring them to me, looking for a way to rescue Santos and his woman without the boat crashing over them.

Santos backstrokes with one arm while he holds the girl

with the other. He doesn't look up until I reach beside him and put the boat in neutral. "Take Casey first!" he says, making the girl raise her left arm. I reach for her just as a swell lifts us, and carries her out of reach. We come together after it passes, the boat almost drifting over the floating couple. Before another swell overtakes us, I bend over the side of the boat, grab her by her wrist and yank her out of the water.

She yowls at the sudden shock of having her entire body weight suspended by one arm. I pull her in, ignoring her groan when her body accidentally strikes the side of the boat, dropping her on the cockpit floor where she collapses, gasping, coughing, retching. Another swell lifts the boat and I rush to the side looking for Santos. Seeing nothing, I race back to the wheel, reach for the throttle.

"NO!" Elizabeth mindspeaks. *"He's at your stern."*

I find Santos clinging to the bottom of one of the outboard motors, seemingly oblivious to the idling engine's grumble, vibration and exhaust—trying to gain enough purchase to climb into the boat. Unaware of my surveillance, he struggles on, maintaining his grip around the motor shaft with one arm while he tries to grab the cowling with the other, the boat smashing up and down, his body colliding again and again with the still propeller.

"Not a very smart place to put yourself," I say.

Santos looks up. "I didn't think you'd be stupid enough to put the motors in gear."

"It wouldn't have been a very pretty sight if you were wrong." I extend my arm, help him clamber over the stern. He drops to the floor next to Morton, holds her in his arms.

"She'll be fine," Santos says. As much for her benefit as mine, I think.

I throw the motors in gear and concentrate on turning the Grady White, working my way back to the safety of my harbor.

Santos feels us turning, and says, "Wait! What about my Hobie?"

"It's already out there." I tilt my head toward the ocean. "It will probably drift to shore, somewhere up the coast, in a few days."

"No." Santos stands, steadies himself against the back of my chair and looks out to sea. "Look, I appreciate your help. God knows I didn't expect it. But we don't need you to bring us all the way back to shore. If you can take us to my boat and help me right it, I'm sure I can get us home safely."

I shake my head. "It's just a boat," I say. "Anyway, don't worry—I'm not taking you to shore, I'm bringing you to my island."

Elizabeth meets us at the dock, three, large white-cotton bath towels in her arms. She waits while Santos and I help Casey Morton out of the boat, then hands towels to both of us. She unfolds the third one and stares at the woman—Morton shivering, barely able to stand. "You poor dear," Elizabeth says, shaking her head at Morton's blue lips, the purple bruise on the woman's forehead and the numerous cuts and tears to her wetsuit. "We'll get you inside and warm right away."

I raise my eyebrows at my bride's newfound solicitude, watch as she tenderly wraps the towel around the woman. *"Elizabeth,"* I mindspeak. *"You wanted me to save them. I did. Now what?"*

She glares at me, puts one arm around Morton's waist and guides her toward the house. "Come," she says over her shoulder. "Let's get all of you by the fire."

After the wind and cold and spray on the water, the warmth in the great room borders on oppressive. Still, I sink to a seat not far from the fire and sigh, delighted to let the heat overwhelm me. Elizabeth guides Santos and the woman even closer, clucking over their wounds. Casey Morton ignores her, stands by the fire, shivering, her eyes glazed, her arms folded around herself. Santos wraps his towel around her, holds her and repeats, "Don't worry, baby. You're okay now."

"You'll both feel better once we get you some dry clothes," Elizabeth says. "And some warm food inside you. Peter, would you go downstairs to the freezer and bring up some steaks?"

"Aren't we being a little too solicitous?" I mindspeak.

Elizabeth flashes me a false smile. *"Humor me."*

I nod, head for the door. As I leave the room, my bride turns her attention back to our guests. "Oh, where's my hospitality? After all that time in the water . . . you must be dying to get the taste of saltwater out of your mouths."

When I return a few minutes later, four frozen steaks in my hands, I find all three of them sitting at the oak dining table, a blue ceramic pitcher before them, Santos and Morton sipping from almost empty, large crystal mugs. I eye the pitcher. *"Elizabeth, the Dragon's Tear wine?"* I mindspeak. *"What the hell are you doing?"*

"It's done," she says, then turns to them. "Finish the rest. You'll feel better."

Casey Morton upends her mug and drains it. Santos sniffs at his, stares at the clear liquid. "It tastes a little greasy," he says.

Elizabeth shrugs. "I'm sure it's not what you're used to. We live on an island. Our water comes from a cistern."

He nods and drinks the remainder of the liquid in his mug.

Elizabeth smiles, motions for me to sit down next to her.

Santos looks around the room. "I have to tell you, I don't understand why you objected to my coming out here. There wasn't anything in the harbor. I haven't seen anything suspicious in the house. . . ." He smiles. "I mean it's odd in here. I don't think I'd like to live the way you do . . . but I don't know what you were trying to hide. And I got to give it to you—if you wanted Casey and me out of the way, you certainly could've just sat on your hands and watched us drift out to sea. . . . Maybe the note was wrong."

"Note?" I say.

Santos shrugs, looks at the floor. "I guess I'm trying to apologize to you both. . . ."

Casey Morton's legs give way. She slumps to the floor, in a sitting position, her eyes open. "Casey!" Santos says, kneeling next to her. She nods, staring into space.

He turns, glares at me, says, "What the hell?" then topples to his side.

I stare at him and the woman, wait for them to move, to make a sound, but neither one does. *"Now what?"* I ask Elizabeth.

She smiles, snuggles close to me. *"Now we keep them."*

Shaking my head, I move a few inches away from her. I think how much easier it would have been to let them float to their deaths, and wish my bride had consulted me before she acted. *"Keep them? For what?"*

"For the child," she says. She takes my hand, lays it on her stomach. *"After I deliver, your son and I will both need fresh meat. These two were going to die anyway. We can keep them in the cells below. This way we'll have plenty of time to fatten the woman. We can use her and the man as servants until my time comes."*

"That's months and months away." I stare at her, realize how much rounder her stomach's become, remember how much her breasts have swelled, her nipples darkened and thickened. *"You won't be ready until May,"* I say, trying to reassure myself with how much more time we have before our responsibilities change.

"Until then I want someone to help me in the garden. . . ."

"I could do that."

"As if you don't have enough to do," she says. *"I don't need you to do any more."* Elizabeth stares at Santos and Morton slumped on the floor in front of the fire, like two mannequins abandoned by a careless window dresser. She grins. *"We have them now for that."*

23

Father told me that when he built this house, he took pains to make sure that sounds traveled very little. *"Especially from the cells on the bottom floor,"* he said. *"I found I always lost my patience with the noisy ones. There were times, I have to admit, that I dispatched some of them more quickly just so I could have some peace and quiet. You can't imagine how dreary it can be to have to listen to hours and hours of human tears and whining."*

Thanks to Father's foresight and the thick stone cell walls his masons built, Elizabeth and I both sleep late the next morning, undisturbed by any noise generated on the floor below us. As usual, I wake first. Leaving my pregnant bride still lost in her dreams, I stop outside our bed chamber, near the spiral staircase, when a few muffled sounds drift up from the cells.

Glad to know the effects of the Dragon's Tear wine have abated, curious to see the condition of our guests, I descend the stairs—the muted noises growing louder, taking form. Casey Morton sobbing and groaning.

When I near the bottom, she stops. I stand in the shadows, out of view of the cells, and listen to the rustle of bodies moving, the metallic clinking of chains. Jorge Santos murmuring in the darkness, "Casey, honey, relax. . . . We'll get through this."

She shrieks instead, loud enough to make me wince, the scream fading only as she runs out of air. Then she begins to moan again, ignoring Santos's assurances, her cries building in volume. Before she reaches another crescendo, I flip the wall switch, turning on all the ceiling fixtures at once—their bright lights erasing all the shadows, shining through the iron-barred doors of each cell. Casey throws one manacled hand over her eyes to block the glare, cowers on her cot and yowls.

I step into my captives' line of sight. Jorge Santos, still in his wetsuit, his left forehead covered by a purple welt from his accident the day before, sits on his bed, blinks from the light as he stares at me. Iron chains attached to an iron ring around his neck and iron manacles around each wrist and each ankle limit his range of motion to only a few feet on either side of his bed. He makes no effort to fight against his shackles. Not so Casey Morton in the cell next to him, separated from Santos by a two-foot-thick stone wall and similarly restrained. She jumps from her bed, tries to move as far from me as she can, tugging and yanking on her chains to no effect.

Already the manacles have rubbed her wrists red, almost raw. Before she hurts herself further, I yell, *"Stop!"*

Casey freezes, staring at me, gasping air like a frantic animal, her blond hair tangled and spiked, her bruises and cuts from the day before covering her face in an irregular pattern of welts and scabs. Blood has caked on the side of her wetsuit where a gash in the black material offers a glimpse of the white skin and the dark red wounds beneath.

Fear, I decide, will do more to still her than any soothing talk. I almost growl my words. "Casey, I keep a pack of wild dogs outside. Do you remember seeing them chase your boat when you and Jorge sailed close to the island?"

She nods.

"If you don't quiet down, I'm going to have to put a few of them in the cell with you. Do you understand?"

She nods again, looks at the floor.

I move on, stand in front of Jorge's cell. "I think your friend will be quiet for a while," I say.

"You're a prince," Santos says, his tone acid. He examines his chains. "Is this what you did with Maria? You drugged her and held her here until you killed her?"

"No." I fight the temptation to explain how I feel about his sister's death, to dismiss it as an accident. "I never drugged Maria. I never had her down here."

"Maybe . . ." Santos shrugs. "At this point I guess there's no reason for you to lie." He locks eyes with me. "But I know you know what happened to her."

His eyes possess the same shape, the same color as Maria's. I find he reminds me too much of her. It irritates me that I still care about his sister's death, and it bothers me that Elizabeth has engineered events in a way that forces me to be reminded of her constantly. Better, I think, that he and the woman had died. I look away.

Santos irritates me more by adopting a smug expression, almost a smirk, as if he's won a point in a contest of wills. "I notice that you didn't deny that you killed her," he says.

Sighing, I shake my head. "No, I didn't deny it. I didn't say I did it either. I don't think discussing Maria now serves either of us very well. . . ." I let my voice deepen, turn menacing. It's time, I think, to remind him his fate depends on my good will. "It certainly doesn't serve you."

"Maybe not," Santos says, refusing to be intimidated. "But it's hard to ignore that your sweet, young wife drugged my girlfriend and me. And"—he holds up his wrists to show off his chains—"I do have a problem with being locked up and chained to my bed." Santos pauses, looks as if he's considering something, then nods his head. "As a matter of fact, I have to admit, I've already decided. I'm going to have to kill you both."

I grin at the incongruity of my prisoner threatening me.

"And how do you plan to do that? Don't you think the chains and the locked cell will get in your way?"

"Well, I didn't say it wouldn't be a challenge." Santos laughs.

His laughter catches me off guard and I let myself join him, wishing things could be different, wondering how hard it will be to control this man. Our mirth lasts only a moment, then fades into silence—Santos glaring at me, me returning his stare.

In the next cell Casey Morton grumbles, "How can you laugh? You know the bastard's going to kill us."

"Are you?" Santos asks.

"Not unless I have to," I say. I see no reason to explain their eventual fate. "Of course, the two of you are going to have to stay here. You'll be expected to help maintain the household and the grounds—"

Santos whoops and laughs. "You're fucking nuts! This is America. You want to make us slaves?"

I frown, consider rushing into the cell and striking him—beating him until he learns humility. "Enough! You need to speak and act with more respect. Look around you. Test your chains. You and your friend have no options. You're going to have to learn to accept that."

"And if I don't?"

"There are dogs outside that would like the opportunity to meet you," I say. "Or I could leave you locked up without food or water. I could hurt the woman or you dozens of different ways. I could kill her and let you live . . . or vice versa." I shrug. "Or I could kill you both. Or you could cooperate and live fairly comfortable lives."

Santos looks around his cell. "You think this is comfortable?"

"It could be made more so."

"We need to get out of these wetsuits," the Cuban says.

"It can be done," I say. "But first, you mentioned a note yesterday."

Santos grins as if he has the upper hand. "We need food and dry clothes. And Casey needs for her cuts to be taken care of."

I nod. "First tell me about the note."

"It came in the mail from the attorney that bailed me out, the one I didn't hire. He said it was from his client in California."

Scowling, I say, "Go on."

"There wasn't much to it. It said, 'You're on the right track. Peter DelaSangre killed your sister.' Then it said, 'If you ever need help bringing him to justice call,' it listed a number, a local one. . . ." Santos pauses, shakes his head. "I can't remember it now . . . and then it said, 'Please call any time day or night.' There wasn't any signature or name."

"Did you ever call?" I ask.

He smiles. "No, I wanted you to myself." Santos pauses again, his grin turning smug, then says, as if he's earned some new concession, "Casey and I should stay in the same cell."

"No." I shake my head. "I don't think so."

"Okay, I guess you're in charge," Santos says, his tone acid again. He holds his hands up, palms out, in a mock gesture of surrender. "So it's whatever you say, Boss . . . for now. Just don't forget . . . things can change. And when they do, you're dead."

This time I chuckle. The man has no concept of my powers and abilities, nor of Elizabeth's. I have no doubt, if given the chance, he will attempt to slay me and I have no fear that he will succeed. "Whenever you think you can kill me," I say, "Please feel free to try."

"I will . . . later," Santos says. But he cooperates when I unlock his cell and readjust his chains so I can lead him into the hallway. Morton surprises me by cooperating too, shuffling out of her cell, waiting next to Santos while I chain them together. Santos whispers something to her, but she saves me the need to quiet them and stares away, saying nothing in return.

Father taught me that keeping humans captive calls for constant vigilance and careful technique. *"As weak as they are, they are most dangerous and most determined once they are taken captive. They become like rodents in a cage. They never stop trying. I've had ones who dug through stone; others who worried at their chains so much that the metal failed. You must always keep them bound in some way, alternate their cells on an irregular schedule, inspect their walls and floors, examine their locks for tampering. Never show mercy, never trust them. Whenever you do, they'll turn on you."*

I fetter Santos and Morton the way Father taught me— with only twelve inches of chain between their feet, their wrists bound by shorter chains, Santos's right ankle shackled to Morton's left, his neck ring connected by a short chain fastened to hers. They have no choice but to move slowly, shuffling in tandem with each other, their chains clinking as they ascend the stairs in front of me.

Their clangor precedes them, wakes Elizabeth shortly before we reach the second floor. *"Peter?"* she mindspeaks. *"Why are you bringing them up here now?"*

"They're a mess. They need to shower and change. . . ."

"They're slaves. Take them outside and hose them down," Elizabeth says.

"That's unnecessary," I say. *"We've plenty of extra rooms, more than enough showers they can use. . . ."*

"They're not our guests."

"But it wouldn't hurt to treat them as well as possible."

"Honestly, Peter, sometimes you make no sense. They're just humans."

Elizabeth joins me as I lead them into one of the other bed chambers. I'm relieved to see that she's chosen to be both in human form and clothed. I doubt that Santos and his woman would be as cooperative if they saw either of us in our natural states.

"You," Elizabeth says to the woman. Morton looks at her, then stares at the floor, waits to hear what Elizabeth wants. She remains still as my bride unchains her and helps her out of the wetsuit and the bathing suit beneath it. She stands naked before us, slightly trembling.

"So thin," Elizabeth mindspeaks. She holds Morton's empty chains in one hand, runs the fingers of her free hand over the cuts and bruises of the woman's face, then turns her so she can examine the long gash on Morton's side where one of the Hobie's wires cut into her. "After you shower, I'll put some herbs on this," Elizabeth says. "It will heal quickly."

Casey nods. The woman's docility surprises me. She accepts Elizabeth's continued inspection—Jorge and I watching them.

"Do you like her?" Elizabeth asks. *"Would you want to make love to this blond woman? Or is she too thin for you, her breasts too small?"*

Santos shifts beside me—clinking his chains, shaking his head—but I ignore him. *"I only want to make love to my wife,"* I say and turn my attention to Elizabeth, her swollen stomach. *"Maybe once I would have found one like this of interest. . . ."*

"She isn't an animal!" Santos shouts. He whirls toward me, throwing his arms over my head, wrapping the chain between his manacles around my neck, choking me, grunting as he tightens his grip.

Instead of fighting off his attack, I immediately thicken my neck muscles, preventing the iron links from blocking my air or cutting my blood flow. Santos tries to tighten his hold and groans when he finds that, no matter his effort, he can't. I almost feel sorry for him as he strains to no avail, wait for him to see the futility of his actions and give it up.

Morton, her eyes wide, watches our struggle, but provides no help. Not so Elizabeth. She quickly tires of waiting for me to end it. "This is stupid," she says. Twirling Morton's empty chains over her head, she steps closer to us and crashes them into the side of Santos's head. His grip loosens and I push the chain from my throat, and knock him to the floor.

I put my foot on his chest to hold him down. "Look at this," I say to him, my finger on the bright red bruise his attack left around my neck. He glances, then looks away. "No, I want you to watch." I bear down on my foot, so all my weight presses on his chest and let up only when I'm sure I have his attention.

"I won't punish you this time," I say, massaging my swollen throat. "You haven't learned yet how strong we are." I relax my muscles, will my flesh to heal. "No attack of yours will ever succeed." I point to my neck. "This is why."

His expression changes from defiant, to bewildered, to amazed as my neck narrows and the redness abates, then disappears. "What the hell are you people?" he asks.

"Your captors," I say. I step off him, motion for him to rise. "All you need to know is that we have the power to do with you as we wish. Now stand and wait while we tend to your friend."

He gets up, ignores the thin, red rivulet of blood running down the side of his face, dripping onto his wetsuit. "If you say so, Boss," he says.

Casey Morton needs no prodding. She does whatever Elizabeth tells her, accepts her chains again after she showers, waits to see what else we require of her.

Jorge, too, now follows instructions. He makes no moves

when I unchain him, doesn't object to Elizabeth undressing and examining him. She runs her palm over his chest hair. *"He's much hairier than you,"* she mindspeaks.

I shrug. *"I thought you liked my bare chest."*

"I do." She grins. *"Remember, I haven't seen as many naked men as you've seen naked women."* Elizabeth cups his testicles in her hand, makes no effort to hide her curiosity as she examines him. Santos endures it, looks away. *"You're larger than him. Still, I wonder how he would be—"*

"Elizabeth!"

Her smile widens. *"Jealous? Why, Peter, you know I'm yours and yours alone. It's just that sometimes I wonder about human men. After all, he's not one of our people. It wouldn't really be cheating."*

"It would be to me," I say, wishing again we hadn't seized these two, realizing how many months we have to go before our child's birth and Santos's and Morton's demise. Far too long, I think, if Elizabeth intends to go on in this vein.

"Why, Peter"—she giggles—*"your face is red."*

24

The evening news carries a report of Santos's catamaran being found, floating upside down, off the shore of Miami Beach. The commercial fishermen who recovered the boat repeat for the cameras that they saw no signs of anyone floating nearby. Both Jorge's and Casey's pictures are flashed on screen. Tapes of Mrs. Santos weeping over her missing son and the Mortons stoically appealing for boaters to help search for their daughter run for days on every broadcast.

At the office, Arturo gloats, and says, "Good riddance. At least that's one problem that's solved itself."

Jeremy approaches me later, asks, "Peter? Did you have anything to do with their disappearance? Not that it matters, as long as they're out of the way."

I give him a blank stare until he retreats from my office.

We keep our prisoners in the house while the search goes on, let them rest and heal in their cells. At first we dress them in my old clothes, Elizabeth's being far too small for Casey Morton. They look almost comical as they shuffle along, barefoot, in chains—my shirts and pants too baggy, too loose, too long for both of them.

Elizabeth grunts when she sees them. *"My slaves back in Jamaica were better dressed than these two. At least they had shoes,"* she mindspeaks.

"Your shoes are too small and mine are too large," I say.

"We'll have to buy them new ones and new clothes on the mainland."

Casey continues to be the passive one, silently following orders, shuffling from room to room as she cleans, never complaining about her chains. But she proves useless in the kitchen. "I don't eat meat," she explains when Elizabeth tells her to prepare steaks, blood rare for us and however Santos and she like for them. "And I hardly ever cook." Morton points to Santos. "He's the one who's good at that."

"You'll have to eat what we give you," Elizabeth says. "You're too thin for your own good." She instructs Santos on what to prepare, ignores his grumbling that the chains get in the way.

When the food is ready, she insists that Casey eat her entire steak, and sits next to her at the oak table in the great room, prodding her to continue eating.

"I wouldn't force her to eat so much," Santos says. He needs no such encouragement, wolfing his meat down almost as quickly as Elizabeth and I do ours. Then we all three sit and wait as Casey takes one small bite after another.

Santos puts his feet on the chair across from him, slouching in his seat, like any other man relaxing after a good meal. He looks around the room, notices the blue ceramic pitcher on one of the shelves. "Hey, Boss, that's what your wife poured for us, when we first came here, isn't it?"

I nod.

"What is it? I've never heard of anything like that."

"Peter, there's no need to tell him about it," Elizabeth mindspeaks.

"And there's no harm in it either," I reply. *"What good would the knowledge possibly do for him?"*

She sighs and turns her attention back to Casey, nagging her to take yet another bite.

"It's a family recipe," I tell him. "Elizabeth makes it herself."

Santos knits his eyebrows, looks from the pitcher to me and back to the pitcher. "Why?"

I smile at him. "Sometimes it's useful. You saw what it did to you."

He shakes his head grimly.

Elizabeth says, "Good. You're finished."

We both turn to see Casey's plate empty. The blonde sits still, her eyes glazed, her white skin paler than usual.

"She hasn't eaten meat since she was twelve years old," Santos says.

Casey nods, then belches, and leans over to her side and begins to wretch, spewing Elizabeth's hard work all over the floor.

Santos glares at Elizabeth. "See, I told you. If you hadn't made her stuff herself . . ."

My bride shakes her head, shouts, "Stop!" at Morton, who continues to empty her stomach.

"Do something," Elizabeth says to me.

She looks so bewildered, so frustrated, I have to stifle an indulgent grin. I hold my hands up. *"We can't control their stomachs,"* I mindspeak.

"Clean it up!" she yells at Santos.

The Cuban gets up to do as he is told. He turns to me, says, "I warned her," and I nod. Elizabeth glares at me. If she could, I'm sure she would make me clean it up too.

As the weeks pass, I become used to sharing our home, letting Santos and Morton lighten my burdens. Elizabeth and I go on shopping forays to Good Will and the Salvation Army, bringing home armloads of clothes for our prisoners. I let Jorge make up grocery lists and we stock the kitchen and freezer with all types of foods and condiments that would never tempt my bride or me.

Growing a little more tired of her pregnancy each day, Elizabeth spends more time in bed. She only ventures outside during the day to oversee Casey as she works in the garden or to accompany me when I go to the mainland. She takes to napping early, every evening, before we hunt.

I find I enjoy having Santos work by my side. The man likes to talk and, as long as we avoid any discussion of his sister, has a seemingly endless catalogue of stories about his coworkers and ex-girlfriends. To my delight, I learn he likes to play chess—the only human game Father deigned to play—and we fall into the habit of playing a game each evening, after dinner, before I lock him and Morton back in their cells.

Elizabeth and I never leave the two unsupervised outside their cells. It becomes routine for me to unlock their doors each morning and lock them again each evening. As time passes without any resistance on their part, my bride and I both decide to lessen the amount of chains Santos and Morton must bear. In their cells, I reduce their load to a single chain attached to an iron ring set in the wall, but long enough to allow them to range the width and breadth of their confines.

Casey learns to surrender control of her diet and finally eats as my bride wishes. Slowly her body thickens and curves appear where bones once were noticeable. Elizabeth too continues to grow bigger, the child strong and kicking within her. Even at night, after my bride has changed into her natural state, her new girth can't go unnoticed. *"Do you still desire me?"* she surprises me by asking one night.

"I thought you didn't want to anymore."

Elizabeth shakes her head. *"I didn't before. I do now. Mum told me I might—for a while—after the baby grew some. Do you still want to, Peter?"*

"Of course," I say and I find myself making love to her again as often as when we first met.

* * *

Sex, I find, is on Santos's mind too. He brings up the subject one afternoon, shortly before the end of January, when I have him follow me outside to help me do routine maintenance in one of the arms rooms.

Even though I can't imagine any way the man will ever have an opportunity to try to break into the room, I make Santos face away before I approach the narrow crack in the stone on the arms door's side. I check to make sure his eyes are elsewhere before I thin my arm and work it into the crevice, feeling for the release lever, smiling at the loud click as it opens.

After my arm regains its shape, I allow the Cuban to turn. Jorge whistles when I lift the crossbar and throw open the room's thick oak door. I watch as he examines the ancient weapons stored on the shelves, the extra cannons in the back of the room, the bags of shot, the sealed, lead canisters filled with gunpowder. "Did you once have an army out here?" he asks.

I grin and shake my head. "Not an army," I say. "But my ancestor believed in maintaining a strong defense. That's why he kept so many rifles and cannons here."

Santos picks up one of the longarms, examines it and puts it back in place. "Muskets, Boss," he contradicts me. "These have smooth bores. That makes them muskets. If the barrels had grooves cut inside them, then they'd be rifles."

"Oh," I say. "I take it you know your way around these."

The Cuban reaches for an old, massive, naval, blunderbuss, rail gun, and grunts from its weight as he lifts it. He nods. "Not that I'm used to handling real ones. Every one of these are collectors' items. You could make a fortune selling them." He studies the piece, looks into the muzzle. "The ball this fires has to be as large as a child's fist."

"Not quite," I say, pointing to the golfball-size, lead balls stacked on a shelf a few feet away.

Santos hefts the piece again before he puts it down. "No wonder they mounted these on the rails. The recoil would knock even a large man on his ass." He picks a flintlock pistol up, cocks it, sights it on me. "Tempting," he says, laughs. "Too bad it's empty."

I smile. "You'd just be wasting your time. It wouldn't kill me anyway."

"None of it?"

"Maybe one of the big pieces . . . if you got lucky. But trust me, you could never aim it in time to get me."

He grins too. "Boss," he says, "you never know until you try."

We spend the afternoon inspecting every piece, applying grease wherever needed. Santos tells me about the big guns in Saint Augustine. "They're easily twice as large as your cannons. One man couldn't move them. God, you can't believe how the ground shakes when they fire."

"Maybe, one of these days, we'll fire the one I keep outside," I say.

"I'd like that," Jorge says.

We finish shortly before dark and linger on the veranda, watching Elizabeth direct as Casey weeds the garden. The woman's blond hair has grown out enough to permit a ponytail and it sways as she works. Her newfound weight has settled mostly to her breasts, hips and buttocks. Jorge shakes his head as he watches her. "Man," he says, "this has to qualify as cruel and unusual treatment. Even prisoners in Raiford get conjugal visits."

His comments come back to me later that evening, after Elizabeth and I have made love. Pregnancy has quieted much of her wildness and sex has become for us a gentle thing, a slow coming together of our bodies, a movement as measured as calm waves lapping at the shore. The very gentleness of it somehow heightens our passion and makes our eventual orgasms almost painfully explosive.

Although I prefer my mattress to Elizabeth's bed of hay, I find it hard not to linger beside her afterward, tails entwined, feeling her warmth, waiting for the baby to move beneath my touch. I find it the most loving time we spend together, one of the few times my bride likes to talk.

"Jorge complained today that we give him and Morton no opportunity to have sex," I say. *"When I lie here with you and share with you what we share, it seems a shame to me to deny them the chance to experience something like this."*

She nuzzles her cheek against mine. *"Peter, they're just humans. When will you learn that how they feel means nothing?"*

"I like Santos. I don't see anything wrong with keeping him happy. It makes it easier when he cooperates."

"True," Elizabeth says. *"But Morton cooperates too—without any kindness from me. Fear can work every bit as well as friendship. . . . Actually, I think it works better."*

I think about it. Morton remains an enigma to me. She does as she's told, volunteers nothing about herself. Except for whispered conversations with Santos, she remains silent. For the most part, she answers to Elizabeth, who limits her involvement to as few brusque orders as necessary. I wonder if different treatment would bring the woman out. *"I prefer the other way. Even humans have value. The man entertains me."*

My bride sighs. *"Don't get too attached to him, Peter. The man will disappoint you. Even if he doesn't, he'll be dead before summer begins."*

I mentally count eleven months from impregnation, an unnecessary exercise, since Elizabeth's assured me many times she will deliver sometime in June. Then I calculate the remaining time. *"Only four more months,"* I say.

Elizabeth shifts in the hay. *"It feels like an eternity. I'm so weary of carrying this extra weight, so fed up with being constantly hungry and tired. I hate it especially when I'm in my human form. I don't know how their women cope with the way their bodies bloat and sag. . . ."*

"I know." I stroke her with my tail. *"But it will be ended soon enough, without hopefully much further aggravation,"* I say. *"Which gives us all the more reason to keep the humans content."*

Elizabeth laughs. *"You're shameless! If you want to let your pet have sex, do it. It doesn't matter to me."*

Santos raises his eyebrows when I tell him to forget taking the chess board out after dinner the next night. I grin at his uneasiness. "Something's come up," I say. "I need to take you and Casey downstairs earlier than usual this evening."

The Cuban shows no expression. I've no doubt he's trying to figure out what I have in store for them and how he can resist it. It makes it hard for me to stop smiling. I follow them down the spiral stairs, Casey in the lead, Santos behind her. As usual the woman begins to march into her open cell as soon as we reach it. "No, Casey, not tonight," I say.

She freezes, takes in an audible gulp of air. Santos turns and stares at me. Both of them look so apprehensive I break out laughing. It only changes their expressions to puzzlement. When I regain control of myself, I undo Casey's chains and say, "I thought it might be nice for you two to have some time together, alone, in Jorge's cell. . . ."

A big grin breaks out on Santos's face. "Boss, you son of a bitch! You had me going. I thought something terrible was going to happen." He laughs. "Son of a bitch! You actually listened to me."

Grinning too, I nod.

Casey Morton glares at us both. "You're giving me to him?" she asks, frowning. "First this man almost drowns me, then you take me prisoner. You make me a slave and that bitch of a wife of yours makes me eat all types of shit. Look at me!" She stamps one foot. "Look how fat she's made me! Now you expect me to fuck whoever you want, whenever you want? Fuck you, you pig!" She looks at Jorge. "Fuck you too, you bastard!" The blonde spins on her heels and stomps into her own cell.

Santos chuckles. "That's the first time she's acted like herself since we got here," he whispers. "I appreciate what you're trying to do here. Really, Boss. But I think it will go better if you lock me in her cell. I need some time to talk her down."

I undo his chains before he enters her cell. "You have two hours before I come back," I say, locking the cell door behind him. "After that you'll have to be in your own cell."

"Don't worry, Boss," he whispers to me, beaming. "When I have to, I can work really quick."

The next day Casey smiles as she goes about her work. For the first time since her capture, she speaks openly with Santos as they toil together. She even mutters, "Sorry for my tantrum last night," to me.

"*See,*" I tell Elizabeth. "*Isn't her behavior better this way?*"

Elizabeth grimaces, humphs. "*I don't know. I think I like it better when they're sullen. You're like my sister, Chloe. You always want the humans to like you. No matter how they act, they never will.*"

I wish later on that my bride could see how grateful Santos is. Elizabeth may be right, but the man certainly beams when he sees me. He grins even more when I say, "From now on, as long as you two continue to do everything as you should, I see no reason why you shouldn't visit each other a few times each week."

"That's good, Boss," he says. "Real good. To show you

how much I appreciate it, I want to cook you something special tonight—an old family recipe."

"I don't know, Jorge," I say. "You know I prefer plain meat."

"Sure, Boss, I know that. But you've never tasted my mother's *Carne' Diablo*. Trust me. You'll love it."

Elizabeth wrinkles her nose at the smell of it while Jorge toils at the skillet on the stove. I understand her reaction. The great room reeks from the aromas of cooking spices and seared meat. My eyes tear from the acrid smoke his cooking produces.

"I can't believe you're going to eat his food," my bride mindspeaks. *"I'd rather eat dirt."*

"I don't want to hurt his feelings, Elizabeth. I'll taste the dish, then take my regular steak."

"What if he's done something to the food?"

I look at her. *"Poison? He makes food for us each day. . . ."*

"He takes the chill off our meat. We would know if he altered it. With all those spices he's using, you wouldn't be able to tell if he poured battery acid over the whole concoction."

"I think you're being overly cautious," I say. *"Still, there's an easy way to allay your suspicions."*

When Santos brings the skillet to the table, he holds it in front of me first. *"Carne' Diablo,"* he announces, and begins to shovel some onto my plate with a fork.

I hold up one hand, stop him and make a show of examining the contents of the pan, the thick reddish-brown sauce still bubbling from the heat—fumes rising as I stir my fork around the simmering strips of beef. "You and Casey first," I say.

He grins. "Sure, Boss. You want to make sure I didn't slip any ground glass into it, huh?" Santos takes the fork, stabs a piece of meat and chews on it as he serves Casey. "Eat," he tells her. "The man wants to see that it won't kills us."

He spears another piece, chews on it. "That enough, Boss? You feel safe now?"

I nod, look away as he serves me and wait for him to sit down before I taste the dish.

"Come on," he says after he sits. "It's only food. Give it a try."

The aroma almost overwhelms me. I harpoon a small piece of meat with my fork and nibble on it. Even in such small quantity, the flavor explodes in my mouth. "Delicious," I say, stab another piece and wolf it down. I consume bite after bite, Jorge smiling as I eat—and I wonder why I've never tried anything but plain meat and fish my entire life.

Santos cautions me. "Take it easy, Boss. It's spicier than you think." But I don't stop until just sauce remains on my plate. Only then do I feel the heat that's building inside my mouth, my throat, my stomach. I grab my glass, drain the water in one sustained gulp then, momentarily speechless, motion for more.

Casey and Santos both guffaw at my antics, even as they run to the kitchen. Elizabeth rolls her eyes. I gasp and wait. Thankfully, the Cuban and the woman soon return, each carrying a large flagon of water. I grab one from Casey, drain it at once. When I grab the other, a look passes between the two of them and I pause before I drink it down. But the heat begins to return and I dismiss my suspicions and gulp down that water too.

"I told you to take it easy," Santos says.

"True." I nod. "You did."

"Next time you'll know how to pace it out."

"If there is a next time," I say.

"Come on, Boss. You liked it. You know it was good."

Now that the heat has subsided, the aftertaste seems to penetrate every tastebud I have. "It was good," I admit.

"And you'd like me to make it for you again. Wouldn't you, Boss?"

I smile and nod.

The winter wind, surprisingly gentle this year, blows in small huffs against the windows. The hearth remains cold, the evening too warm for a fire. Momentarily full, relaxed, I stay in my seat and watch while Casey clears the table and Jorge sets up the chess board. Elizabeth rises, kisses me and goes downstairs to nap.

Later, I know, after the humans are locked in their cells, my hunger will return. Elizabeth and I will take to the sky to hunt and to feast on fresh meat and warm blood. But for now I'm content. Casey turns on the television, settles down near us to watch a game show. Jorge chooses the white pieces, as he does each evening. Opens with his queen's knight to the queen's rook's right.

I smile. The move never works for him. The man opens aggressively then invariably turns timid, playing a defensive game, predictive and routine. Checkmate is already in my sight. In truth, I beat him each night. I wonder why he never loses heart.

25

February passes, then March, with Elizabeth growing larger and more moody each day. By the beginning of April, she refuses to change into her human shape at all. *"It's too uncomfortable,"* she tells me, lying in her bed of hay. *"When I take that form, my back hurts, my bladder feels as if its going to burst."* She pats the scales on her swollen midriff. *"At least in my natural state, there's more than enough room for our son."*

I see no reason to argue with her or to try to bring her out of our room. Whatever oversight Casey requires, I can give. She knows well enough by now how to tend the garden. Because of the help Santos and his woman provide, I have more than enough time to maintain our bedchamber and to tend to Elizabeth's needs—bringing her food from the kitchen, changing her hay.

It shames me to admit neither I nor the humans miss her presence very much. Santos cajoles me into buying rods and reels and we begin to set aside a little time each day for fishing in the harbor.

"My father used to take me fishing with him," Jorge says. "I was still little when he died. He used to swap rods, give me his when a fish took his hook. He always made a big deal saying he couldn't reel them in like I could. Sometimes at the end of the day, he'd build a fire for us and we'd cook our catch and eat it before we went home. Then, when we got home, we'd pretend at first to my mom, that we hadn't caught anything. I always giggled and gave it away." The Cuban shrugs. "Every time I fish, I think of him."

I nod, and think about my father. It surprises me to realize he did much the same thing. "When I was little, mine used to take me hunting. He would pretend he didn't see the prey, let me take it down first. Or sometimes he would make believe he needed my help, call on me to finish the kill. . . . My proudest day was the first time he sent me out alone, knowing he trusted me."

Santos asks, "What did you hunt?"

"Just game," I answer.

I begin to delay returning the humans to their cells at night so they can join me when I watch movies or other shows on the TV. Even when they don't like the broadcasts, they're never as indifferent as Elizabeth can be. I find that their company somehow enhances my enjoyment.

One night when there's nothing we want to watch, Santos suggests we play music. "Not that classical stuff," he says, turning on the FM radio, finding a Cuban station, dancing with Morton. When he sees me watching them, tapping my foot in time to the beat, he motions for me to join them, teaches me the steps. To my surprise, Casey allows me to take turns dancing with her, even joining in with Jorge and me when we laugh.

Except for going for food and other necessary supplies, I stay on the island. I tell myself, I don't want to have to lock Santos and Morton in the cells any more than needed. But I know the truth. I've never felt less lonely in my entire life.

Arturo calls a few days later, and asks, "Peter, is everything okay? You hardly ever come in anymore. Jeremy keeps asking when you're coming to shore. He complains he can never plan when to see you."

"Everything's fine," I say. "I just don't see much reason to leave the island these days."

"We need you here. There are decisions that need to be made."

"You can always call me."

"Peter, it's not the same. You know that. Jeremy's already made comments that, since we never resolved the attacks on you, you may be scared to come to the mainland."

I laugh. "Jeremy wishes I would be scared."

"Yes, he does," Arturo says. "I'm worried, with you gone so much, that he may try something again."

"Have your people watch him."

"They already are."

I shrug. "Then I have nothing to worry about."

Arturo calls again the next day. "You can start worrying now."

"Why?" I ask.

"My California friends inform me, your Chinese buddy is back in the country. They say he may be on the way to Florida."

"Can't they take care of him?"

"They don't know where he is."

I sigh. Life has been too pleasant for me to allow it to be roiled by threats. "Well, let me know when there's something to be done."

"Peter, there's more—"

"Damn it, Arturo, what?"

"My sources came up with a name, Xian Lo Chen. On a hunch I went back and read the newspaper reports on the fire. One of the people burned to death was listed as a Benny Chen, an executive with a Mainland Chinese fan factory. I think Xian Lo may be a pissed-off relative."

I shake my head. "Arturo, I want you to take care of this

for me. I don't want to have to deal with some crazy Chinese bastard right now."

"What the hell's come over you? This isn't how you usually handle things."

I sigh. "And you usually take care of what I want. If you need me to hold your hand so badly, I'll come in next week."

"That would be good," Arturo says. "I'll let Jeremy know we're having a meeting."

"Do what you think is best. Just get rid of Chen for me."

I hang up, irritated that I let Arturo pester me into leaving the island. I wonder how he would react if he knew what my life has become. I smile at the thought. He'd be shocked to find who I spend my days with—and so much of my nights.

My preoccupation with Santos and his woman still concerns Elizabeth. *"I shouldn't care. They're going to die soon enough,"* she says. *"But you need to harden your heart to them. I've seen Chloe weep for days when Pa killed one of the servants. I don't want your humans' deaths to hurt you so."*

The thought of their imminent demise weighs on me. I hate that the joy of my son's birth will bring on the sadness of their deaths. I turn inward, try to find a solution which can leave me happy. None presents itself.

I wake early the next Friday morning to a day without a cloud in the sky, without a ripple on the ocean. Rushing outside to the veranda, I luxuriate in the sun's mild warmth, glance from ocean, to bay, to sky—take in the shades of blue, the streaks of green, the almost-purple of the deep water offshore. I breathe in deep, savoring all the varied, salt-tinged smells carried by the morning breeze. Then I remember my promise to Arturo and groan.

The day is too splendid to waste inside an office. Arturo and Jeremy will have to understand. I have better things to do than to spend the day in their company. I'd rather sit outdoors and talk with Santos. Certainly, I think, he won't object, if I tell him to forget his chores and join me for a day of fishing in our harbor.

I call the office. Emily answers. "Oh, Mr. DelaSangre," she says when I ask for Arturo. "You know Mr. Gomez doesn't come in this early. Mr. Tindall's here, of course. He's in a meeting but if you want him, I'm sure he'll come out."

"Not necessary," I say. "Just tell them something came up. I can't make it today. Tell them I'll call next week."

"Too bad, sir, we were all looking forward to seeing you."

"Another time."

"Mr. DelaSangre . . . before you get off, I think you'd like to know a letter came for you yesterday. It's marked personal and confidential. I thought it might be important. . . ."

I shake my head. "I doubt it. It's probably a sales pitch. Open it, read it to me."

"If you think it's okay, sir," Emily says. "Just one second."

I wait, listen to the rustle of paper, the opening of a drawer. Picture her getting her letter opener, sliding it into the flap.

She mutters, almost to herself, "No return address. Postmarked from Malibu . . ."

California! I think. Before I can say, "Stop!" I hear the rip of paper. A blast sears across the phone line, half deafening my ear. Only silence follows. "Emily!" I yell into the dead phone. "Emily!"

Nothing.

"No . . . No," I mutter, dialing the office. The phone rings. No one picks up. I call Jeremy's private line. That too goes unanswered.

I dial Arturo's cell phone, try him on and off for fifteen

minutes before he finally picks up. "I was talking to Jeremy. He called me on his cell phone. All the regular lines are out at the office. We have a problem," he says. I've rarely heard his voice so somber.

"I know, I was on the phone with Emily."

"Oh, Peter, sometimes things are really shitty."

"Emily?" I ask.

"She's dead, Peter. Jeremy says it was one hell of a letter bomb."

"Damn it, Arturo, all she was doing was opening a letter for me. She's no part of what you or I do. . . ."

He sighs. "If it wasn't her, it could have been you or one of us. These people seem very determined."

I think of the couple locked in the cells beneath my house. "At least we know it isn't Santos."

"You might wish it were. This Chen character seems to have a good idea of your comings and goings. That letter was timed to arrive just before our meeting."

"If Chen is the one."

"Whoever it is seems to know a hell of a lot about you. Peter, Jeremy says maybe we were wrong to push you to come to shore. I think he's right. I think you'd be better off staying on your island until we get all this resolved. You call me with what you'll need. I'll bring it out to you."

26

What does a hunter do when he's hunted? How does an attacker cope with being attacked? Every fiber of my being now cries out for me to take action, to take revenge, to strike and slash and kill. I no longer want to stay put on my island while others solve my problems.

I call Arturo each morning, but Chen remains a ghost, a rumor, a name with no details, no history. One day he's reported in Chicago; the next, he's seen in New York.

"My friends say he's unreachable, deep in Chinatown," Arturo says, after a week's gone by. "The Chinese gangs are very protective of him. We'll have to wait until he shows himself down here. If he does."

Elizabeth wants me to travel north and take care of it myself. As much as the idea tempts me, I reject it.

"Father said more have died from action without thought than from sensible defense," I tell her. "He always lectured me, 'Know your enemy before you attack.' I don't know anything about this man or his friends. Until I do, I'll wait for him here. No matter how much I'd rather be out hunting for him."

Arturo agrees, encourages me to turn my attention to my island, my home. Jeremy calls, saying, "Don't worry, Peter. We'll handle things here. Arturo will take care of your problem. Just relax and enjoy."

I frown. "I want that man dead," I say. "I want to know where Chen is—where he's going."

"Trust us, Peter," Jeremy says. "Arturo and I will handle everything. Let us do the worrying. You just stay put, take care of yourself."

Jeremy is hardly ever solicitous of my needs. I find I prefer his normal surly self. "What makes you so nice all of a sudden?" I ask.

Tindall barks a short, harsh laugh. "I think we're all safer when you stay away, Peter. You know how close to Emily's desk my office is? When that letter bomb went off, I thought I was dead meat. Hell, my ears are still ringing from that damn bomb blast. The truth is, Peter—the next time someone tries to kill you, I don't want to be anywhere near you. As long as this bastard is out there, let us watch your back for you. Stay on your damn island, enjoy yourself—please."

I laugh and hang up. No matter Jeremy's reasons, the advice is good, I think. Father chose this island and built this house to be able to withstand any attack. I can't think of any place on the mainland where Elizabeth and I would be as safe.

Resolving to follow Jeremy's advice, I decide to live as normal a life as possible while I wait for the mysterious Mr. Chen to show his hand. Certainly I won't pass any window or go outside without examining the water for suspicious boats. And I'll pay more attention to the barks and growls of the dog pack, listen for any sign that intruders may have tried to land on the island's shore. But Elizabeth and I will still hunt each night and I'll still tend to my chores each day.

My cell phone rings a few weeks later, while Jorge and I are in the midst of servicing the Grady White's Yamaha engines. I put down my wrench and answer it.

"Peter? I've got good news," Arturo says.

"Chen's dead?" I ask.

"No, not yet. But he is on the move. My people managed to find out he was flying down here yesterday. They missed him at Miami International by only a few minutes. Our sources say he's hiding somewhere in South Miami now. It's just a matter of time before we locate him."

"You're sure?"

"Positive," Arturo says. "I have the surveillance films from the airport. Only one Asian got off that flight. Two others met him at the baggage claim. We know what all of them look like. I gave their pictures to our people and to our friends at Metro Dade police. The cops have a bulletin out on all of them. If any of them goes anywhere, does anything, either the police or one of our people should spot him."

"Good," I say, grinning, relieved that something's finally being done. "Call me when you know anything further."

I hang up and turn to Santos.

He stops lubricating one of the outboard's prop shafts, stares at me, grease streaked on his face, and studies my expression. "Good news?" he asks.

"Yes," I say. "If I were a drinking man I'd break out a bottle."

"So what *do* you do to celebrate?"

Turning my head toward the veranda, I stare at the cannon pointed seaward and remember my late-night celebration a few days before I left to find my bride. "Jorge," I say, "it occurs to me, we've never fired the cannon like I promised."

"No, Boss, we never have." He resumes greasing the shaft.

"It occurs to me that we should."

"Sounds good to me." He pauses, then says, "Why don't we do it late tomorrow afternoon? Afterward, I'll make *Carne' Diablo* for you again."

I wonder why he's being so thoughtful. Still the man cooks food for me all the time. It's not so unusual a suggestion. So I smile and say, "Good idea."

* * *

That night Elizabeth surprises me by inviting me to her bed after our hunt. *"Gently,"* she cautions me and we make love as lightly as two feathers rubbing together. Afterward, she sighs and pulls me close to her. Her stomach contorts as the child rolls and kicks within her.

She smiles. *"Your son wants to come out,"* she says.

"So soon?" I ask.

"Silly, it's less than two weeks until June. Your son could come any time after that."

So soon, I think, picturing the looks of terror on Casey's and Jorge's faces when they realize their fate.

"Aren't you happy?" Elizabeth asks.

"Of course I am," I say.

"We'll have the house to ourselves again. No more humans to bother you. Just me, you, and our son." Elizabeth grins. *"I can't wait. I'll get my old body back and we can begin to enjoy ourselves again."*

I nod.

"I know in some ways I've been a disappointment to you, Peter. But I hope not too much." Elizabeth strokes me with her tail.

I look at her. Even swollen as she is, I find her beautiful. *"You've never disappointed me,"* I say. *"We were brought up differently. We've just had to learn about each other."*

"Peter," she says, looking into my eyes, *"do you remember, on the boat, when we talked about love?"*

"Yes."

"I told you then I wasn't sure what love was."

I nod.

"I've been thinking a lot about it these past few months. The child's nearness has made me examine things. I'm sure now, Peter. I love you."

They are words I never expected to hear from her. Momentarily, I wonder if I've been disloyal to her, spending so much of my time with Santos and Casey, enjoying it as much as I have. But just being beside her, hearing her words, reaffirms her importance to me. *"I love you too,"* I answer.

We lie side by side, in that netherworld between consciousness and sleep, listening to the rhythm of each other's breaths. *"Peter?"* Elizabeth rouses me. I move enough for her to know I'm listening. *"In the morning when you wake, would you do something for me?"*

"Of course."

"The gold clover necklace that you gave me before we married is on the dresser top. I know it's silly. I know it doesn't fit me in this form but I'd like to wear it. Could you fasten it around my wrist so it won't fall off? Promise me?"

"I promise."

We drift toward sleep again and I remember my other promise, the one I made to Jorge Santos. *"Santos and I will be firing one of the cannons tomorrow afternoon. I don't want the sound to surprise you."*

"It won't, Peter," she says, snuggling against me. *"Just be careful playing with your silly toys."*

In the morning I wake and change to my human shape. Leaving my bride's side, I immediately look for the gold clover necklace. I carry it back to Elizabeth, kneel beside her and carefully wrap it, twice, around her right wrist, just above her taloned paw. It makes me smile that she wanted to wear it and I take my leave, kissing her on the snout, taking care not to wake her.

I pause before I leave the chamber, watch her sleep, let the love I feel for her well up inside me. Resisting the impulse to wake her and pledge my love aloud, I go out the door. Later, I think. There will be plenty of time for that.

Santos and Morton both seem somewhat subdued when I release them from their cells, as if their thoughts remain elsewhere. I think nothing of it, my mind on Elizabeth and the child. I don't permit myself to think of the humans' impending deaths. I decide to confront that when necessary.

In the late afternoon I go out to the veranda, survey the sky, nodding at the low gray clouds, the gusting wind—smiling at the roiled surface of the sea. No boats are anywhere in sight nor, in this weather, would I expect them to be.

Sure our activities will go unheard and unobserved, I open the arms room, then fetch Morton and Santos. The woman sits on the wall and watches while Santos and I roll the cannon back. I let him prepare and load the charge. We both stand by to let Casey light the fuse.

They both shout when the cannon fires, belching flame and smoke. I join in their hurrahs when the ball strikes, sending up a white plume of water a quarter-mile offshore.

Jorge grins, and asks, "Again?"

"Why not?" I say and we take turns loading the ship killer, then firing it. I run Santos back to the arms room six times for more ammunition, all of us turning giddy, laughing as we load the cannon, our ears ringing, our faces smoke blackened.

"Peter," Elizabeth mindspeaks to me. *"Don't you think it's time to stop? If you keep this up, some passing boat will surely notice and inform the authorities."*

I think of all the bribe money the marine patrol takes and laugh. *"As if they'd care,"* I tell her, sending Santos to the arms room one last time, thinking how tired he must be when he takes longer than usual to return and load the cannon.

After Casey lights the fuse and the cannon fires, I send Santos and Morton inside. I close and lock the arms room out of their sight. Then, still grinning from the pleasure of firing the big gun, I follow the two humans indoors.

* * *

I insist that Jorge prepare Elizabeth's steak first. When it's ready, I leave him and Casey in the great room to prepare our dinner while I bring my bride hers.

"Did you have a good time?" she asks as she sits up.

"Very good," I say, sitting in the hay next to her, placing her plate between us.

"I missed you."

Her confession surprises me. *"I thought you liked to be left alone during the day."*

"Until recently I have. But the baby's making me feel so many things now. I find I want you near me."

"Then I'll come down right after dinner," I say.

"Can't you just stay?" Elizabeth asks.

I shake my head. *"Jorge's making* Carne' Diablo *especially for me tonight. I wouldn't want to disappoint him."*

"You and your pet human." Elizabeth holds up her arm, and admires the necklace wrapped around it. She sighs. *"If you think you have to go, then do so. Just be careful with that food. Remember what it did to you last time."*

27

"Hey, Boss! You ready for your dinner?" Santos greets me as soon as I walk into the great room.

I sniff the acrid smell of spices and meat sizzling in his skillet, grin and sit at the table. "Bring it on," I say. "Let's see how I handle it this time."

"Indeed, Boss," he says, smiling, serving me first. "Let's see if you can take it tonight."

He and Morton sit across the table, eat in tandem with me. This time, I space my bites, sip water between every few. Still I feel the heat building as I proceed. One bite strikes me as particularly hot, scalding my throat, making me cough. I take a gulp of water, say, "It's delicious. But did you make it spicier tonight?"

Jorge and Casey exchange glances. Both smile at me. "Not so you'd notice, Boss," he says.

I return to my meal, take bite after bite, sip after sip. By the time I finish, my mug sits empty and the heat still burns inside me. I shake my head, say, "It's still too damn hot. I need some more water."

"No problem, Boss. Coming right up." Santos and Morton both rush to the kitchen.

To me it feels like it takes forever for them to return. The heat builds, sears my throat, eats at my insides. Finally, they come back, each carrying a flagon as before. I rip them from their hands and gulp the entire contents of one, then the other.

"Better?" Santos asks.

I sigh and nod, the heat abating, a calming glow growing within me. My mouth feels greasy and I run my tongue against my teeth, wondering why they feel so slippery. A thought crosses my mind and I shudder, then look toward the shelves on the wall. I can't find Elizabeth's blue ceramic pitcher anywhere on them.

My mouth falls open. I struggle to close it. Santos's face and Morton's loom in front of me, studying me. Both grin as if they've won the lottery. I want to ask them if it was the Dragon's Tear wine, but I can't form the words.

"Did it work?" Morton asks.

"Test it," Santos says.

She picks up my fork and jams it into my right forearm. I try to scream, will myself to change. Nothing. Casey yanks the fork out, studies the blood on its prongs, the red liquid flowing from the four puncture wounds on my arm.

"Well, Boss," Santos says, "you can't say I didn't warn you." He forms a fist with his right hand and strikes my face with all his force. The impact throws my head to the side, turns my vision blurry. Still, I can't move or make any sound.

I concentrate on my thoughts, but even they seem to form and dissolve of their own accord. I ignore the sound of Jorge and Casey talking, let their words wash by me.

". . . kill him," Jorge Santos says and I return my attention to the world around me.

"I don't think you can," Casey says. She points to the wounds on my arm, now mostly healed. If I could, I would laugh. Even drugged and near comatose, my body still possesses the ability to heal itself.

"Son of a bitch!" Jorge mutters. He walks to the kitchen, returns with a long carving knife, stands behind me. "You killed my sister, you prick," he growls, grabs my hair, yanks my head back and slices through my neck.

Even dulled as my senses are by the Dragon's Tear wine, the pain that sears through me—as intense as if he had used a red-hot blade—brings tears to my eyes. But I can't even gasp.

When he releases me, my head sags forward. I watch as my blood gushes onto the tabletop. Within a few moments, the flow stops. Casey says, "I don't like this. He's already healing. Let's just get out of here."

"No," Jorge says. "Not before we kill them both." He saunters to the far wall, takes down Father's cutlass and returns.

"What makes you think that will do any better than the knife?" Morton asks.

"I don't." Santos takes an exaggerated fencing posture, lunges forward, runs the blade through me once, twice. Cleans my blood from the cutlass by wiping it on my pants leg. Watches as my wounds close in minutes.

"We just don't have the right weapons," he says, smirking. "I know where we can get them."

"Let's just leave," Casey says again.

"You forget the dogs," Santos says. "We'll have to do something about them too. Kill them all."

"How?"

"Some help wouldn't hurt," Santos says. He looks around the room, points when he sees my cell phone. "Casey, honey, please get that for me."

He looks into my face as he dials the phone. "Oh," he says, "I guess when we talked about the note, I neglected to tell you one thing—I remembered the number after all." Then he walks away, says into the mouthpiece, "This is Santos, I'm calling about Peter DelaSangre. . . ."

His voice drops and no matter how I strain, I can't hear any more of the conversation.

Later, they help me up and lead me out of the room to the spiral staircase. To my surprise, I shuffle forward on command and continue moving as long as I receive constant attention. Jorge provides this, prodding me along the way with the cutlass. "I should just push you down the stairs, you evil bastard," he mutters in my ear.

Casey shushes him. "We don't want to wake the bitch up," she whispers and we proceed past the second floor in silence.

I try to call to Elizabeth, but can't form any sounds. I attempt to mindspeak to her, but the thoughts escape me. I lose track of where we are, only regain awareness when Santos slaps my face.

"Get in the cell!" He guides me forward, but Casey grabs my arm.

"Not mine," she says. "It's too large and comfortable for him." She pulls on me, makes me walk farther. She stops, points. "This one, it's smaller."

"Fine," Santos says. He shoves me, knocking me to the stone floor next to the cot. The Cuban holds me down while Casey rifles through my pockets and produces my keys. I pay no attention to the clank and jangle of chains and manacles as they undo their fetters and bind me in them.

Jorge slaps me again. I realize I'm on the cot—my neck, my wrists, my ankles chained. I make no effort to test my fetters. The Dragon's Tear wine shackles me more completely than they ever could.

Casey Morton looks down at me, spits in my face. "I hate you!" she says. She begins to cry and pummels my face with her fists, striking again and again, saying, "I hate you! I hate you! I hate you!"

Jorge pulls her back. "Casey, honey, stop," he says. "We don't know how long we have until the wine wears off. Let's get what we need from the arms room and finish these creatures off."

"How can we get through the door? You told me yourself,

there's no visible lock. No way you can see to release the crossbeam."

"That was before." Santos beams. He puts his face to the bars, directs his words at me. "Today, when we were firing the cannon I finally had a chance to examine the mechanism." He clangs the cutlass blade against the steel bars. "There's a release lever that can be reached through a crack in the stone. You just need something skinny and strong to reach it." Santos laughs, thrusts the cutlass through the bars. "This will do, I think."

They turn off all lights on the floor, leaving me in total darkness. Without the slightest glimmer of light, even I can't see through the blackness. I'm tempted to sleep, but I fight the impulse. Elizabeth is in danger. I concentrate on reaching her. To my amazement, I do, finding myself in her dreams, her mind more open to me than any day since our wedding. The Dragon's Tear wine, I think. I try to call her name, but can't form the word.

Dogs bark outside. I hear them with her, see her room as she does as she blinks her eyes open. I feel her confusion too as we hear the sound of metal scraping stone, the metallic click of the crossbeam lever releasing, the groan of the arms door being yanked open, the clank of heavy objects being moved on the veranda.

"Peter?" Elizabeth mindspeaks. *"I hear things. What is happening?"*

I try to tell her. The words almost form, but slip away before they gel. "Danger," I want to say. "Save yourself."

"Why don't you answer me?" Elizabeth asks. *"Peter, please!"*

She rises and I watch through her eyes as she walks to the bedchamber's outside door. *"No!"* I imagine myself yelling, but no sound, no thought escapes me. Elizabeth opens the door and Casey Morton screams.

Elizabeth roars and I see Casey's horrified countenance just as my bride does.

"Casey! Move!" Jorge Santos shouts and the blonde jumps to one side. He lifts a massive weapon to his shoulder and aims it at Elizabeth. She stares at the barrel's black muzzle and I recognize the weapon as a rail gun. I try again to warn my bride, but she rushes forward without hearing me.

The gun explodes before her, Jorges Santos flying back from the recoil. Elizabeth screams as the ball rips through her right eye socket. Her mind goes blank.

Cut off from her, I lie motionless in the dark, alone with my thoughts. Grief engulfs me. I attempt to move, to curl into a fetal position, but even that is refused me. I can't blink an eyelid or moan. It is wrong, I think, to be denied the ability to weep.

28

Time passes or doesn't move at all. It's impossible for me to tell. All I know is the hard slab of the cot beneath me, the weight of my chains. I strain to see anything of my surroundings, but view only darkness. I listen, but hear only the stillness around me. I know Santos will come to kill me. The man could never leave knowing the murderer of his sister still lives.

I struggle to move, concentrate on controlling just one finger—the small one on my right hand. I will it to respond. It trembles and, if I could, I would smile. I will it to move again and it flexes. I turn my attention from finger to finger, slowly bringing each to life. My eyelids resist and then succumb to my desire to blink.

My successes make me hopeful and I try once more to mindspeak. *"Elizabeth!"* I call. *"Elizabeth, please answer me!"*

A sob escapes from my lips when I receive no reply. I lie still again, give way to the solitude of my existence.

Something . . . a wisp of energy . . . a glimmer of a thought touches me. I concentrate, try to reach out, strain to receive whatever may be out there.

"Elizabeth!" I call again.

A feeble reply brushes my consciousness. *"Peter?"*

I open my mind to her, attempt to merge with her, like I did before. I recoil from the pain and confusion I find, her anger as she rejects me. *"Elizabeth,"* I mindspeak. *"Please."*

It takes all my energy to understand her thoughts. *"Peter, where have you been?"* she asks. *"Where are you now?"*

"Oh, Elizabeth, you can't believe how happy I am to hear you. . . . I was afraid he killed you."

"Very nearly. He hurt me badly, Peter. Where are you? I need you. I think he and the woman are still near me. Please, Peter."

"Lie still. Don't let them know you're alive," I say. *"I'm below, locked in one of the cells. At dinner they tricked me. They served me Dragon's Tear wine."*

"Oh, Peter! I warned you."

"You did and you were right. But now we have to stop them."

"I'm healing quickly. It won't be long before I'm much stronger, Peter," she says. *"I can hear them now. They're talking about you."*

I attempt to raise my arm. It refuses to budge. I force a sigh. It seems control of my thoughts will be easier than command of my body. *"Elizabeth, I'm afraid it will be awhile before I can leave my cell."* The idea of leaving her alone angers me. I try again to merge with her thoughts. This time she doesn't rebuff me.

Elizabeth emits a mental gasp when I join with her. Together we listen.

"We could use more firepower," Jorge says. "They should be here soon. But for now, we need to rely on ourselves. We don't know where the woman is or how many more things like this are around. We still have to kill DelaSangre. Bring me three more rail guns and I'll load them for us."

Casey Morton grunts her assent.

"They still don't realize what we are," I say. *"That has to*

be to our advantage. Can you open your good eye just a skinch?"

Elizabeth does and together we watch Santos nearby, working in the flickering yellow glow of two lit torches, pouring powder into one of the large guns.

"Peter?" my bride says. *"I can do it. I'm growing stronger. In a little while I'll be able to stop them. . . ."*

"No! *Not without me."* In my cell I try to lift my arm again. It rises a half-inch before my strength fails me. *"If they think you're dead, they'll leave you alone and concentrate on searching the house, trying to find the person they imagine you to be. By the time they give that up and come for me, I'll be recovered enough to elude them. Then we can both end this."*

"What if they go for you first? I won't be able to help you there. It would be better if I acted sooner, alone."

"I know Santos. We've played chess for months. He always goes on the defensive. He knows I'm locked in a cell. He'll want to find and eliminate you first."

"What if you're wrong?" Elizabeth says. *"It* is *possible you know."* Irritated, she twitches her tail.

I feel her movement. *"Stay still!"* I warn her again.

"Did you see that?" Casey asks Santos.

Jorge, intent on working the ramrod, driving the charge home, says, "Huh?"

"I think the thing's tail moved."

"Casey, it's just an involuntary movement," he says. "We blew half its head off. Nothing would survive that. . . ."

The high-pitched growl of a small outboard motor interrupts their conversation. Santos and Morton both look seaward. Out in the dark, the dogs greet the noise with a chorus of barks and growls. Santos says, "I think the cavalry's arrived."

Casey stares at the water and snorts, "Some cavalry! Four middle-aged men in an inflatable dinghy."

The dog pack's noise turns to bedlam and, in my cell, I can picture them on the beach massing for an attack. Staccato bursts of machine-gun fire cut through their clamor, turning their growls into yelps, their barks into howls.

Santos grins. "With that armament, I think they're help enough."

As the bursts and dog yelps continue, Santos goes on loading the rail guns.

"Why bother?" Casey asks.

Jorge shrugs. "Just in case," he says.

In my cell I wince at each machine-gun blast, worry that all my dogs will be destroyed forever and wonder, if we survive, whether I'll ever be able to replace them. All too soon the gunshots stop and the night becomes quiet again.

"Damn!" I mutter. I clench my fists, open them. I'm able to raise my arms almost to shoulder height, then drop them. Soon, I think. If only I have enough time.

I groan when the first man steps into Elizabeth's view. Tall and thin, grinning, looking like a charter captain in his yachting cap, T-shirt and khaki shorts, Jeremy Tindall approaches Jorge, his hand out, and says, "Mr. Santos, I believe." Three shorter, more muscular men follow behind him, their faces obscured by the shadows.

I pray that Arturo isn't one of the others.

"You should have killed him long ago," Elizabeth mindspeaks.

The other three men emerge into the light and I let out a sigh of relief when I see that all are Asian. Tindall nods toward a gray-haired Chinese man dressed much like him. The man is older than the others and carries a large, black Colt automatic in his right hand. "This is General Chen," Tindall says, "and these"—he points to two fatigue-clad men armed with AK-47 machine guns—"are his assistants."

Santos shakes Tindall's hand, nods to the others, who nod back to him. "Glad you're here. We can use the help."

Casey points at Elizabeth. "It isn't bleeding anymore."

"What the hell is that?" Tindall says. He backs away, as do the others, muttering in Chinese.

"I'm not sure," Santos says. "But whatever it is, it's dead." He turns to Casey. "If it would make you happy, take my blunderbuss. Shoot it again." The Cuban cocks the newly loaded weapon, holds it out for her.

"I've never fired one of these," Casey says, and takes the rail gun, holds it with both hands by her waist.

Santos begins to pour powder into the wide barrel of yet another gun. "Just point it and pull the trigger," he says. "Worst thing happens, you'll miss, and since it's dead already anyway—who cares?"

The blonde scowls at him. "Sometimes you're such an asshole! What if it's alive?"

She pokes the barrel of her gun into Elizabeth's left haunch. To my relief, my bride stays still.

Tindall and the Chinese step closer. The two assistants hold their AK-47s at rest. "I'd be careful if I were you," Chen says, and points his pistol in Elizabeth's direction.

"Looks dead to me," Santos says, dropping a golfball-size lead ball into the barrel of the blunderbuss, ramming it home. He cocks the hammer, primes the flashpan with gunpowder.

"Maybe . . ." Casey says. She prods Elizabeth again with the gun barrel then points it straight at my bride's midriff.

"NOT THE CHILD!" Elizabeth mindspeaks, roaring, sweeping her tail in front of her, knocking Casey down, the blonde's gun flying from her hands, the woman screaming.

Chen empties his automatic into Elizabeth as he backs up, Tindall behind him. His men rush in front of him, fumble with their machine guns, preparing to protect him.

Elizabeth roars, ignores Chen's bullets, kills one man

with a single slash across his neck, yowls as the other man empties his clip into her. She leaps forward and seizes him in her mouth, shaking him until he no longer moves.

"Son of a bitch!" Santos shouts. He shoulders his gun, fires, the ball whizzing by the side of Elizabeth's head.

Crying, Morton tries to crawl away, saying, "Please, please."

I feel the agony of Elizabeth's wounds. I know the hunger that courses through her, the need for food to speed her healing. I share her anger at her attackers. Elizabeth bellows and I revel as she rakes Casey's body with her talons, rips her open. I smell the rich aroma of fresh blood as my bride breathes it in, savor it as she does.

The blonde screams again and Elizabeth attacks once more, biting a huge hunk of flesh from Casey's leg, swallowing it in one gulp.

Santos drops his now empty rail gun, watching my bride. Elizabeth eyes him as she tears another piece of flesh from the dying woman. She looks for Tindall and Chen, but they've disappeared from sight.

"THE MAN!" I feel my bride's hunger and need for energy, but I see the danger too. *"YOU HAVE TO STOP THE MAN!"*

"He's nothing," Elizabeth says.

The Cuban dives for Casey's discarded gun.

Elizabeth sweeps her tail at him, knocks him down.

Santos grabs the rail gun by the tip of the barrel and scrambles back, pushing with his feet, scooting on his rump. Elizabeth, growling, stalks him until he backs into the wall of the house. Unable to retreat any farther, he yanks the rail gun toward him just as my bride rushes at him, and slashes out with her left claw.

He blocks her with the gun—its barrel slamming into his forehead with the full force of Elizabeth's blow—then pivots the blunderbuss and fires it at point-blank range.

Fire and smoke erupt in front of Elizabeth. The noise deafens her. The massive ball passes through the side of her neck, shredding flesh, shattering her spine, splintering her shoulder bone. I bellow in my cell at the same time as Elizabeth roars in pain on the veranda. She staggers backward, collapses against the parapet, her eyes still open, her mind still aware.

Santos, almost as stunned as she, sits across the walkway from her, his back still to the house's wall. Casey lies on the deck between them, her blood coating the wood planks, her breath coming in spastic gasps. The Cuban stares at Elizabeth, waits for her to roar forward and finish him.

"I can't, Peter. I can't move. . . ."

"I know," I say, feeling what she feels, knowing as she does how badly she's injured. I struggle to sit up, my body finally beginning to comply. *"Don't give up. Your body can survive this."*

She sighs. *"He won't let me."*

"It won't be much longer before I can move well enough to find my way out."

"It will be too late, Peter."

Together we watch Santos. He stares at her, shakes his head, mutters, "Son of a bitch." Then he crawls toward her, stopping by Casey, putting his lips on her forehead—a farewell kiss, I suppose. He lingers a moment, then continues on, stopping just out of Elizabeth's reach. Santos examines her again, shakes his head once more. "What are you doing with that?" he says, reaching forward.

"Oh, Peter," Elizabeth mindspeaks as the Cuban undoes the gold chain that I just this morning wrapped around her wrist.

Santos holds it in his fist. Still staring at Elizabeth, he scoots back to the wall and braces against it, pushing himself up with his legs. The Cuban pauses, inspects the gold clover charm, kisses it and fastens the chain around his neck. Never taking his eyes off Elizabeth, he sidles away from her, works his way to the arms room.

Tindall and Chen come out of the shadows. Chen stoops over, picks up an AK-47 lying by the side of one of his dead men. He checks the magazine, finds it's empty and reloads it. Then, chambering a load, he points it at Elizabeth.

"Don't bother," Santos says. "I have something better."

I try to change shape, but the Dragon's Tear remains too much with me. I look around the cell, try to recognize anything that might help me free myself. The dark defeats me. I tug at my chains. They resist me. *"Try to escape, Elizabeth,"* I say. *"Before he comes back!"*

"You know better, Peter. I can't."

"You have to force yourself to heal. You have to try, even if it takes your last bit of energy."

"No," she mindspeaks. *"It might kill the baby."*

"Elizabeth," I say, *"Without you, what chance does the child have?"*

"I won't risk hurting my baby!"

I try to think of something to say to inspire her, to spur her to act in her own interest. I worry that Elizabeth's injuries have weakened her ability to reason.

Santos returns carrying a cannonball under one arm, a canister of powder under the other. He ignores Elizabeth's scrutiny, goes about the business of loading the cannon.

Frantic, I struggle against my shackles.

"I couldn't let that woman harm the baby," Elizabeth mindspeaks.

"I understand."

Once the cannon's loaded, Santos looks at Tindall. "You could help you know," he says.

Chen laughs, keeps his rifle trained at Elizabeth. "Jeremy doesn't like to get his hands dirty," he says. "He's used to others doing his work for him."

Tindall scowls at him, walks over to Santos. "Just show

me what to do," he says. He grunts and groans as he helps Santos inch the ship killer around, until the black, gaping maw of the cannon aims straight at Elizabeth's head.

Santos stares at her. "I don't know what the hell you are," he says. "But this should finish you." He walks away, toward the arms room.

"Peter, I don't want to die," Elizabeth mindspeaks.

I pull at my chains as best I can, knowing I lack the strength to escape yet. *"I know, my love,"* I say.

"Your love . . . I like that. Peter, I was so young. . . . I was learning. I would have made a good wife for you after the baby was born."

"I'm sure, love. I'm sure you would have." In the dark, I feel tears wetting my cheeks, do nothing to wipe them away.

"Promise me, you'll say good things about me to our son."

"Of course," I say, not quite sure she realizes what she's saying.

Santos returns with a torch he's taken down from the wall.

Elizabeth sighs, says, *"I would have been a very good mother."*

The Cuban lowers the torch's flaming end to the touch hole and the roar of the cannon penetrates the house, reverberating in my cell.

29

Rage alternates with sorrow. I know my bride is dead. For the first time since our marriage, I can't find her touch. I have no sense of her. It's as if I've lost my sight, or my hearing. I am truly alone now, without hope, my future shattered.

Jorge Santos is to blame. I imagine making him die slowly, in great agony.

I yank on my chains but still they resist me. The manacles cut into my wrists and I welcome the pain.

Tears come again and I welcome them too. I understand now how Father felt when Mother died. Like him, I've lost my life's companion. And my child before he's ever known the world. I want to howl and tear my hair. Damn Jorge Santos!

And yet I can't blame the man completely. I am the murderer of his sister. I have been his captor. His woman, if she isn't dead, lies dying on the veranda of my house, mortally wounded by my wife. If anyone has good reason to kill, it is Santos.

And I have no doubt he intends to kill me. I know the man. I calculate how long it will take him to come for me.

As he does when he plays chess, he'll hesitate before he proceeds, fret that his position might be insufficient. With me imprisoned, he'll think he has the time to take every precaution.

First he'll make sure at least two rail guns are loaded. He

won't bother with more, the guns are too large, and more of them would burden him too much.

Besides he has Chen and Tindall as his allies. Though Tindall, I'm sure, will prove worthless. He'll lag behind, argue for caution. As a miliary man, Chen will urge a quick assault. He'll feel safe enough to proceed as long as he holds a loaded machine gun.

But Santos will insist only he knows the house. I'm sure he'll feel the need for further protection before he ventures inside. He'll tarry long enough to load a few pistols too, stick them in his belt. Only then will he search the upper floors for Elizabeth. Only when he doesn't find her, will he come for me.

In truth I'm tempted to let him. My wife and child are gone. I sigh and lie down on my cot. The thought of life alone on my island fills me with dread. Santos, at least, has a mother to return to. I have no one.

I let the dark envelop me. I become nothing lost in nothingness, air floating within air, time lost for all time. I would float away if my chains didn't weigh me down. I would sink if the cot wasn't underneath me. This, I think, must be how it feels to die.

Perhaps I will.

My breathing irritates me. I hate the sound of my heart beating. I want complete silence. I try to still myself, achieve total calm. And still, the quieter I become, the less I move, the more something tweaks at my consciousness. A lingering thought? An emotion my subconscious refuses to stop feeling?

No matter how I try to dampen my senses, it intrudes. Finally, unable to ignore it, I concentrate on identifying it, disregard everything else. The sensations I receive frustrate me with their vagueness. It's almost like mindspeaking but not quite—as if it's slightly merged with the type of closeness Elizabeth and I shared. No words, no images, just feelings—

fleeting impressions of occasional movement, occasionally restricted by something soft (a wall?), sometimes flashes of content, always the overwhelming sensation of moist warmth.

Elizabeth must be dead. I know it. I feel it. Yet my heart races at the thought that some remnant of her consciousness may be left, that some possibility may remain for her resurrection. I reach out for her, mindspeak, *"Elizabeth?"*

The answer stuns me. No words to it, no thoughts, just the feather-light touch of another presence brushing against my mind—not my wife but my unborn son.

Henri! My child may yet be saved. The realization changes everything. If I fail, if I permit Santos and the others to win, not only do I die but so does my son. Time, which meant nothing a few moments ago, means everything now.

I curse myself for wallowing in self-pity rather than recognizing the possibility of saving more than myself. By now they must be searching the floors above me. I must take action immediately. I turn my attention back to my surroundings, see nothing. Outside, at least, stars or a partial moon usually give me enough light to see through the darkness. But here in the cell with no lights on anywhere, blackness engulfs me.

The chains that bind me remain too strong to break, but for a creature who can change shape at will that hardly matters. I test whether the effects of the Dragon's Tear have abated enough, concentrate on narrowing my right hand and wrist.

My body seems almost indifferent to my wishes. It conforms to my shapechanging ever so slowly. I concentrate, ignore the pain the change requires and pray Santos's search of the house takes longer than my escape.

Finally, I'm able to slip my hand out of the right manacle.

My left hand and wrist go easier and I escape that fetter

too, turn my attention to my ankles and feet. Only the slave collar remains. That proves the most difficult, as I elongate and narrow my head enough to slip free. I stand as soon as I throw the last chain off and almost topple back—the sudden rush of rising, coupled with the remaining effects of the Dragon's Tear wine and the total dark looming around me disorient and confuse me. I weave in place a few moments, focus my thoughts on where the cell door may be.

When I reach it, I find barely three inches of space exist between each thick iron bar. I almost cry when I think how difficult slipping my body out will be. Surely, I think, it can be done, but I've never attempted such a thing. I back up, pace a few steps. Taking deep breaths, steeling myself for the attempt, I pace a few steps more and walk headfirst into a wall that I didn't expect to encounter.

Then I remember Casey's insistence on putting me in a smaller cell. I grin, shake my head, take more deep breaths to clear my mind, then test my assumption by putting my back to the wall and walking forward until I touch the opposite wall. Just five steps! I almost laugh out loud. Santos will be so confused when he arrives to find the locked cell empty. I grab the end of the cot and yank on it, raising it, opening the passageway to the treasure room below and the door to the dock beyond it.

In their desire to place me in the smallest, least comfortable cell, Santos and Morton, who had no knowledge of the secret passage, unwittingly assured my escape.

Once on the stairs, I close the passageway behind me, take the steps two and three at a time. I waste no time turning on lights. I know the way. Rushing through the corridor, ripping my clothes off, I reach the door to the outside and throw it open. I wrinkle my nose at the stink of sulfur the expended gunpowder has left on the evening air, and change shape.

I leap toward the sky and travel from the dock to the veranda in a few wingbeats. My poor defiled Elizabeth lies broken and lifeless against the parapet. Casey Morton still lies a few yards away, amazingly still alive, gasping weak, ragged breaths.

Looking out to sea, I grin at the Grand Banks, pitching and bobbing at anchor, a quarter mile off shore. I knew Tindall wouldn't dare risk bringing it any closer.

I search for Santos and the others, make sure they're not lurking somewhere waiting to ambush me. But that is just caution. I'm sure they're still busy inside. Finding me gone will make them expect an attack behind every doorway.

My child remains my primary concern. I open my mind to him and thank the fates when I sense his presence. His mother's body has cooled and that change in his environment has sent the first tendrils of fear into his awareness.

"It's okay. You'll be fine," I mindspeak to him, knowing he won't grasp the meaning of the words, hoping he understands the love and reassurance behind them. *"I'm your father, Henri. I'm here to take care of you."*

I shudder as I slice Elizabeth open with my talons. If I could find another way I would, but my son must be saved. Reaching inside her, I search for the sac that holds the baby, find it and cut him free, lifting the slippery creature. My son mewls at the shock of open air.

Cradling him, trying to warm him against my body, I marvel how well-formed the child is—except for his tail, not much larger than a human baby. Henri moves his head and I find myself staring into his emerald-green eyes. I see him and sense everything he feels at the same time and the transfer of love between us makes my legs weak. Poor Elizabeth, I think, what a shame that she couldn't experience this.

I hold the child up to the sky and he mews, opening his mouth, clumsily opening and closing his wings. I feel his pangs of hunger, understand what is required for his sustenance. This was why my bride wanted our captives on hand, so the child's needs could be served.

The baby mews again when I place him on Casey Morton's chest. But soon he senses the live flesh beneath him and begins to feed. The woman trembles once, at his first attack, and then finally, thankfully, breathes her last breath. I let Henri feed alone a few minutes until, realizing how much energy I've expended, I begin to feast beside him.

A gust of wind blows over us and I wrinkle my nose at the stink it carries to me, the acrid aroma of human perspiration. I keep my head down as I stare upwind with one eye and spot Santos inching forward in the shadows, a rail gun in each hand, two ancient flintlock pistols stuffed through a belt on his waist.

He must have exited the house through one of the bedrooms on the other side, I think, and circled back toward us. I tense my muscles, but continue to feed, watching him, waiting to see where the others are, waiting for them to act.

Santos stops, lowers one gun to the floor, raises the other to his shoulder, aims and a takes a deep breath to steady himself before he tightens his finger on the trigger.

I grab Henri, leap away at that moment, and take to the air, the ball passing where I just was. A machine-gun blast goes off to my rear, Chen following my flight from the shadows, chasing me with his bullets until his clip empties.

"Damn! Fuck!" Santos yells. He throws the spent gun down, lifts the other, searches the dark sky for any sign of me.

But Henri is my first concern. I spiral around the house, wondering where best to put him. On my second circuit, I decide he'll be safest inside. Holding him close to my body, I crash through the picture window in the great room, grab pillows from the couch and use them to make a place for Henri in the far corner of the cupboard. Leaving him hidden there, I rush down the spiral staircase to my room.

I find the doors to the veranda still open, just as Elizabeth left them when she rushed out. I grin, thinking of the humans' faces when they see me. They'll be looking for me to attack from the sky, not to burst out from the room.

I linger, hidden in the room's shadows while I watch Santos, Chen and Tindall on the veranda, and listen to their conversation.

"Now what do we do?" Tindall asks.

Both Santos and Chen stare at him. "We?" Chen says. "Where's your weapon?"

"You know I don't use those things. I'm a lawyer. I fight with words. . . ."

"So when that thing comes back, we'll stand back and watch you sue it," Santos says. Chen laughs.

"Laugh all you want. Remember, it's my boat that will take us away from here. Where would you be without me?" Tindall says.

"Don't remind me, Jeremy," Chen says, pointing his AK-47 in Tindall's direction. "Without you, my company would still be doing business with Caribbean Charm. Without you, my colleagues in China and I would never have lost so much money in the fire. Without you, my son, Benny, would still be alive. Without you, my men would be home with their families."

Tindall's face flushes. "Don't give me that shit. My son's dead too, you know. I didn't hear you or any of your colleagues object to setting up that company. You wanted to come after DelaSangre as much as I did. Without me, you'd never have known anything about his movements." He turns to Santos. "Without me, your ass would still be rotting in jail. Who the hell do you think arranged your bail?"

"I did," Chen says.

"But you never would have known about Santos without me."

"Shut up, both of you!" the Cuban says.

They turn, staring at him.

"We have to search the house again—and the island. We have to find that thing and the DelaSangres, kill them all."

Seeing all three men so preoccupied in their conversation, I choose this moment to attack.

"Shit!" Santos shouts as I explode through the open doorway.

Tindall lets out a high-pitched scream, sees the other dead man's machine gun still lying on the ground, grabs it and runs away.

Chen stands his ground, fires at me, the AK-47 bucking in his hands, the muzzle flashing, almost every bullet striking the armored plates of my underbelly, penetrating them—each impact causing an explosion of pain.

I bellow, rush toward Chen. Santos raises his gun, tries to aim at me. But I'm too much a moving target, slashing out at Chen as I pass, taking to the air to swoop back and slash again. My talons rip flesh and muscle. Chen grasps his slit throat, gargling indecipherable words as he falls.

Santos follows my movements with his gun. Still flying, I veer, then circle away from him, leaving him to aim at an empty sky. Moments later, I return, approaching from his rear, swooping down and slashing his back open as I streak past. To his credit, he finally manages to get off his shot.

The massive lead ball strikes me in the back, between my wings. I bellow, struggle to maintain control of my wings, even as pain and weakness overwhelm me. I try to roar, but groan instead and crash to the ground—just feet away from Santos.

"Ha!" he yells. Then the pain of his injury strikes him and he sags to the floor.

We both lie still, man and dragon, side by side, moaning from our injuries.

Santos struggles to a sitting position first, glares at me.

"Fuck you!" he says, reaches for one of his pistols, pulls it from his belt and fires.

The ball hits, but hasn't the power to penetrate my scales. Before he can fire the other pistol, I whirl and smash him with my tail, throwing him across the veranda, stunning him.

While he lies on his back, dazed, a trickle of blood seeping from the side of his mouth, I drag myself across the veranda toward Chen's body. Once there I rip him open, take bite after bite, feeding on him, letting his meat nourish me and help me heal.

I keep an eye on Santos while I feed and concentrate on mending my wounds. He doesn't move, but he watches me, his eyes widening with each bite I take. Planning his next move, I'm sure, looking for any advantage he can find.

I've no intention to give him any. It is time, I think, to end this thing. Time for him to know just who and what I am. I flex my wings, stretch my limbs, feel the renewal of my energy and roar, breaking the night's calm with my sound. Santos winces, prepares for my attack. Instead I shift into my human form. Naked, I walk over to him, remove the remaining pistol from his belt and hold it in my right hand, pointing it at him.

The Cuban moans as he forces himself into a sitting position. "What the hell are you?"

"Tired," I answer. I have no desire to do a song and dance for this human. The glint of the torchlight on the gold clover-leaf chain around his neck catches my attention. I hold out my free hand. "Give me the chain."

"Sorry," the Cuban says. "I don't think I can do that. It belonged to my sister."

"I know. I took it from her after she died."

"After you killed her," Santos corrects me.

I look at the man, the human, and understand the loss he

feels. But I no longer feel guilt for what occurred. I shrug. I am what I am, I think.

Tindall emerges from the shadows, comes into the torch-light, the AK-47 in his hands.

"Shoot him!" Santos shouts.

Jeremy points the machine gun at me. "I always knew you were some sort of monster, but I never imagined this."

I stare at him, wonder if he has any idea how to use the weapon in his hands, wonder how many rounds are left in the machine gun's magazine. "Put the gun down, Jeremy," I say.

He shakes his head. "Then you'll kill me. You put *your* gun down."

If I try to shoot him first and fail, I chance leaving my child in jeopardy. It's a risk I find myself unwilling to take. I know Jeremy. If he thinks there's a way out, he'll take it. I nod, lay my pistol on the ground. "Have I ever tried to kill you before, Jeremy? You've certainly given me reason enough to do so. Put the gun down."

Santos screams. "Damn you, shoot him!"

Tindall pauses, seems to reconsider, but then his eyes harden and he stares through the gunsight at me.

Before he can squeeze the trigger, I say, "Think, Jeremy. You've seen me survive wounds that would kill any man. What makes you think that your bullets are any more powerful than the others? Are you sure you want to risk this?"

"What choice do I have?"

"Jeremy, what good would it do me to kill you? Who can replace you at the office? You know I need you," I say. "We've always worked out our differences. Put down the gun. I promise I'll let you leave."

"You asshole," Santos mutters. "What good are his promises?"

"Have you ever seen me break my word?" I ask.

Tindall shakes his head, says, "I didn't want it to come to

this, but you left me no choice. The Red Army owns Chen's factory. They were furious he lost so much money. Chen promised them he would take revenge and recover their investment. He threatened to kill me if I didn't help him. I had to. Besides, you killed his son and mine. You shouldn't have, Peter."

"Maybe so," I say. "But it's time now to put the gun down."

"Don't!" Santos growls.

Tindall takes careful aim again. I suck in a breath, wait to see whether his finger tightens or not.

No one speaks. Only the crash of the waves, as they rush and retreat from the shore, breaks the silence of the night. I stare at Tindall, at the rifle's black muzzle. Somewhere in the dark a dog whimpers. A gust of wind rushes across the veranda, sends the torchlight's flames into frenzied spasms, the shadows dancing all around us in sympathy.

Finally, I shake my head, deciding it's time to push this worthless creature, see if he thinks he can withstand my power, see if he actually possesses any courage. "Jeremy, shoot or put the damn thing down," I growl.

Tindall adjusts his position, seating the rifle butt a little more firmly into his shoulder. His eyes harden, his jaw clenches and I prepare to jump to the side as soon as I see the first twinge of muscle movement in his hand, wondering if I can move and change fast enough. But then sweat breaks out on his forehead, streams down his face and the rifle barrel begins to waver ever so slightly.

"Put it down, Jeremy," I say again. "We both know you're no assassin. It's time for you to go home."

Trembling, shaking his head, the thin man slowly lowers the AK-47 to the ground.

Santos groans. I smile at him, then look at Tindall. "Go back to your boat, Jeremy," I say. "We'll settle this later."

"Thank you, Peter," he says, backing away. "You won't be sorry. Thank you."

As he makes his way across the island, I hear the growls and barks of the few remaining dogs. Glad some have survived, I whistle them back, to make sure they allow him safe passage.

Once I hear the outboard motor cough to life, I turn to Santos. "Get up," I say. "I need your help."

He winces and moans, but still manages to struggle to his feet. "That man is a fool, isn't he?"

"Aren't you all?" I ask.

My child yowls loud enough for his wails to reach us outside. I glance at the third-floor windows, wishing I could rush upstairs to hug and reassure him. But there are things I still must do to make him safe.

"Jesus!" Santos says. "What is that?"

"My son," I say. I point to Elizabeth's remains. "And that's my wife. You killed her."

Jorge flexes his shoulders, grimaces at the pain the movement brings. "I don't suppose you're going to let me go, huh?"

I shake my head, then look seaward, follow the white foam trail of the inflatable's wake, calculate how long it will be before Tindall reaches the Grand Banks.

"Come on," I say. "We don't have much time."

"Why should I help you?" Santos says.

Why indeed? I think. I look at the man, standing upright despite his wounds, defiant even though he knows he has little hope. "You want to get away?" I ask.

He nods.

"After this is over, I'll give you the chance."

"Like the one you're giving Tindall? I told him not to trust your promises."

"You'll get a fair shot," I say. "I told Tindall he could

leave and I let him. I told him we'd work it out later." I smile. "This is later."

Santos laughs bitterly. "Okay, DelaSangre, let's get this over. I can't wait to see what you think a fair chance is."

I bring the powder and ball and watch him load the cannon. Together we turn the old ship killer, aim it for where Tindall's inflatable will be in a few minutes.

"It's going to be a tough shot." Santos shakes his head.

"I thought you said you were good," I say. I go to the arms room, bring back Father's ancient spyglass.

"It would be easier to hit the trawler."

"No," I say, extending the telescope, studying the dark water, finding the white churn of the outboard's propeller, the silhouette of the motor, the dim form of Tindall's back slightly forward and above it. "A shallow trajectory should do it."

I hand the spyglass to Santos, go for a lit torch while he gets a sense of what I suggest. Finally he says, "I think you're right."

Santos checks the wind, sets the elevation on the cannon, shows me just where he thinks the ball will hit.

"I'll tell you when he comes into range," I say, taking the telescope, handing him the torch, both of us keeping our eyes seaward, following Tindall's movements.

Santos stands by my side, a flaming torch in his hand. He stares at the ocean, waits for my command.

I wait until the inflatable is within a few dozen yards of the trawler. By now I'm sure Tindall thinks he's reached safety. I smile. *"Now!"* I shout.

The cannon roars, belches flame. The ball, traveling almost parallel to the water, strikes the outboard motor first, turning it into a thousand flying metal fragments, sparking the fuel line and the gas tank at the same time as it strikes Tindall.

Tindall and the inflatable both disappear with one brief flash of fire.

Santos, still staring out to sea, whistles, then mutters, "Wow."

The night settles around us. The sea breeze washes away the sulfur stink of the cannon's smoke. In the house, Henri has quieted. I sigh and stare at the sea. Any time before this night, I know, I would have laughed and grinned with Santos, celebrating the success of our jointly executed cannon shot.

Santos turns to me. "Now what?" he says.

I sigh again. Death lies all around us, blood stains the veranda's floor and still, one more life has to be taken. I can think of no other way. Father was right. No human can ever be trusted. But as easy as it would be, I have no desire to simply execute this man.

"Go get one of the rail guns and load it," I say, walking over to the ancient flintlock pistol I placed on the deck, picking it up.

"You sure I can't get one of the machine guns?" Santos says.

"I'm sure."

He wanders the veranda, collects one of the spent blunderbusses, takes it to the arms room for ball and powder and returns to load it within my view. "We're having a duel, is that it?"

I nod. "I promised you a fair chance."

"What if you lose?"

"I won't," I say, thinking how easy it is to read his movements.

"You never know, DelaSangre, you never know. I almost had you tonight, twice, and you know it."

"Just load the damn thing."

When he finishes ramming the load home, he looks at me and shrugs. "Well, it wasn't all bad. . . . Another time, another place, who knows? After all, you thought we were friends, didn't you?"

Santos cocks the rail gun, primes the flash pan and aims at me.

It shames me to realize I once thought some sort of friendship had formed between us. I raise the pistol, cock and aim it. "My kind and your kind can never be friends."

"And what kind are yours?" he asks.

I look into his eyes, wait for Santos to signal his intent. He doesn't turn away. He doesn't flinch. His bravery earns him the right to a response, I think.

But Santos doesn't wait for my reply. He sucks in a steadying breath and, sure of what that signals, I squeeze my finger on my pistol's trigger —just an instant before he squeezes his.

My gun flares at the same moment I spit out the answer to his question. "Dragons."

30

Since Elizabeth's death, Henri and I have lived alone. I find little reason to leave my island, to seek any other company. My son's very presence, his constant need for my attention make it impossible for me to succumb to loneliness and grief. For this I'm grateful.

At first the thought of raising a child by myself terrifies me. I have no background for this, no training. Elizabeth knew what to do. Her mother taught her from birth just what was expected of her. "She even allowed me to help take care of Chloe, after she was born," Elizabeth told me. "Babies are easy."

Only childbirth itself frightened her. "It's when our women most often die," she said.

I call Arturo Gomez and tell him a much-modified story of my son's birth, Jeremy's perfidy and Elizabeth's death at the hands of him and his henchmen. "At least, Henri came to no harm," I say. The Latin offers to rush me books on human childcare and, out of curiosity, I allow it.

But as I read Spock and Lear and the others—during the times Henri sleeps—I shake my head over and over again. I end up disregarding and discarding all of the books. Mine is not a human child. Mine has different needs.

Elizabeth had laughed when I suggested buying a bassinet for the baby. I understand now just why. After all, no manufacturer has ever designed diapers with a dragon-child in mind. I find that hay—as she suggested—makes the perfect bed for my sleeping son. It conforms to his sleeping shape. When fouled, it's simple to replace.

Arturo offers to find a nursemaid for the child. I stifle a laugh at the suggestion. The Latin knows we're different, but he has no idea just what we are. Besides, I know no one else can ever take care of my child as well as I can.

Even if there were a way for a nursemaid to cope with such a creature as my son, I wouldn't surrender the closeness Henri and I have. With Henri, I can share his thoughts. When he cries from hunger, I can sense his pangs. When fear grips him, I can see what scares him. When he looks at me, the love that pours from him almost staggers me. And when I look at him—especially when he sleeps, quiet and innocent and oh so vulnerable to all the dangers of the world—the love I feel for him brings tears to my eyes.

I find it ironic that had Elizabeth lived, she would have been the one to tend to our child's needs, to grow as close to him as I have. In a way, her death has brought me an unintended blessing. Not that I wouldn't undo it in a moment if I could.

Not a day goes by that I don't visit her grave—the ground still bare where I buried her, adjacent to her beloved garden. I report to her the growth of our child, pledge I will keep my promise. I will teach Henri about his mother.

I tend to Elizabeth's garden too, make sure all is cared for as she would have wished. When Henri grows older, I will bring him here often and tell him stories about her.

I don't know when I'll tell him how she died. He certainly will never see anything to make him wonder about it. Within days after Elizabeth's death, no reminders of her disaster remained. The bodies of Jorge Santos, Casey Morton and the other humans now decay somewhere in the depths of the Gulfstream.

Every remnant of their blood and Elizabeth's has long since been eliminated, the veranda sanded and refinished.

Even the cannon that took my bride's life has been discarded. It now lies rusting at the bottom of our island's tiny harbor.

Tindall's Grand Banks is lost somewhere at sea, wherever its motors and the heading I programmed into its autopilot delivered it. When last I saw it, the empty craft was following a direction that should have taken it between Cuba and the Bahamas—out into the vast Atlantic.

No sign of Jeremy, of course, has ever been found. Not that anyone seems to miss him. As soon as the Coast Guard search was called off, his wife and sons sued in court to have him declared legally dead. Arturo says they're already arguing over his estate.

Good old Arturo. He and my new attorney—Jeremy's oldest son, Ian—handled all the paperwork expediting Elizabeth's death certificate and arranged for all the necessary papers to record Henri's birth. A new will was written, money shifted and trust funds set up. Thanks to their machinations, within days after my child's birth, his future was secure.

The future becomes a very important thing after a child is born. I spend a lot of time thinking about it, making plans. All children, I suppose, want to correct their parents' mistakes by doing differently themselves in the rearing of their own children. In this I'm no exception.

I've come to agree with Father that Mother erred when she insisted I be so exposed to humans and their ways. I spent far too many years wishing I had been born human, yearning for their company, wanting their approval.

I hate that it took so long for me to embrace my heritage. Yet I don't want Henri to grow up like his mother, bereft of all exposure or interest in art and music and literature. Humans may never be our equals, but there's much they create that I want my son to be able to appreciate.

He will never be sent to school with their kind. If necessary, I'll teach him myself on our island. I want him to grow
up, proud to be what he is, yet aware of all the world has to
offer.

It takes until Henri's third month of life for me to be sure
just how I intend to pursue our future. For his own good, I
decide, he should have a mother to nurture him too. Most
certainly, it will also serve me if I find another wife.

Human women no longer hold any fascination for me.
Father told me long ago, *"Once you've experienced a
woman of our own kind, you'll never again want to touch a
human female in that way."* I find I agree. But finding a
woman of the blood is never easy. The thought of the long
search it will require fills me with dread.

My son, on the other hand, fills me with joy. Already he
has grown enough so that some of his thoughts form almost
as words. During his waking times he fills the air and my
mind with an endless stream of baby talk. His scales are still
baby soft, his color a light tan overall. He has yet to shift
completely into a human shape, but when he sees me in
mine, he tries.

Sometimes the results leave me laughing, the infant half-
human in appearance, with a tail protruding in the wrong
spot or an ear strategically misplaced. I open my mind to
him and gently think him back to his natural shape. It melts
my heart when one day he forms an entire baby face, complete with a cleft like mine, but far smaller, on its chin.

I often lie on the hay beside him and let him crawl over
me, grabbing and tickling him, laughing in tandem with his
giggles. Always at some moment during our play, he grabs
the gold clover-leaf necklace I recovered from Jorge Santos
and now wear around my neck any time I'm in my human
shape. He loves to toy with it, the glistening emerald in its
center fascinating to him.

"It was your mother's," I tell him. I'm about to say, one day it will be his, when a better thought occurs. It shames me that I haven't thought of it sooner.

The next morning, I compose the letter I've long dreaded writing. I tell Charles and Samantha Blood that their daughter died in childbirth. The truth, I decide, will serve no one. I assure them she gave birth to a wonderful baby boy.

I write a second letter too, this one to Chloe. In it I tell her much the same thing but add, "Your sister loved you very much. She wanted me to make sure you had something of hers. I'm sending it along with this letter. Perhaps, one day, I'll have the pleasure of seeing it around your neck."

Gomez arranges for the letters and the necklace to be delivered to the Bloods' agent in Kingston, Claypool and Sons, the same one who took receipt of my gift of gold to Charles Blood. I give Arturo other instructions too. He raises his eyebrows when he hears them, but knows better than to argue.

In the evening, after the sun has set and the moon has risen, I carry my son out to the veranda. He sniffs the sea air and babbles and laughs when the evening breeze gusts at us. I hold him over my head and he spreads his immature wings, too small and chubby yet to take him into the air.

"One night," I mindspeak. *"I'll take you into the sky with me and we'll hunt side by side."*

He babbles something in return and I grin at him, pull him close. But he squirms and struggles until I release him and expose him to the warm night wind again.

Somewhere, out over the water, a large fish jumps and crashes back into the sea. Waves show up white against the dark of the ocean as they rush at the shore. The sounds of their endless crash and retreat seem as much a part of me as the beat of my own heart. I stare up at the stars, the dark clouds scudding by overhead, and smile. One day Henri will love this island as much as I do, I think. One day, I hope, Chloe will too.

I'll have to wait a few years, until my son's old enough to control his shapes and actions. But I have more than enough time. Arturo's already located an estate inland from Montego Bay, near Cockpit Country. Henri and I will be able to move there long before Chloe reaches her first oestrus.

Charles and Samantha Blood will be furious, but they will just have to cope with it. With me living close by, I'll be able to catch the first scent of her first heat. I will have her before any other suitor can be aware of her existence. After that, we will be bound for life. Short of killing me, her parents will be unable to prevent our union.

I dislike that I'll have to win her in such a devious way, but I see no other choice. Even if I could find another woman of the blood, there would be no guarantee she would be compatible with me. Chloe likes so many of the things I value.

When I think of her, the same image of her human shape always forms in my mind—a young, dark girl in shorts, riding her horse bareback, galloping alongside our car as we depart the valley. Chloe grinning, her naked legs pressed against her mount's sides, her hair streaming behind her, her body moving in perfect rhythm with her horse's strides.

The child squirms in my arms, making no secret he wants to be put down on the deck. *"Not so fast,"* I tell him. I'm not ready yet to give up his touch.

In a little while, after he falls asleep, I'll leave him and take to the air. I look forward to the sensation of flight, the adrenaline rush of the hunt. Most of all I look forward to Henri's excited reception when I return, the closeness of feeding beside my son.

I think of how horrified any human would be, if they saw us, and I smile.

Another salt-tinged breeze washes over us and Henri squeals. I embrace him, rub my cheek against his and say to him the words my father said to me so many times as I grew up—words I hope my dragon-child listens to more carefully than I ever did.

"We are what we are."

See what's coming in April...

❑ ORBIS
by Scott Mackay
For millennia they seduced us with their visions of hope, and a mythology that became our religion. Now, the Benefactors are about to be unmasked for what they really are—and mankind may not have a prayer.
45874-5

❑ ANGRY LEAD SKIES
by Glen Cook
Private Investigator Garrett has agreed to play body-guard for a kid who is being threatened by creatures that defy description. But before Garrett can make heads or tails of the story, the kid is abducted—and the chase begins.
45875-3

❑ BATTLETECH #54: *STORMS OF FATE*
by Loren L. Coleman
As the civil war within the Federated Commonwealth rages on, someone plans a strike that could put it all to an end.
45876-1

To order call: 1-800-788-6262

The next generation in the bestselling Civil War series...

WILLIAM R. FORSTCHEN

DOWN TO THE SEA
A Novel of The Lost Regiment

The union of interstellar exiles founded by Andrew Keane and the 35th Maine has been at peace for nearly 20 years. Keane is president again, and survivors of the once deadly Hordes have been reduced to a status similar to that of contemporary American Indians, which they don't enjoy. Meanwhile, the empire of the Kazars, far to the south and torn by civil war, still reaches north to menace the humans.

0-451-45806-0

To order call: 1-800-788-6262